A MAIDEN TO REMEMBER

Love's Addiction
Book Three

Marie Higgins

ARE YOU SIGNED UP FOR DRAGONBLADE'S BLOG?

You'll get the latest news and information on exclusive giveaways, exclusive excerpts, coming releases, sales, free books, cover reveals and more.

Check out our complete list of authors, too!

No spam, no junk. That's a promise!

Sign Up Here

www.dragonbladepublishing.com

Dearest Reader;

Thank you for your support of a small press. At Dragonblade Publishing, we strive to bring you the highest quality Historical Romance from some of the best authors in the business. Without your support, there is no 'us', so we sincerely hope you adore these stories and find some new favorite authors along the way.

Happy Reading!

CEO, Dragonblade Publishing

**Additional Dragonblade books by
Author Marie Higgins**

Love's Addiction Series
A Wallflower to Love (Book 1)
A Governess to Protect (Book 2)
A Maiden to Remember (Book 3)

Ellie Middleton has exactly one month to find a husband. If she doesn't, her father will betroth her to a vile man. Although her heart still belongs to the soldier who died in the war, she is willing to enter a loveless marriage. Out of options, Ellie does the unthinkable when she runs into her brother's friend, Vincent Wallace, the Earl of Trenton, and boldly makes *him* a proposal of marriage in name only. Will the rogue accept the bargain she's offered?

Vincent Wallace has no desire to marry and tie himself to one woman. However, he doesn't like the idea of Ellie settling for just anyone, either. He can't get her off his mind, and he desires her more than any woman he's ever known. But when he is threatened to stay away from Ellie or die, Vincent doesn't know whether to release her and allow her to be happy or fight for the woman he has fallen in love with.

CHAPTER ONE

MARRIAGE! ELEANOR MIDDLETON shuddered. The mere thought left a bitter taste in her mouth.

Ellie faced her father, determined not to allow him to guilt her into doing something she wasn't ready for. As usually happened once a month, her father had called her into his study to have that *talk*. She geared herself up to give him the same answer she'd been giving him for three years now.

The plea in her father's expression, and the sadness misting his gray eyes, twisted her heart. There was no doubt he cared deeply for her, but why couldn't he comprehend her plight as well?

"My dear," he said calmly as he held her gaze. "It's time for you to wed. If you wait any longer, men will think you're not looking for a husband."

Ellie took a deep breath for courage and released it slowly. She mustn't get angry. He thought he was doing what was best for her, although she knew it was her stepmother urging him to do this.

"Father, I must tell you the same thing I told you last month. I'm not ready. Why can't you understand?" Knowing this conversation would take longer than she wanted, Ellie turned and sat on the edge of the sofa cushion with her back straight.

He wore a different expression this time when she turned him down. Before, his shoulders drooped in defeat, but today, he pulled them back and lifted his chin. *Oh dear!*

The impulse to jump up and run to safety became overpowering, but she would not relent. Although her hands were clasped and resting on her lap, she wished to have a handkerchief to hold on to—or wring the life out of.

The day had started out lovely. Ellie awoke, ate breakfast, dressed, and strolled through her stepmother's flower garden. Inhaling the sweet scent of the roses always lifted her spirits. But as soon as she stepped inside the house, a servant informed her that her father and stepmother were waiting to talk with her in the drawing room.

Ellie hadn't dared ask why. She knew.

"My dear," her father said with a gentle, caring voice, as he leaned forward in his black leather chair. "It's been three years since Lord Adam died. I think by now your heart would be healed."

Clenching her teeth, Ellie held back her temper. She took deep breaths, trying her hardest not to spout out the angry thoughts clashing in her head. Obviously, her father had never been so in love, only to have the ideal person that one imagined spending the rest of their life with just suddenly taken from their grasp, never to be seen again. Yet her father expected Ellie's heart to be healed by now? No. Perhaps her heart would never heal.

She would *never* be that woman she'd been while Adam courted her. They were so happy and in love. Adam was unlike any man she'd ever known. How could she find someone to replace him when there was no such man?

Finally, she felt as though she could speak without saying something she might regret later. "Father, Augusta." She glanced at her stepmother, who sat beside her on the sofa, before focusing on her father. "I'm deeply touched to know you care about my welfare. However, my heart hasn't mended. Forgive me, but I'm just not interested in marriage at this point."

Grumbling, her father pushed his fingers through his thinning brown hair with streaks of gray, as a grimace tugged at his mouth.

"No, Ellie, this will not do." His voice lifted. "Augusta and I have given you ample time to recover. We both feel that three years of mourning is long enough. You *will* find a husband. Immediately."

Anger rose inside of Ellie, and she dropped her gaze to her lap, taking in deep breaths. She wasn't in *mourning*, not like her father had suggested. She'd stopped wearing black and gray gowns nearly a year and a half ago. Why didn't he understand?

"Father, I must remain true to my heart." She tightened her fingers on the handkerchief. "You had once promised I could marry the man I loved and admired, just as you allowed Justina to marry the man she loved. Why can't you give me the same privileges as my older sister?"

Silence stretched in the room for a space of several minutes. A gentle wind from outside blew through the opened window. The sheer drapes flapped softly. The refreshing fragrance of the roses outside drifted through the air, slightly calming Ellie. If she wanted to be fully relaxed, she would still be strolling through the garden right now. Instead, she had to tolerate her father's insistent request.

Hesitantly, she raised her attention to her father. He drummed his beefy fingers on the armrest of his chair, as his mouth pulled into a straight line. It appeared that he wasn't going to give in this time. She must prepare a stronger excuse as to why she wouldn't marry.

If only Justina were here. Ellie's sister had been married for two years already, and she missed having her around in times like this. Justina would know what to say to help their father change his mind.

"I'm sorry, Ellie, but whether you feel you are ready or not, your stepmother and I agree that you must start looking for someone to marry as soon as possible. Time is of the essence."

She shook her head, desperation sinking in her chest. Would

she lose the argument this time? Perhaps she wasn't trying hard enough to argue the case. She must win.

Unshed tears stung her eyes, so she blinked to keep them hidden. "I don't understand. Why is it so important for me to start looking for a husband now?"

"You see, my dear"—Augusta's overly sweet voice drew Ellie's attention to the slender, fancily dressed woman—"the longer you wait to wed, the more apt you will be to become a spinster."

A surprised laugh bubbled up in Ellie's throat, and she couldn't hold it back. "Are you jesting? You are worried about me becoming a spinster?"

"Well, it's more than that, dear." Her stepmother patted Ellie's hand. "The longer you wait, the more men will wonder what is wrong with you because you have not married sooner. Men will not want to court you. They will lose interest, and if one man loses interest, they all will."

The thin woman looked at Ellie with such seriousness in her brown eyes. A few silver streaks highlighted her fading auburn hair. The woman had married Ellie's father barely over a year ago, but Ellie hadn't been able to consider Augusta her mother yet.

"Oh please, Augusta." Ellie rolled her eyes as she pushed away her stepmother's touch. "You cannot believe that will happen. I have it on good authority that Miss Evelyn Cummings waited four whole years after her fiancé died before she married, and her reputation wasn't ruined."

"However," her father added in a stern voice, "Miss Cummings was *not* the daughter of a nobleman."

"Exactly." Scowling, Ellie gave him a sharp nod. "And because my father is a duke, I'm quite certain that men will still be vying for my attention even after I become a spinster. After all, they all know I come with an impressive dowry."

The fierce glint in her father's gray eyes had Ellie holding her breath. Perhaps she shouldn't have raised her voice just then. But she couldn't hold back her feelings any longer.

Slowly, her father stood as he folded his arms across his wide chest. His gaze locked on Ellie and wouldn't budge for the longest pause of silence she'd had so far during this conversation. She swallowed hard and tried to keep calm, and at the same time, she must not cower. Especially in this particular cause.

"Ellie Marie Middleton," he growled.

Her hopes sank. Panic grew inside of her. Never had her father been this adamant and used her whole name. Usually, all she had to do was show him some tears and he bent to her will. Could he have grown immune to her tactics?

"You *will* start looking for a husband, because in four weeks' time, if you haven't found a man to marry, I will sign betrothal papers for you to wed Lord Stone."

Shock vibrated through her. "Lord *Stone*? Are you referring to Augusta's nephew, Edgar Stone?"

"Indeed, the very man." Her father arched a dark, bushy eyebrow but kept his harsh expression. "He has been hinting about courting you, and I believe it is time I allowed it."

She sprang from her chair and grasped her father's arm. Her world as she knew it closed in around her, making her feel as if she were drowning. Even her vision became tunneled as dread pulsed through her head. She couldn't lose control now. She must fight for her life. "No, Father. Not him. He is a vile man."

"Your stepmother and I believe he will make you a fine husband."

Panic tightened her throat. "A *fine husband* isn't supposed to strike women and beat them to a bloody pulp. A *fine husband* should have patience and understanding. Edgar possesses none of those traits."

Augusta gasped and shook her head. "Those are just rumors, and you of all people should know not to believe them. I have known him for years, being my older sister's son, and he treats every woman like a queen."

Ellie wanted to scream at her stepmother. The woman was so

very wrong about her nephew. Ellie had known women who'd gotten close to Lord Stone and ended up with bruised eyes. She had witnessed the way he yelled at an older woman, which had stirred fright into Ellie. If a man could treat an elderly woman in such a way, she didn't have to imagine what he would do with a wife if he became displeased. But obviously, her father and Augusta wouldn't be swayed.

"Father, you are missing one important detail. I don't love him. I never will." Tears burned her eyes, but she tried not to let them show. She wouldn't cry and beg like a young girl any longer. She was a woman full grown at the age of twenty and four, and so must act the part.

"If love is what you seek," her father replied, "you have four weeks to find that man. I will not relent this time, Ellie. Your pouts will not influence me, I assure you."

She yanked away from him and glowered. She would bet money that Augusta had something to do with this. Ever since Ellie had met Edgar Stone for the first time at her father's wedding to Augusta, the mention of that disgusting man's name sent shivers up her spine.

"Fine." She heaved quickly, trying to hold in her anger, but it wasn't working. "If that is the way you want to play, then I suppose I have no other choice. I shall find a man to marry in four weeks, because I will *not* marry Lord Stone."

Ellie spun away from her father and marched toward the door. It didn't matter that she had not been excused by him—she didn't want to stay in that room any longer. The stubborn man just wouldn't listen to reason. Well, he would *not* get his way. Not this time. She would find someone else to marry, even though she knew her heart would never be involved.

Her heeled shoes clicked on the marbled floor as she strode quickly down the hall, heading for the grand stairs that would take her toward her room on the second floor. Sulking was necessary at this moment, only because she needed to mourn the fact that her life would never be the same. She would have to find a husband and live in a loveless marriage forever. She had given her heart to Adam Haddington, a soldier her father hadn't exactly approved of, but he accepted Adam since she loved him. And now that Adam had fought for his country and was killed, she would never know happiness again.

Her steps gained speed as she rounded the corner...and ran head-on into a human form. Her head whacked against something hard, and pain exploded in her temple. Stars danced in her eyes as she tried to focus on the person she'd just hit.

Dizzy, she stepped back and swayed, but two strong arms wrapped around her, holding her upright. A manly scent of pine mixed with leather filled her senses.

Blinking, she tried to focus on the man's face that was only about four inches from her. Deep blue, worried eyes held her stare. His lips were moving, but she couldn't hear anything due to the buzzing in her ears.

Slowly, he walked her to a settee and set her down with his arms still around her waist. She wasn't certain she liked how personally he held her, but she allowed it, fearing that without his arms, she would crumple to the floor.

Taking profound breaths, she hoped to fight against the light-headedness assailing her. What could have caused her to act this way? But then she noticed he rubbed his red chin as a smile touched his mouth.

"Are you all right?"

His words were clearer this time, and she nodded. "I shall be in a moment." She touched the sore spot on her forehead and cringed. This was going to leave a mark, she just knew it. "Forgive me for running into you."

Finally, his face didn't appear so fuzzy, and she could see the man more fully. He was handsome, but still, he couldn't hold a candle to Adam's rugged good looks. Yet as she stared at him, a prick of familiarity passed through her mind.

"It's not your fault," he said. "I shouldn't have been standing so close to the corner of the hall." He rubbed his chin again. "I must confess, you have a hard head."

She glanced toward the hall where they had collided. "Why were you standing there?"

"I was admiring the painting. It's really quite lovely."

"Uh, thank you." She licked her dry lips. "I actually painted that."

His eyes widened, as well as his smile. "Then allow me to pay you a compliment and tell you how very talented you are, Miss Middleton."

"I thank you," she repeated. "But I must know, *why* were you standing there to begin with?"

He chuckled. "I was waiting for your brother to join me. We are going riding this afternoon."

Ellie ran her gaze over him one more time now that she was more alert. There was a slight wave to his dark blond head of hair, especially the thickness gathered at the back of his neck. His blue eyes held a touch of gray and nearly sparkled when he smiled. Indeed, he was dressed for riding with his black coat over a tan waistcoat and white shirt and cravat. Stretching across his legs were beige riding trousers that snugged against his muscular thighs quite tightly. He wore black riding boots, making his attire complete.

Embarrassed of where her attention had wandered, she snapped her gaze up and peered into his eyes again...eyes that were so incredibly dreamy to stare into. He peered at her as though he held some kind of secret. His stare also slid over her, and the longer he looked, the wider his smile grew. Apparently, he must be enjoying the view.

She shook herself and focused on the matter at hand. What could she possibly be thinking? Now was not the time to act like a featherbrained ninny who swooned over a handsome man. Obviously, she acted this way because of her head injury.

"Pardon me, but have we met?" she asked.

He chuckled again. "Indeed we have. We were but children at the time." He stood and bowed. "I'm Vincent Wallace, Earl of

Trenton."

The Wallace name hit her, stunning her nearly as hard as when her head had whacked against his shoulder. They were children together, and she had disliked his cocky attitude way back then. Vincent and Ellie's brother, Dominic, were chums for years. Both grew to be rakehells, and because their fathers were titled lords, nobody thought to scold their behavior. A few years ago, it seemed as though Vincent's family had dropped out of Society as well, because she hadn't heard the name Wallace mentioned in the *ton*'s circles.

She stiffened her back and rested her hands on her lap, trying to appear proper again. "Yes, I do remember you. Tell me, Lord Trenton, when did you receive your title?"

"Because my father died and left the earldom to me."

"Please accept my condolences for his passing."

"I thank you."

He sighed heavily and glanced back up the hall. She followed his gaze. Her brother had yet to appear. Even the servants were conspicuously absent.

When Vincent returned his focus to her, she noticed a different expression cross his face.

Slowly, he sat beside her...very close beside her.

"Tell me, Miss Middleton, what have you been doing since we last saw each other?" His gaze dropped to her left hand before he stared into her eyes again. "I see you are not married."

Ellie really didn't want to converse with a man, especially one with his reputation for seducing women. However, she realized he would be a fool to try anything on his friend's sister. At least, she *hoped* he had those scruples.

"If you must know," she told him, "I was engaged three years ago, but my fiancé died in battle." Her throat tightened as memories swam in her head. It was like reliving that painful time all over again.

"Yes, I was informed about Adam Haddington's death. He was a brave man to have died in such a way."

She nodded as her throat tightened. Adam had been her hero in all ways. "You are very kind indeed."

"Are you being courted now?" he asked in a soft voice as his fingers trailed to her hand, rubbing small circles on her wrist.

For the nerve... Gasping, she yanked her hand away and stood. "That, my lord, is none of your concern."

He rose with her, still standing so very close that she could smell his manly scent, and especially his breath that smelled like grapes.

"Forgive me for intruding on your personal life, Miss Middleton. I was only trying to make small talk."

She was quite bored with their conversation and didn't have any qualms about ending it now. Besides, she needed to go to her bedchambers and lie down with a cold rag on her head in hopes of helping the headache pounding in her skull disappear.

As politely as she could, she smiled and gave him a nod. "I shall let you return to waiting for my brother so I can attend to other things. It was...um, *nice* to see you again, Lord Trenton. I hope you and my brother have a pleasant time during your ride."

He bowed. "And it was delightful to converse with you again, Miss Middleton." He stepped closer and placed his hand on her arm. "Please, tell me we can talk at another time. I'm very interested how you can paint so well. I've thought about trying my hand at the art, as well."

Was he jesting? She couldn't possibly meet up with him again, especially because of what she knew about his lifestyle.

"Perhaps one day." She withdrew from his touch. "Now, if you'll excuse me?"

Taking quick steps, Ellie moved away from him, heading for the stairs. Lord Trenton thinking *she* would want to spend more time with him was utterly ridiculous. As soon as she could rid herself of this headache, she would have to formulate a plan on how to find a good man to marry. And of course Vincent Wallace would not be on that list.

She reached the grand stairs and took two steps before pausing. Curiosity nudged her, and she couldn't stop from peeking over her shoulder toward him. The insipid man was actually watching her, with his mouth stretched wide in a sinful grin, no less.

Ellie grumbled under her breath and focused back on the steps as she headed toward her bedchamber. When she reached the second floor, curiosity got the best of her again, and she had to look to see if he was still watching. Sure enough, he had stepped closer to the stairs and stared up at her, grinning as if he enjoyed the view.

Her heart did a silly flip, so she hurried around the corner to remove herself from his sight. Although she was desperate for a man, she would *not* choose one with a sordid reputation for seducing women. That was all she needed, a husband who cheated on his marriage and embarrassed his wives.

"Trenton, my good man. Sorry to keep you waiting."

Her older brother's voice echoed from below, and she stopped in the hall. Once more, she was inquisitive and wanted to know why her brother had chosen to become friends with Vincent Wallace after all these years.

"No need to apologize," Vincent's deep voice replied. "Your sister kept me company."

Sucking in her breath, she flattened her back against the wall, waiting to hear her brother's reaction.

Laughter rang through the entryway, and she scowled. Her brother could be quite rude at times.

"Oh, I bet that was an interesting conversation," Dominic remarked.

She bunched her hands into fists and scowled. Her brother's sarcasm was inappropriate. He had never understood her and never would.

"Actually, it was very fascinating," Vincent said. "She has blossomed into quite a vision of loveliness."

Ellie's face warmed from the compliment, and at the same time, she wanted to throw it in her brother's face for being so inconsiderate. But that was what older brothers did, or at least that was what Dominic had done all her life.

"Oh my good man," Dominic said with laughter in his voice. "I'll forgive your blindness for now because I assure you, once you get to know her, you will think differently. She has a reputation of late for being an ice queen."

Ellie gritted her teeth. The nerve of her brother. No wonder their father was worried that she hadn't been married yet. Dominic probably started the rumors, which of course led to the earlier conversation with her father and Augusta.

"But enough about my sister," Dominic continued. "What is new with you, Trenton? How are you and your sisters faring since your father died?"

Immediately, Ellie pictured his sisters, who were at least five years younger. Their names were Laura and Lilly—twins.

"As it is," Vincent said, "I'm struggling to keep my father's estate running. Unfortunately, he was a poor gambler, and it's evident by the way he kept his manor. It has been a challenge to oversee my sisters' welfare because of problems with the estate."

Very interesting... Ellie peeked around the wall and down to the first level. Dominic and Vincent were almost to the front door. She wanted to hear more, but she didn't dare follow. It would be humiliating if Vincent caught her spying.

Once her brother and Earl of Trenton left the manor, she breathed a sigh of relief. Now she could get back to her sulking. However, her mind spun with ideas, which eased her pounding headache.

She hadn't been friends with Vincent's sisters, only because they were so much younger, though they were sweet girls. He had even been a charmer as a child, and that only worsened when he matured.

Sad to think Vincent came to obtain a title only to have very little funds to go with it. Ellie didn't know what their circumstances had been before he inherited an earldom, but he would certainly need funds in order for his sisters to have a decent dowry and marry well.

Ellie reached her chambers, and as soon as she stepped inside, her mind clicked. The realization nearly stunned her.

She had the money to help him out, and in return, he could help her with her situation. If she could convince him to marry her—knowing it would be in name only—she would be willing to help his sisters find husbands, as well. Not only would this help Vincent, it would save Ellie from being forced to marry someone like Edgar Stone.

Another thing that encouraged her was knowing Vincent Wallace's estate wasn't very far from here. She definitely needed to be close to home to continue doing what she'd done since her father married Augusta. If Ellie didn't watch the odd woman closely, who would? She suspected Augusta had married the duke for his money, because already she had spent a fortune.

Suddenly, the weight of panic eased from Ellie's shoulders, and she smiled. Indeed, this would work. Of course, with Vincent being a rakehell, she would have to tread lightly on his lifestyle and not get in the way. But she could live with that as long as he allowed her the freedom she required to do whatever her heart desired, and as long as he didn't know *everything* she did during the day.

Ellie nodded and rushed to her closet. Waiting for her brother and Vincent to return would be torture, but this would give her the time she needed to plan out how she could convince a rogue to marry her.

CHAPTER TWO

V INCENT'S MORNING RIDE was pleasant, but not as exciting as seeing Ellie Middleton again after all these years. He could scarcely recall his conversation with Dominic, yet Vincent remembered every word, every movement, and every time Ellie's eyes sparkled.

Confusion tugged him different ways inside his head. He couldn't decide if she was the angel his best friend, Adam Haddington, had once claimed her to be, or if she was truly Satan's own daughter and the *Ice Queen* that some men in Society had labeled her.

During their short conversation, he could see the haughty woman he'd always known her to be. He also detected a spark of fascination in her pretty brown eyes when she looked upon him. Being a rogue, his first reaction was to try to melt the Ice Queen to see if he could steal a kiss.

He'd been charming women since he was fourteen, so he knew when he had captivated a sweet maiden. From the rumors he'd heard, Ellie hadn't even looked at another man since her beloved had died. Vincent grinned. That made her ripe for the picking.

But since he blamed himself for Ellie's fiancé going off to battle and being killed, Vincent doubted she would want to have anything to do with him once she discovered the truth. Perhaps he just wouldn't ever tell her the connection he had with Adam Haddington, and pray she never found out.

For five months, he'd been so involved in his father's estate, and trying to repair the damages his parent had made before he died, that Vincent hadn't the time or the energy to woo a lady. Now that he was nearly penniless, at least the estate was livable. Vincent needed to find a way to make more money so that he could give his sisters a sizable dowry, which would hopefully entice a man to ask for their hands in marriage. Thankfully, Dominic had good advice on where to invest in speculations.

Without money, Vincent feared that his sisters would end up working for a living. Their parents—God rest their souls—had tried to give their children the best of everything. Unfortunately, they had never taught Vincent how to be a responsible guardian for his sisters. Failure from his accomplishments left a bitter taste in his mouth.

He stopped his horse and dismounted at the stable. The only stable hand that Vincent could afford hurried out to take the horse. Without a word, Vincent handed the man the reins before turning toward the manor.

Gently, he slapped the riding crop against his leg as his mind wandered back to Ellie Middleton. He would have to watch himself around the brunette beauty. She wasn't the type of woman he was used to charming, and because he was friends with her brother, that made her unattainable. And, of course, she was his friend's fiancée, which should make her completely inaccessible.

However, that was three years ago, and as long as Vincent could just tease the lovely woman, he would definitely try to see how things turned out between them. He would only pour on his charm just enough to tempt her, as long as he didn't completely *fulfill* his mission. At least it would bring some entertainment into his busy life of trying to make money and managing his sisters' lives.

As he entered the manor, the uplifting voices of his sisters captured his attention as they chatted excitedly. Another female voice entered their chipper conversation. Who could possibly have come to visit them this afternoon?

He quickened his step toward the sound of the flighty females, which led him to the drawing room. His sisters sat sipping their tea, and their visitor, who daintily held her teacup, was faced the other way so he couldn't ascertain her identity.

Laura saw him first. Her eyes widened, matching her smile. She stood and motioned for him to enter.

"Vincent, you're back. You will never believe who has come to pay us a visit."

The soft brunette ringlets framing the other woman's head looked familiar, as did her straight frame. He walked further into the room, and their guest placed her teacup on the side table before turning his way.

Stunned, he halted, and his breath caught in his throat. What was Ellie Middleton doing here?

She stood and curtsied. "Lord Trenton, it is good to see you again."

She wore a different dress this afternoon. The one she had on this morning gave her a more girlish appearance, but this one made her look like a desirable woman. The light green sensation with a white lace overlay covered her body and showed much more of her womanly figure. The bodice had a deeper square cut, giving him a glimpse of her ample bosom and the tops of her creamy shoulders.

"And it's good to see you again," he replied. He motioned to her chair. "Please sit and finish your tea with my sisters."

"Will you not join us?" Ellie asked sweetly.

A nudge in the back of his mind told him to tread carefully. The woman before him now was acting so different than she had this morning. Earlier, she couldn't wait to get out of his company, yet now she was practically begging him to stay.

"Regretfully, I must decline. I have budgets to add up in my books, and I just don't have time for this social visit."

Her bright smile dropped. Could she actually be disappointed that he was leaving?

"But please," he continued, "stay and visit with my sisters. It has been quite a while since they have had such delightful company."

Ellie nodded. "If you insist."

"I do." He glanced at his sisters. It was good to see happiness brightening their faces, especially given how forlorn their expressions had been of late. Although younger than Ellie by at least five years, Laura and Lilly still needed friends, no matter their age. Perhaps with Ellie's help, she would be able to reform his sisters into women. Heaven knew they needed female companionship. They dressed as though they were still in the schoolroom, instead of women in their nineteenth year.

He moved his attention to Ellie. He prayed she would want to assist him with his sisters. According to Dominic, Ellie didn't have much of a social life and spent most of her time in her room painting. That was probably why it surprised Vincent to see her at Trenton Hall. But he wouldn't question fate.

"Now, if you'll excuse me." He bowed to Ellie before leaving the room.

Conversation picked back up inside the sitting room, and the giggles from his sisters were heard all the way to his study. As he sat at his desk, he stared at the columns in the books, not seeing anything. Nothing registered in his head because his ears were fixed to listen to sounds of Ellie's laughter. Surprisingly, every time he heard the musical lilt of her voice, he sighed and smiled. And each time, he tried shaking her from his head so he could concentrate on his task. Unfortunately, it didn't work.

Was she doing this for show? His friend, Adam, had thought the sun and moon set with Ellie, yet now most men didn't want her to even look at her. Which woman was she really?

Time passed by quickly, and soon enough, the echo of women's heeled shoes clicked on the floor in the entryway. Vincent snapped out of the dreamlike state he'd been in since seeing Miss

Middleton, and jumped out of his chair. He rushed out of his study, and then stopped. He didn't want to interrupt his sisters as they said their goodbyes to their guest. And he definitely didn't want them to see him sneak out of the house to find Ellie before she left the grounds. Of course, he would have to make running into her appear accidental.

He waited until he was certain his sisters had gone upstairs before he darted out the side door. Ellie was at the stable as his servant assisted her into the buggy. Vincent slowed his steps, so she wouldn't think he was hurrying.

He walked to the broken-down fountain in the front of his yard and stopped. He studied the chipped stones and rubbed his chin, pretending to be in serious thought. The structure would be lovely once he could repair the damage. He trained his ears to listen for Ellie when her vehicle neared. Certainly, she would see him now.

Just as he had planned, she started on her way down the drive, but then pulled the single-horse buggy to a stop near Vincent.

"Lord Trenton," she called out.

Trying not to grin with satisfaction, he moved away from the fountain and strode her way. "Greetings again, Miss Middleton." When he stopped beside the buggy, he gave her a charming smile. "Did you have a pleasant visit with my sisters?"

"Indeed I did. I hardly recognized them from when I saw them last. It was a very good visit."

"I want to thank you for coming to see them. As I mentioned before, they don't receive many visitors. I'm certain they cherished the afternoon with you."

"Lord Trenton? Would you like to take a drive with me?" She patted the space next to her. "I feel the need to talk about your sisters with you, and how I might be able to help."

His hopes shot up, and he didn't hesitate to climb into the vehicle beside her. "I'll confess, I'm most eager to hear what you have to say."

She chuckled as she urged the horse on. "I'm pleased that I didn't have to beg you to ride with me."

"Oh, my sweet Miss Middleton." He casually slipped an arm behind her, resting it on the seat. "Turning a beautiful lady down is not something I do very well."

A teasing grin stretched her mouth. "Yes, that is what I've heard."

"Besides that"—Vincent waggled his eyebrows suggestively—"there might be other things you will have to *beg* me to do, and I look forward to that."

She laughed, but he could tell it was forced.

"You don't say," she said before returning her attention to the road.

"So, Miss Middleton, what was it that you wanted to discuss with me about my sisters?"

"I would like to help them prepare for the Season."

Vincent narrowed his eyes on the woman beside him. Was she a mind reader? But there must be something she needed in exchange. Why else would she want to help a rakehell? He couldn't wait to find out what it was.

"And how would you do that?" He scooted closer to her, keeping his arm resting on the seat behind her. He softly ran the tip of his fingers along her back. She didn't seem to mind, thankfully. "I'm not sure if you have heard the rumors, but thanks to my gambling father, I cannot afford a dowry for my sisters, so there really is no need for them to have a Season."

"I have heard that rumor, but I might have a solution for you."

She went silent as she guided the horse to a small meadow and stopped in the shade of a large oak tree. She sighed, hooked the reins over the rail, and turned toward him. Vincent wasn't certain he liked the look in her mischievous eyes.

"Miss Middleton, I find myself anxious to hear what you have to say."

"What I suggest will not only help you and your sisters, but it will be of great assistance for me, as well."

He nodded, suspecting there was a hidden meaning in all of this. "Continue."

She inhaled deeply, and as she released the air, her shoulders relaxed just a bit. "You are in need of funds to run your estate and to assist your sisters in obtaining a dowry. I can give that to you on one condition." She swallowed noisily. "I need you to become my husband, but in name only."

A small breeze blew against his face, and he thought something had lodged in his ear. He couldn't possibly have heard her correctly. "Beg pardon? Did you say you want me to become your *husband*?"

He waited for her to laugh or make some snide remark over what he thought he'd heard. Instead, she lifted her chin stubbornly and nodded.

"Yes, that's what I offer."

Confusion filled his head, and he leaned back, giving him more room to breathe. But her flowery scent billowed around him, dazing his mind momentarily. Marriage?

"Surely you jest, Miss Middleton."

"It's not a joke, my lord. I'm quite serious."

"Why would you want to marry me? I'm certain you've heard the rumors about my lifestyle."

"Indeed I have." She lifted her chin a notch higher and seemed to take a subtle breath. "However, I'm willing to overlook that. You need something which I have, and in return, I need you to marry me."

An indecent thought crossed his mind, and he hitched a breath. "Miss Middleton, are you perhaps…in the motherly way?"

A blush exploded across her face as she shook her head. "Absolutely not! How could you even think such a thing?"

Vincent shrugged. "Usually when women are desperate to marry, they are in that type of delicate condition."

"Well, I assure you, I'm not in that *condition*. Far from it, in fact." She fidgeted in her seat and twisted her hands in her lap.

"Lord Trenton, the truth is, my father is pushing me to marry within the month, and if I'm not wed, he will sign a marriage contract with my stepmother's nephew, Lord Stone." Her voice tightened, so she cleared her throat. "Needless to say, I'll do anything to keep from marrying him, even sink low enough to ask a rogue to become my husband."

Sink low enough? Vincent was certain she was being rude, but he wouldn't comment on it yet. "And you know no other man to ask to be your husband?"

She shook her head. "I haven't spent a lot of time in social circles since my fiancé died."

Dominic had mentioned this during their ride, but Vincent wasn't sure he believed it. Why would a beautiful, unmarried woman pine after a dead man for three whole years?

Nevertheless, Vincent couldn't accept her offer, as tempting as it was.

"I'm sorry for your plight, but I must deny your request. I enjoy being a rogue, and so I'm not likely to settle down with just one woman."

She blinked quickly. Did he detect tears in her eyes? Impossible.

"I have thought about that, as well," she said softly. "I shall give you leniency for your continued lifestyle as long as you promise to do it discreetly. And you must allow me to be my own woman, and let me do whatever I wish—as long as it's discreetly, of course."

"You...you want to have affairs behind my back?"

Her face reddened again. "Absolutely not!" She licked her lips. "All I wish is to be allowed to continue my painting and to visit my father's estate whenever I like."

For some reason, he didn't believe her. Why would any woman say such a thing? They wanted their husbands to be faithful, yet Ellie was being contradictory. Was there something else that she wasn't telling him?

"Let me get this straight." He adjusted himself in his seat.

"You will allow me to continue my affairs, while I allow you to run the household as you please, and paint to your heart's content?"

"Correct."

He studied her pretty face. She appeared to be quite serious, but he still felt there was something else she wasn't telling him. "Miss Middleton, does your brother know what you want to do? And what about your father? Does he know?"

She squared her shoulders. "They don't, and I would appreciate it if you would keep this a secret and not tell them, or anyone, for that matter."

"So you're saying that you want me to pretend to be in love with you, just as you'll pretend to be in love with me, to convince your family that we should wed?"

She lowered her attention to her hands again. "Yes, I suppose that is what we will have to do to make it believable."

By the way she squirmed slightly in her seat, he could tell how uncomfortable this subject made her. It made him squeamish, as well. If she had the courage to propose to *him*, Vincent was certain she would have the courage to do other things as well. Although he should refuse her again, he wanted to tease a little first. After all, he hadn't been classified as a rogue by mistake.

Vincent glanced toward the house, but they were far enough away that his sisters wouldn't see what he was about to do. He tried not to let the grin of excitement show on his face.

"Miss Middleton, what you say does have merit. However, I think we would have to be very convincing in order for your father to agree."

Her gaze snapped up. Panic showed on her face. "What...do you mean?"

Carefully, to not surprise her, he brought up his hand and gently cupped the side of her face. She stiffened, but she didn't pull away.

"I think we need to practice first. Don't you agree?"

"P-practice what, exactly?" Her voice shook.

"Practice staring into each other's eyes as if we are so in love that we forget about the rest of the world. I think we need to also practice the art of kissing."

She gulped down a hard swallow. "*Art* of kissing?"

"Yes indeed. Didn't you know kissing is considered an art form?"

"No."

"It is." He scooted closer. "Shall I teach you, my sweet lady?"

Beneath his palm, her skin grew hot, and he felt the throbbing of her heartbeat. Her breaths came faster, causing her lovely bosom to rise and fall quickly. Just seeing, and feeling, her emotions jumping inside her made him restless.

One of the things he enjoyed about seducing a woman was the first kiss. He cherished the little whimpering sounds they made as he kissed them, as well as feeling their bodies tremble from his gentle touch.

Vincent leaned his face closer to hers until her hot breath blew across his face. "Will you allow me to demonstrate the art of kissing, my precious?"

When her tongue sneaked out of her mouth and slid across her lips, his heartbeat jumped. She was going to let him, and he almost couldn't stand the wait.

"I-I suppose…if it's going to help us make it more believable."

"I assure you, it will." He slid his fingers along her jaw and tilted her face, positioning it for his takeover. Slowly, he guided his touch down her neck. She closed her eyes, and her lips parted.

As he placed his mouth over hers, he took things slowly. She sat very stiff, but the longer he moved his lips across hers, the more her body relaxed. Thunder pounded in his ears from the excitement of it all, but he didn't want to frighten her.

He withdrew, only enough to look into her eyes. They were closed, but slowly flickered open. Her mesmerizing coffee-colored gaze searched his. He couldn't see passion laced in her eyes yet, and he promised himself he would make her feel the excitement. Her curious stare told him she wanted more.

So, he would give it to her.

He wrapped his arms loosely around her as he captured her mouth again. Gradually, her body softened enough to press against him. Finally, she was willing and would allow him to continue. Being very gentle, he nipped at her bottom lip, and when her mouth opened wider, he slid his tongue inside. A tight sigh squeaked from her throat as she melted against him.

He tightened her in his embrace, holding her so very close to his body. Using his tongue, he tried to teach her how to kiss, and it seemed she was eager to learn. She hesitantly copied his movements, but within seconds, her actions became bolder. Excitement grew inside him, and now it was him who wanted more.

A throaty moan escaped her. His pulse beat faster, and he couldn't hold back the passion any longer. The kiss turned heated, and he yearned to touch her in a more personal way. Hoping not to upset her, he slowly slid his hand over her shoulder to rest on her bare neck. The silky smoothness of her skin felt wonderful beneath his fingers. The beat of her heart matched the same quick rhythm as his.

Vincent inched his palm down from her neck to her heaving bosom, but just as he neared the very thing he was after, she hitched a breath and pushed him away.

Dejected, Vincent kept calm instead of yanking her back into his arms as he wanted. What could have possibly made her interrupt his lessons? She seemed to be enjoying herself just as he was.

"Forgive me, but...I'm not ready for that." She took deep breaths as her attention flitted around them.

"I understand," he said, even if he didn't. "I won't rush you."

She licked her lips and adjusted herself in the seat as her trembling hands took hold of the reins, but she didn't urge the horse forward. Instead, she sat stiff and proper as she stared at the animal.

He really didn't know what else to say. The mood was broken, and he doubted he'd get it back. Perhaps the only thing to do now was let her down nice and easy while rejecting her proposal.

"So, Lord Trenton, are we in agreement, then?"

Her voice wobbled with uncertainty. Vincent really felt like a jackanapes for denying her, but he just couldn't go through with it. Even thinking about marriage made him feel suffocated. It was almost certain she would learn that he was responsible for her fiancé's death, and she would hate him.

He would have to find a different way to come up with the funds for his sisters' dowries.

Sighing, he shook his head. "As much as your offer sounds very tempting and would help out my sisters tremendously, I cannot accept your deal. I'm not the marrying kind of man, and I will never be."

Ellie's expression changed to confused, and then to hurt, and finally to anger. Her eyes darkened as she scowled.

"You knew all this time that you wouldn't accept? Yet you continued to kiss me…that way?"

He lifted one shoulder. "Pretty much, yes."

"Oh!" She slapped his chest. "You are the cruelest man I've ever met. I cannot believe I wanted your help. Indeed, I must have gone insane for a moment. Now get out of my buggy." She pointed toward the road. "And I never want to see you again."

Perhaps he deserved her anger. But it was a passionate kiss, nonetheless. For certain, he would think about her for quite a while, wondering if she would ever give him a second chance.

CHAPTER THREE

NOW ELLIE HAD exactly three weeks to find a man to marry. Why hadn't her father planned this startling news closer to the beginning of the Season? Perhaps then she could have found someone. Especially since Vincent Wallace had smashed and spat on her hopes. What had she been thinking to consider him? His reputation hadn't lied.

As her maid dressed Ellie for the upcoming ball tonight, she stared blankly at herself in the mirror. For one full week she hadn't been able to get Vincent's kiss—or his refusal—off her mind. Adam had been a wonderful kisser, but never had he been bold enough to do what Vincent had done.

Remembering the way the earl made her heart skip and left her breathless had been a shock to her system. Then, when he touched her neck and slid his hand down further, her body had wanted to know more of the sensual feelings awakening inside of her. Luckily, her mind argued and won, which was why she stopped him. She didn't ever want to forget about Adam, yet while kissing Vincent, the man she'd professed to love until her dying day had disappeared in her mind. She couldn't have that.

To add insult to injury, Vincent had had the audacity to turn down her offer. If that wasn't a slap in the face, she didn't know what was. At least he'd followed her wishes by not seeing her again. Thankfully, she'd only wasted one day on him, but she didn't have any energy to go into town and try to mingle, either.

Tonight would be different. Her family had plans to attend old Lady Cruthers' annual ball, which was a premier event of the Season. Ellie had missed it the past three years, but she couldn't miss it now. She prayed she found a man soon.

"I think you look mighty pretty in that gown, Miss Ellie." The maid beamed. "Do you want me to style your hair the same as I always do?"

Ellie opened her mouth to say yes, but her thoughts skidded to a stop and turned in a different direction. For her to catch a man's eye, she must not dress the same. She must dress more daring, just as she had when she went to Lord Trenton's home last week.

Stop thinking of him! Ellie pushed the image of his handsome face out of her mind and peered into the mirror at her maid. "Actually, I don't want ringlets. I want the bulk of my hair to be wound in a coil at the back of my neck, and small tendrils around my ears and underneath the bun. Also, I want baby's breath woven throughout my hair, but not overly so."

Her maid's eyes widened, and she nodded in approval as she followed Ellie to her vanity. Before sitting on the stool, she glanced over her gown, this time making certain it met the expectations she had for herself tonight. She must have been thinking straight when she picked it out, because the deep rose gown with a black lace overlay was perfect for tonight's occasion. Even the low, square-cut bodice fit perfectly with her mood. She would wear a pearl necklace with matching earbobs.

Tonight, she had only one goal in mind. She would flirt and tantalize every man she met. With any luck, she would find someone perfect to play the part of her husband.

Time passed quickly, and soon she entered the ballroom alongside her father and Augusta. Ellie's palms moistened inside her elbow-length black gloves as her heart raced with fear. She worried that she wouldn't find anyone, but most of all, she feared that she might see Vincent again. After all, he was now a noble, and probably attended functions like this to introduce his sisters.

Should she smile and act polite in front of him, or should she ignore him as if they'd never met? The latter seemed safer.

Ellie stood beside her father as he introduced her to everyone who greeted them. Her father's friends had available sons, and her dance card filled up quickly. More at ease now, she relaxed and tried to enjoy herself. Since she'd practically been a recluse for three years, it seemed odd to stand in gossip circles and pretend like she knew—or cared—what everyone was talking about.

Augusta stood next to Ellie as she forced a smile while listening to the henwits her stepmother considered friends. Ever since her father announced that he was going to wed Augusta, Ellie had kept a leery eye on the woman. The widow seemed too fake from day one. Her sweetness poured like molasses over Ellie, leaving her irritated. Honestly, she couldn't understand what her father ever saw in that woman. Ellie's mother had been the most beautiful, loving person, with a heart full of kindness for everyone. Not once had her mother acted fake. Not like Augusta.

"Did you hear about the Earl of Trenton?" one of the ladies in the group asked.

Ellie's mind snapped to the conversation. She couldn't help but travel back to the week she wanted to forget, but couldn't. Strange, but she could still smell his scent of pine and leather and hear his baritone voice as he laughed, as if he was standing right by her. If she could recall all of this, why then couldn't she remember how much she loathed him?

"Good evening, Lord Trenton," Augusta said. "I didn't know you were at the ball. It's nice to see you out and about now that you are settled into the estate."

Ellie snapped back to reality. What had her stepmother just said? She swept her gaze across the other ladies in the circle. Their attention was on someone standing behind her.

She spun around and faced the man she hadn't wanted to see.

Vincent was handsome in his fine black coat and matching

trousers. The dark blue waistcoat over his pristine white shirt and cravat made his blue-gray eyes twinkle.

Anger rose inside her. Why couldn't he have stayed home?

Wearing a ridiculously charming smile, he greeted all the women in the circle. Pausing, he met her stare and bowed.

"Miss Middleton. It's a pleasure to see you again. As always, you look ravishing."

She gritted her teeth. Why would he say *that*? Was that the very phrase rogues used when seeing a woman they had rejected recently? Well, two could play at his game. It was better to go along with him than to have the old biddies at the gathering wondering why Vincent made the duke's daughter upset.

She curtsied. "And may I say how handsome you're looking tonight? It's certainly good to see you again."

"Lord Trenton," old Lady Pratt said quickly, "why don't you mark your name on Miss Middleton's dance card? I'm certain she wouldn't mind saving a dance for you."

"Uh, well…" Vincent's gaze moved quickly between the older woman and Ellie.

She should let him suffer a few minutes longer, but she couldn't wait to throw her popularity in his face. "As enjoyable as dancing with you sounds, unfortunately, my dance card is full tonight. Perhaps next time."

He nodded. "Perhaps. Now, if you'll excuse me, I need to make introductions for my sisters."

"Enjoy your evening, Lord Trenton," Ellie said sweetly, although her words tasted bitter. "And give your sisters my regard."

"I will indeed." He turned and left the group.

Seething inside, Ellie bunched her hands into fists at her sides, she wished she could leave. She didn't want to talk to anyone, mainly because she was certain she'd spout her frustration at the situation her father had gotten her into. It was hard not to blame her sire, but instead, she must think positive. She would overcome this obstacle before another one crossed her path. And she was determined to get through this with her head held high.

"Lord Trenton is such a charming man, and very handsome," the elder Lady Bothwell said. "Don't you agree, Miss Middleton?"

She tightened her hands into fists. She certainly did *not* agree. "I suppose he is rather charming. But he's a rogue." She flipped her hand. "I would never want to be in his company for longer than a minute."

The other women in the circle giggled behind their fans.

"Oh, but Miss Middleton," Lady Langely said, "don't you know that reformed rakes make the best husbands?"

The henwits released another round of giggles. Ellie rolled her eyes and turned away from the bunch. She didn't care if reformed rakes were good husbands or not. Vincent was no longer in the running, since she'd scratched him off her list last week.

The dancing began, and her mind was kept busy as she tried to move her feet to the steps before they were stepped on by her partner. Unfortunately, she wasn't fast enough a few times.

She chatted with the men, but they all seemed to only focus on themselves. Couldn't *one* of them make her feel giddy—or at least as though she could become good friends with them after they were married? Apparently, she hadn't met that man yet.

The next dance paired her with other partners for a moment, which was nice, since she didn't have to think up a topic of conversation. Again.

For the first minute, she quite enjoyed herself, mainly because the movements were slower and her sore toes could relax just a bit. As she and Mr. Leslie moved to join another couple, her gaze landed on Vincent as he stepped from his dance partner to Ellie. Immediately, the hairs on the back of her neck rose, and she stiffened. His eyes locked with hers. The worst part was she couldn't read his expression. Was he happy to be dancing with her—if only briefly—or was he doing it to taunt her?

Finally, she was back with her partner, Mr. Leslie, and she breathed a sigh of relief. However, she couldn't stop her attention from moving toward Vincent and his dancing partner. Ellie wasn't certain she knew the woman, but she felt sorry for the young lady, especially because, knowing Vincent, he'd use her and then toss her aside like yesterday's leftovers.

Time passed quickly, and soon Ellie was partnered with Vincent again. Holding her breath, she hoped not to inhale his intoxicating and very seductive scent. But it didn't work as she'd wanted.

"Your anger is quite obvious, my precious," he whispered.

His precious? Inwardly, she seethed. She thought not!

"Forgive me, my lord," she said in a low voice, "but I'm not as skilled at performing as you are."

"Oh, so harsh, Miss Middleton." He grinned.

They traded partners again, yet she couldn't relax. Not until that man left the ball, which probably wouldn't happen soon enough. Now she prayed this particular dance would come to an end.

Ellie's wish was not granted, and she was again paired with Vincent too soon. This time, they had to hold hands as he walked her down the line. Would this torture ever end?

"So tell me," he said softly as he rubbed her gloved fingers with his, "have you found a man to marry yet?"

"That, my lord, is none of your concern. I'm sure you'll read a wedding announcement in the *Gazette* before the month is over."

"I'm certain I will."

How she hated it when he got the last word in. "What about you?" she quickly added. "Have you found the funds needed to give your sisters a dowry?"

"Not yet, but I haven't given up searching. I have joined a few speculations, and your brother assures me they will pay off soon."

"Then I wish you good fortune, because you're going to need it. My brother isn't very good at those type of investments."

She ended just at the right time, and was finally paired again with Mr. Leslie. Thankfully, the dance ended soon afterward, and she didn't have to talk to—or touch—Vincent any more.

Exhausted, her feet aching, she didn't want to dance the next reel. She begged her partner to let her rest a spell. He was kind and fetched her a glass of punch, allowing her to sit while they chatted. This meant so much more to her because she actually got to know him a little better without interruptions. Mr. Aaron Hobart was the second son of an earl, but didn't have a title, although he had an inheritance. Right away her mind drifted to another earl she knew…

She mentally shook *that man* out of her thoughts and concentrated on Mr. Hobart. He seemed to have better manners than the others she'd danced with tonight, and although he wasn't outright humorous, he did put her at ease. It wasn't hard to picture him as her husband.

Gradually, Ellie could see a light at the end of her dismal tunnel of husband hunting.

VINCENT COULDN'T TAKE his eyes off Ellie. She was absolutely stunning tonight. No longer did she look like Dominic's younger sister, with freckles scattered across her nose, dirty shoes, and a wrinkled dress, as he'd remembered from their youth. Now she resembled a *real* woman, but not the kind that was easily seduced.

Ellie looked elegant in her red gown. Of course, he knew why she'd dressed this way. She wanted to attract men, which was definitely working. However, Vincent was willing to bet that most of the men who danced with her tonight didn't know how innocent she really was—since Vincent had firsthand knowledge of that.

He tipped a flute of champagne to his mouth and sipped slowly as he watched her sitting with Mr. Hobart, in deep conversation. So far, her dance partners had been a boorish lot, but from the sparkle of interest in her eyes, Vincent could tell she was going to get to know Mr. Hobart much better.

A twisting knot started in his stomach, and the longer he studied the two, the harder the knot tightened. This would not do! He should ask questions about Hobart and discover if this man would be a good fit for Ellie. After all, Vincent knew what lengths women would go to because of desperation.

He tore his attention from the pair and searched for someone who might know about Hobart. Lord and Lady Campbell stood close by. Vincent grinned. Lady Campbell loved to gossip, and during a recent fox hunt, Lord Campbell had enjoyed telling everyone what he'd heard from his wife.

Vincent strode toward them and greeted them with a bow. He started up a conversation about hunting, and at that point, Lady Campbell excused herself and walked away.

When Lord Campbell paused, Vincent decided to ask the question on his mind. "My lord, what do you know about Mr. Aaron Hobart?"

The middle-aged man with a rotund belly raised a brown, bushy eyebrow. "Hobart, you say?"

"Yes, the Earl of Whitehouse's second son."

"The earl is a fine chap." Campbell nodded as he linked his fingers together across his wide middle. "Hobart is a good hunter. He takes after his father, you know."

"I'm sure he does." Vincent chuckled. "Can you tell me why he's not yet married?"

The other man quickly glanced around them before leaning toward Vincent. "From what my wife says, Hobart spends too much time at the gaming tables. Apparently, he's looking for a wealthy wife and won't settle for anything less." The lord took another glance around. "But if you ask me, he'll never be sober enough to find the right woman, even if she's naïve enough to fall for his charms."

Vincent bunched his hands. Ellie was certainly the perfect target for Hobart. Unfortunately, the gambler would have all her money spent within a year or two. She didn't deserve a husband like that.

Perhaps he should warn her. Suddenly, an odd emotion filled him. It was if he could feel his friend staring down from heaven toward Vincent, encouraging him not to let Hobart win. Indeed, Vincent would be a heel if he didn't say something to Ellie.

But she was upset at him. Would she even listen to reason? Vincent's father was a prime example that men should *not* gamble away their money.

When the topic died down, Vincent excused himself and made his way through the crowd toward Ellie and Hobart. The dance would end soon, so he really only had a few minutes to make a comment before the next man claimed a dance from her.

Ellie didn't see him coming, but Hobart did. As Vincent came closer, he nodded. "Hobart? Will I see you at White's tonight? There's another big game with high stakes planned this evening." Vincent winked. "And, of course, plenty of bourbon. Just the way you like it."

"Um…of course." Hobart's face reddened.

Vincent took a quick peek at Ellie. Her cheeks were crimson as well, but it wasn't embarrassment that lit up her face. Her glare nearly burned right through him. It hurt to think he'd upset her again, but this particular situation had to happen in order to keep her from falling into the gambler's clutches.

Without saying another word, Vincent continued through the crowd until he found an empty space against the far wall. This would be a perfect place to keep an eye on his sisters, who, thankfully, had full dance cards, and to watch Ellie to see what other man she might take an interest in.

Two dances later, Ellie made her way on the dance floor with Lord Pettingill. Vincent didn't need to ask Lord Campbell about this particular man. Pettingill was worse of a rake than Vincent, if that were possible. Just last year, he had tried to seduce one of Vincent's sisters, before he even had a title. Thankfully, Vincent stopped the flirtation before the man could ruin Lilly's reputation. After that, Vincent kept his eyes on Pettingill—and the rakehell seduced three other women within a month.

Another little tidbit he'd learned about Pettingill was that he charmed wealthy women into buying him gifts or paying off his debts.

Vincent studied Ellie's expression while she danced and chatted with Pettingill. Her eyes lit up, and she smiled. Dead giveaway that she was thinking about making this man her next conquest. But Vincent couldn't say anything to her in front of the other lord. So how could he go about letting her know that Pettingill wasn't worth her time?

"Oh, Vincent." Lilly grasped his arm, jerking him out of his concentration. "I'm having the most wonderful time. I'm so happy you decided to bring us with you to the ball tonight."

Vincent smiled at his sister. She looked pretty this evening with her lavender gown and her hair done up fancy. But it was the enjoyment on her face that brightened her countenance considerably.

"I'm glad you're having a good evening. I don't want to dampen your spirits, but look over there and see who else is at the party." He nodded in Ellie's direction.

Lilly rose on her tiptoes to look across the crowd. When she saw Pettingill, she gasped. "Oh no! That rake is flirting with Miss Middleton. We must stop it." She tugged on his arm. "Vincent, you must say something to her."

"Actually, I think it's best if she hears it from you, since you were his victim at one time."

Her eyes widened. "Really? You think that is wise?"

"I do, but wait until Pettingill leaves before you say anything to Miss Middleton."

Lilly fidgeted next to him as she aimed her glare at the other lord. Vincent tried not to grin too wide. Pettingill didn't deserve a sweet woman like Ellie. Vincent would like nothing more than to see him forced to wed a penniless waif because he'd seduced her. That would serve the man right.

"They are done dancing," Lilly whispered. "I'll go over and tell her now, before her next partner comes to claim a dance."

Vincent nodded. He flexed his hands by his sides as he watched Ellie to see what she'd do when Lilly came to her.

Ellie's caring smile lit up her face as she took hold of Lilly's outstretched hands in greeting. Lilly leaned into Ellie and whispered something in her ear. Slowly, the lovely smile on Ellie's face disappeared, and by the time Lilly pulled away, both women were frowning.

Something peculiar squeezed inside his chest. His first reaction was to hurry to Ellie and take her outside, to get away from all of the men who were wrong for her, until he realized that *he* was one of those men. He should be satisfied in knowing he was the reason Pettingill wouldn't snatch her up. So why wasn't he happy about it?

Lilly walked away from Ellie. Within moments, she looked slowly around the room. Before her gaze came toward him, he looked away. Would she know he had asked Lilly to tell her about Pettingill? If Ellie asked, he'd admit to it. There was no shame in confessing to want the best for the duke's daughter.

"There you are, hiding in the corner."

A woman's sultry voice snapped Vincent out of his thoughts. Standing in front of him was one of his former mistresses, Lady Livingston—Candace. They'd parted ways as friends, but every so often she reentered his life and tried to sway him to come back. He never did, mainly because he was with a different woman at the time.

Smiling, he took her hand and brought it up to place a kiss on her knuckles. "Lady Livingston, the sight of you takes my breath away."

Although the words were practiced, they weren't true this time. Candace was a very lovely woman who'd been widowed for six years. She appeared the same as when he saw her last, still wearing expensive gowns and costly jewelry, but he could honestly say that no longer was she the loveliest woman he had ever seen. And it seemed her waist had thickened slightly. Laziness could do that to a person. Why he'd said that she took his breath away, he didn't know.

Immediately, Ellie popped into his mind, making his heart soften. Now *she* was the woman who took his breath away.

As quickly as the thought came, he ushered it out. He shouldn't be having thoughts like this about her.

Candace chuckled sensually as she slowly pulled her hand away, purposely sliding her fingers against his palm in a suggestive manner. "Oh, Vincent. You always say the sweetest things."

"It's good to see you. What have you been doing since I saw you last?" he asked.

She waggled her eyebrows. "Trying to replace you, my dear man."

He widened his eyes in shock. "You're still trying? Whatever for?"

"Come now, Vincent. You know you're one man that's not easily forgotten."

He laughed. No woman had ever told him that. "How interesting that you would think such a thing when you go through men almost as fast as I go through women."

"Vincent, have you forgotten how many times I've told you how *special* you are to me?"

He arched an eyebrow. "If you say so."

Candace looked away from him and put her focus directly on Ellie. He held his breath. She must have been watching him long enough to know whom he'd been absorbed in since arriving at the ball.

"I see that Miss Middleton has captured your interest."

He swallowed hard. "She has?"

Candace turned her attention back on him and narrowed her eyes. "Don't play coy with me, my good man. I know you well enough to know when you've targeted a fair maiden to be your next seduction."

He laughed forcefully, mainly because he didn't want Candace knowing the truth. "You think you can read my mind, eh?"

She patted his arm. "Let me relay a little tidbit I learned from her fiancé, Lord Adam Haddington."

"Adam?" The surprise rushing through him lifted his voice. "You knew Adam?"

"I knew him quite nicely, in fact." She winked.

"While he was engaged to Miss Middleton?" Vincent would never believe Adam could have cheated in any way on Ellie.

"No. Once they were engaged, he stopped coming around. However, while he courted her, he told me a few things about the duke's daughter."

It really was none of Vincent's business, so why was he so curious? "Like what, exactly?"

Candace released a deep, throaty laugh. "Adam said she had two personalities. He never knew from day to day what kind of woman she was going to be."

Vincent scowled. He could hardly believe that. "I'm shocked, my lady, especially since Adam was a good friend of mine, and he spoke highly of Miss Middleton."

"To you he did, but he never did love her. He was only marrying her for her dowry."

Another pang shot through Vincent's chest. That couldn't be right, could it? His irritation emerged, and he wished his friend was still alive so that Vincent could throttle him. How could Adam be so cold-hearted? And how could Adam have lied to Vincent, his so-called best friend?

He licked his dry lips. "As you know, men marrying for ladies' dowries isn't that uncommon."

"You are exactly right. That's why Lord Livingston married me." Candace rubbed the palm of her hand down Vincent's chest. "Which brings me to another topic."

Now what did she want? "Which is?"

"Vincent, have we not always been honest with each other?"

Most of the time... "Of course."

"Then let's not stop now. I came here tonight hoping to find you."

He eyed her suspiciously. "Why would you do something like

that?"

"Because I have a very delicious proposal to offer you."

Delicious? Apparently, she wanted to be his mistress again. Either that or she'd learned how to cook and wanted to make him some tasty meal. But he really didn't believe *that.* "I cannot wait to hear what it is."

"Shall I drop by your manor tonight after the ball so we can discuss it?"

He hesitated in answering, only because his sisters didn't need to see Lady Livingston coming to see him in the dead of night. "Actually, no. I shall come to your townhouse."

She laughed seductively. "I'm not at my townhouse. I'm in my country estate. You've been there, remember?"

"How could I forget?" he said convincingly. As he searched his memory, he struggled to find the one where he had been with her at the estate.

"I had an All Hallows' Eve party there." She arched an eyebrow. "Now do you remember?"

Inwardly, he sighed. He recalled the day vividly. Many people were invited to her party, yet she had singled him out to be her next conquest. "Of course I remember."

Smiling, she reached up and patted his cheek gently. "I shall see you later, then."

"Yes, you shall," he said softly, hoping nobody around them could hear.

She lowered her eyelids and batted her eyelashes at him as she waved her fan. The heavily perfumed aroma that always clung to her went with her as she left. Although he already knew his answer to her *proposal,* curiosity got the better of him, and he wondered if there was more to her offer. And, by chance, did it have anything to do with his being an earl now?

It wasn't hard to notice how differently people treated him now that he was an earl. He'd brought his sisters here in hopes that each could catch some man's eyes, and it surprised him when both sisters had filled up their dance cards. But it also worried him. Men would expect some kind of dowry, which Vincent could not provide, yet. With any luck, Dominic's suggestions would pay off soon. Dominic had found the best speculations and had earned quite a bit of money himself.

Vincent relaxed against the wall and searched for Ellie on the dance floor. She wasn't there. Feeling a little panicked, he straightened and glanced over the crowd to find her. She was gone, but her parents were still here.

Not far away, he noticed Lilly chatting with some friends. He stepped around some couples to get to her, then took her by the arm and pulled her closer to whisper in her ear. "Where is Miss Middleton?"

When he pulled back, confusion was written on his sister's face. "When I left her, she said she was going to talk to you." She glanced around them. "Didn't she come?"

His heart dropped. If Ellie had come this way, she would have seen him with Lady Livingston. What were the chances that Ellie had overheard?

Inwardly, he groaned. He hoped that wasn't the case.

CHAPTER FOUR

ELLIE ELBOWED HER way through the crowd, praying nobody would detect the tears swimming in her eyes. She needed fresh air before she became sick. The events of the last hour were enough to cause any woman to go insane. Especially because Vincent Wallace was involved.

She made it to a side door and hurried through it before anyone could stop her. She was certain her father or Augusta would be searching for her soon, especially when her next dance partner wouldn't be able to find her. But it didn't matter. She couldn't stay in that room one moment longer without screaming.

After Lilly had come to tell her about Lord Pettingill, Ellie's anger had surfaced—again—and this time she wasn't just going to brush it away as she had when Vincent ruined her conversation with Mr. Hobart.

The nerve of that man! Why couldn't Vincent just let her be? He obviously didn't want to be her husband in name only, so why was he trying to destroy her chances with other men?

Ellie slowed her steps to not attract attention from the others who were strolling in the moonlight on the back terrace. There was too much lighting out here on the walkway to find privacy. She needed to find someplace where she could hide so that others wouldn't see her anguish.

Phrases drifted through her mind from what she'd overheard

when she came upon Vincent and Lady Livingston. Ellie's heart wrenched, and she held her breath, trying to keep from crying. He wouldn't accept her offer, yet he would meet the widow later tonight to hear *her* offer? Ellie wasn't completely naïve. She knew exactly what that woman wanted from Vincent. And the fool appeared eager to get it.

Finally, she found a grove of trees where nobody stood around, a place where she could hide and release her frustrations. She pressed her forehead against the trunk, brought her knuckles to her mouth, and allowed her sobs to break free. Her body shook as she thought of everything that had happened to her lately. It was her own fault for being this emotional. She shouldn't have expected Vincent to eagerly accept her bargain. She figured he would be jumping at the chance to help his sisters—and her, of course. It hurt to know how wrong she'd been.

She especially berated herself for enjoying his kiss a week ago. Why had she done that when she was still very much in love with Adam? But then, Vincent was a scoundrel of the worst kind. He had taken advantage of her weakness—of her innocence. She'd been an utter fool.

Behind her, the leaves of the bushes rustled, but before she had time to wipe the tears from her eyes, two strong hands grasped her shoulders and pulled her away from the tree, pressing her face against a muscular chest. She didn't need to look at the man's face to know who it was. His familiar, masculine pine scent had left an imprint in her memory, which would probably be hard to erase.

"Shh…" Vincent said in a quiet voice. "Don't cry, my precious."

Her heart twisted again. Why did he keep calling her that endearment? She most certainly wasn't *his* precious.

Taking in a deep, slow breath, she tried to collect her wits before she spoke. If she said anything now, she'd just cry all over again.

His warm palms drew small circles on her back as he gently pulled her closer. Although their embrace was most improper, it was also, in an odd way, comforting. Her mind clogged with confusion. Why did she feel this way? What happened to the hatred she had for him only moments ago?

He was silent, except for his breathing, which brushed the top of her head, and slowly moved down to her ear. A shiver ran through her, which confused her more, since she wasn't cold. But when his lips swept over her temple, she hitched a breath. What was he doing? Was this some kind of seduction? Well, she'd show him his tactics weren't going to work this time.

She lifted her head and gasped. He was entirely too close. Shadows played across his face, making him that much more handsome.

"Are you feeling better?" Tenderness coated his voice.

She expelled a breath as she tried to collect her senses before they went flying all over the place. She wished she could see his eyes, but even those were darkened with shadows. He continued to hold her against his body, and of course inhaling his scent like this made her legs weak.

"I'll be fine once you move away," she finally said, thankful her voice didn't crack.

His mouth stretched wide. "I'm happy to see that your energetic personality has returned."

"Please." She pressed her hands against his chest to push him away. She was only able to take one step back because his arms were locked around her waist. "I don't know why you came to find me, but I wish you'd return inside. I want to be by myself. Can't you see that?"

"What if I want to talk to you first?"

"I'd rather you didn't."

He stroked her cheek. "Lilly mentioned that you wanted to say something to me earlier. Will you tell me what it was?"

Her memory returned in a disturbing flash. Vincent had stood so close to Lady Livingston—a woman with a sordid reputation, no less—and her hand rested on his chest. The look of lust in the woman's eyes resurfaced in Ellie's mind, and to make it worse, Vincent had held the same expression while looking at the widow.

Ellie's gut twisted again. "It's not important any longer."

"Why?"

She rolled his question over in her head. Why wasn't it important? Was it because of what she'd heard him and the widow discussing so seductively? She tried pushing aside the pain from his refusal and focusing on why he had made her upset tonight.

Finally, anger rose inside of her, and she felt more like herself again. She yanked herself out of his arms and took another step back.

"Fine. I shall tell you what was on my mind." She folded her arms and glared. "You have no right trying to ruin my chances with other men. When you refused my offer, I moved on. Why can't you let me find another man to become my husband before my father signs the betrothal papers with Lord Stone?"

Slowly, Vincent nodded as he tapped his finger on his chin. "I understand now. You thought I was trying to interfere when I was only trying to help. I realized you didn't know about those gentlemen, which was why I stepped in. Forgive me for trying to save you from a bad marriage. I didn't want you to be with men who didn't put their love for you first in their lives."

She huffed and stamped her foot. "Why can't you understand that I don't care about love? I gave my heart away a few years ago. There is nothing left of my heart to give to another man. I just want to find a way to keep from being wed to Augusta's nephew. If you knew Edgar, you'd know why I don't want him in my life."

He nodded again. "I've seen Lord Stone strike a woman across the face."

"Which is why I don't want to be living with him as his wife."

Vincent continued to gaze at her, even though she couldn't see his eyes. She wished she could read his expression. Had she finally gotten through to him? Would he leave her alone now?

"I do understand, Ellie. But I also wish you would understand *me*. You are too special to be tied to a horrible husband. That's why I tried to scare you away from Pettingill and…um, that other one."

She rolled her eyes. "Mr. Hobart."

"Oh yes. That's the bloke." Vincent stroked his thumb against her chin before slowly trailing it toward her lips. "I'm not sure you understand the purpose of marriage, my precious. You may want to marry a man in name only, but men wed to have heirs. Even if you convince yourself it's in name only, I assure you, the man you marry will eventually want to consummate the marriage. He will want a child to carry on his name and title. There is no way he would be immune to your beauty for very long before giving in to his desires."

Her face heated from this very improper topic. She should *not* be discussing this with Vincent. However, her mind started clicking, and a question lurked on her tongue. "Is that why you turned my offer down?"

She wished she could see his eyes. Were they filled with panic right now? She just hoped he told her the truth.

After a few uncomfortable moments of silence, he cleared his throat and dropped his hand. "Yes, I suppose that's why I refused. I'm not ready to settle down and have heirs. And just like you, I'm not ready to fall in love."

She sighed heavily. Finally, he let her know his feelings. At least she was relieved he hadn't turned her down because she was hideous or because he didn't like the way she'd kissed him. "Yes, you are correct, Vincent. Eventually, a married man will want to beget heirs. I'm happy to know that's what you were truly thinking when you turned me away."

"Of course it was." He rubbed his palms down her arms before grasping her fingers. "I do still care about you, and I don't want to see you get hurt, which was why I stopped you from getting to know those other two men."

Although she should yank her hands out of his grasp, she kept them there. Why did it feel so comfortable when she knew it shouldn't? "Tell me, Vincent, are you going to help me find my future husband? Is that what your purpose is here tonight? It's obvious that you aren't here to help your sisters find beaus. If you were, you wouldn't be standing in the shadows under a tree with me right now."

He chuckled and brought one of her gloved hands to his mouth, kissing her knuckles. "You wish me to help you find a husband?"

She shrugged. "If you are going through the effort of trying to scare them away, you may as well assist me in finding the *right* man. It would be less work for you. Perhaps you could introduce me to some of your friends."

He laughed again and lowered her hand, but he continued to cradle it in his strong grasp. "I really don't have many friends who are searching for a wife."

"You are friends with my brother."

His brows lifted. "Forgive me, my precious, but I don't think it's proper to marry your brother."

She huffed. "Of course it's not. I was just pointing out the fact that you *do* know men who are available for marriage."

"Not as many as you'd think. Besides, the ones I know are rogues."

"Like yourself?"

He barked out a sudden laugh. "Yes indeed, but worse."

"You think they are worse because none of them actually care about the women they try to seduce?"

His smile vanished. "I didn't exactly seduce you, Ellie."

"I said *tried* to seduce."

Vincent released her hands and stepped toward the tree into the shadows a little deeper. He pushed his fingers through his hair. "I suppose I should apologize for that."

She hiccupped a laugh. "You *suppose?*"

"Fine." He nodded and faced her. "I shall apologize now.

Please forgive me for convincing you to kiss me."

"Sorry, Vincent. I won't accept that apology."

"Forgive me for making you curious about kissing me. Is that better?"

"Actually, no." She braved a step closer to him. "Tell me, Vincent. Did you feel guilty for leading me to believe you were going to accept my offer?"

Seconds ticked by without his answering. He blew out a rush of air from his mouth, breaking the silence.

"I'll admit I said that because I wanted to kiss you. Actually, I wanted *you* to kiss me."

For some silly reason, her heartbeat skipped as flutters jumped in her belly. Why wouldn't these sensations go away? She didn't want to feel them for *him*. "You wanted me to kiss you before you refused me?"

"Yes."

"Because you knew you wouldn't get a chance afterward?"

His smile grew. "Exactly."

"An experienced rogue, such as yourself, couldn't allow the moment to pass without having a very passionate kiss with an innocent woman, am I right?"

His smile shifted, one side lifting higher than the other. Oh how she wished she could see what emotions played in his eyes.

In one large step, he stood in front of her again—a mere breath away. He cupped the side of her face. Why she didn't stop him, she didn't know. Maybe it was because of the way her heart sped faster with excitement. Or it was the way she detected his fast breaths as they fanned her face.

"You thought the kiss we shared was *very* passionate?" he asked in a low voice.

She swallowed the lump of dryness that had suddenly formed in her throat. Even her mouth became parched. "Um, well…didn't you think that it was?"

Slowly, he nodded. "But I'm relieved that you thought the same way."

Goodness! He was leaning closer to her. He couldn't possibly want to kiss her again, not after what happened the last time. And even if he did, she couldn't allow it.

So then why couldn't she tell him to stop?

Before she knew what she was doing, she licked her dry lips in preparation for the moment his mouth fused with hers. All words disappeared in her head, and the only thought crossing her mind was whether he would kiss her. And if she would enjoy it as much as their first time.

Of course you will, silly!

Yet she must push him away. If she allowed his kiss, he'd hurt her all over again. Unless…

Perhaps if she just pretended that this kiss was going to teach her how to woo men, maybe her heart wouldn't be affected. She must think of this as part of her education.

She gulped, trying to moisten her throat. "I-I haven't stopped thinking about it."

A groan escaped his throat as he closed the space between them and placed his mouth over hers. Immediately, he wrapped his arms around her shoulders, pulling her against him. She didn't fight it. She didn't want to. Instead, she slid her hands up his chest and linked them around his neck.

He kissed her differently this time. Wilder. More passionate. She almost couldn't keep up. His mouth slanted back and forth over hers. His hot, velvety tongue slid into her mouth, causing the most sensitive tingles to shoot through her body. His hands moved over her back just as fast as if he searched for something he couldn't quite find.

Breathless, she copied his actions. Never had she been kissed in this manner. And heaven help her, but she liked the out-of-control feeling. Vincent made her feel desirable. Wanted.

However, he didn't want her. And realistically, she didn't want him, either.

The thought destroyed all the passion building inside her. She felt as if she'd jumped into a river in the dead of winter…naked.

She couldn't allow these feelings to rush through her like this. There must be a way to temper these emotions when they were together.

Turning her head, she broke the kiss. "No, Vincent. This cannot happen."

He kept her in his arms, and his breathing was as heavy as hers. After a few moments, his arms loosened, and she stepped back.

"Forgive me. I was caught up in the moment."

"Yes, I know how you feel, but…I cannot let this go on."

He nodded.

She took a deep breath and released it slowly. Once she composed herself, she straightened her shoulders and faced him. "I suppose the dancing is about over."

"I'm sure it is."

She cleared her throat. "My father and stepmother are probably wondering where I am, so I'd better go."

"Indeed."

"And of course you have a widow you'll be meeting soon, so you should be on your way."

His head snapped up, and he peered at her. "How do you know about that?"

"I overheard."

His eyes widened. "How much did you hear?"

"Enough to know you'll be meeting her after the ball. But not to worry, I don't plan on stopping you." She couldn't halt the anger rising to her head, and especially the ache piercing her body. Her head throbbed with so many different emotions. "I just hope her offer is better than mine."

Before he could stop her, she spun around and hurried toward the walkway. Just as she reached the edge of the trees, he grasped her arm.

"Ellie, no. I won't allow our conversation to end this way."

Her heart wrenched—an emotion she was tired of having around him. "Please release me, Vincent. There is no reason for us to end our conversation differently."

"No, you're wrong. I need to know that you don't hate me."

She threw him a glare. "Why? What do you care? You'd rather be with a woman like Lady Livingston." She nodded toward the manor. "So please, begone. I don't want to be the reason she falls asleep waiting for you."

"Ellie, please." Vincent's voice wavered. "Don't do this."

Because they were closer to the light, she could see his eyes a little better. Perhaps it was better that they moved into the shadows again. Seeing the confused pain written on his face was not good for her self-control.

⟫⟪

VINCENT COULDN'T UNDERSTAND his own thoughts. All he knew was that he didn't want Ellie to loathe him. Whether it was guilt over Adam's death or not, there was something deep inside his mind that commanded him to make amends. Even the twisting of his gut influenced his actions.

"Ellie, I want us to be friends. Isn't that what you want too?"

Her gaze bored into his. There was his answer. Yet he wouldn't accept it.

"Why is it so important for us to be friends?" she asked in a tight voice.

"Because we were once childhood friends, and I'm still chums with your brother." He wasn't about to bring up the subject of Adam.

"No, Vincent." She took a step toward the lit pathway. "It has to be more than just that."

In silence, he searched his mind and his heart. Something urged him to tell her about Adam, even though he was reluctant. But perhaps by bringing up the man they had in common, her mind would be eased. Of course, what he truly desired was taking her back into his arms and kissing her to distraction.

He sighed. "It is not often I make enemies with women I have shared a passionate moment with."

Ellie rolled her eyes. "Then count me as the first."

She yanked her arm away from him and stepped out of the shadows and into the pathway leading to the terrace. But when she came to a sudden stop, he moved closer to see what had grabbed her attention. When he recognized the fierce expression of her father, Vincent's world slowly crumbled around him. It was as though he stood on the brink of a collapsing bridge that would break and take him down into the deep unknown.

The older man's arms were crossed over his wide chest, but it was the disappointed scowl that Vincent didn't like. Warning bells rang through his head. Should he run, or at least try to create some kind of excuse to get out of this mess? Although his mind scrambled with plausible excuses to give the duke, his voice refused to work.

"F-Father?" Ellie's voice shook.

The duke's glare switched from his daughter to Vincent. The longer the seconds ticked by, the smaller he felt. His chest tightened, making it harder to breathe.

The duke motioned toward the grove of trees. "Shall we have a private conversation?"

His gaze stayed mostly on Vincent during that question. Helplessly, he nodded. A low groan came from Ellie as she turned and strode back into the shadows. Vincent had no other choice but to follow her. His mind scrambled once more to grasp something intelligent to say, yet he had never been in this situation before, and he didn't know how to get out.

Ellie's eyes were downcast as she wrung her hands against her middle. Vincent gulped, trying to moisten his suddenly dry throat. This hadn't worked as he had planned. Apparently, *nothing* was going the way he had intended.

"Correct me if I'm wrong," the duke said quietly, breaking the uncomfortable silence, "but did I just overhear you and my daughter admit to sharing a passionate moment?"

Vincent tried swallowing again, but the blasted lump in his throat wouldn't budge. "Well, you see, my lord—"

"The truth, Trenton." The duke's voice became stronger.

"We did share a kiss, my lord."

"Just now?" The older man arched an eyebrow. "In this grove of trees?"

"Yes," Vincent said, and Ellie chimed with the same dismal reply.

The duke's glare moved between Vincent and Ellie again. His mouth pulled tight in irritation as his nostrils flared. Vincent had never felt so defenseless as right now.

"You do know what this means, don't you?" Ellie's father asked her.

Meekly, she lifted her watery gaze to her father and nodded. "I do."

Inwardly, Vincent groaned. He knew what it meant, too.

"This is what I propose," the duke continued, linking his hands behind him as he paced in front of Vincent and Ellie. "Lord Trenton will court Ellie for an entire week, taking her out in public so Society isn't surprised when I announce my daughter's wedding." He stopped in front of Vincent. "Does this sound reasonable? I'd rather do it this way than force you to marry my daughter and live through the scandal that will follow."

"Ye—" Vincent choked on the words, so he quickly cleared his throat. "Yes, my lord. That option does appear the better choice."

The duke swung around and faced Ellie. "Is this acceptable to you as well?"

She kept her gaze on the ground. "Yes, Father."

"Splendid." He clapped his hands once. "Then let us get back to the party now that the dancing has ended."

Ellie didn't meet Vincent's eyes as they walked behind her father. Vincent felt as if he'd been in front of a magistrate and been condemned for his crimes. But living as Ellie's husband wasn't exactly torture, was it? His heart argued with his mind. Of course it was. The whole time he would feel guilty about his part in her fiancé's death. He'd fear the moment when she discovered it and would forever loathe him.

Not only that, he wouldn't be able to touch her, since she only wanted a marriage in *name only*. How could he live the rest of his life as a monk?

Inwardly, he groaned. He was doomed.

CHAPTER FIVE

E LLIE DIDN'T KNOW if she was happy or sad.

Her heart danced with happiness knowing that her father wouldn't force her to marry Augusta's dreadful nephew, yet at the same time, pain of remorse squeezed her heart at knowing a man was being forced to marry her. That wasn't what she had wanted. If only Vincent would have accepted her bargain in the first place, they could have entered the marriage on their own terms.

She couldn't sit still as she waited for Vincent to pick her up for a ride in the park. Her father thought that would make a good start for beginning her week of being courted. Augusta sat calmly on her rose cushioned chair while she sewed on a sampler, but Ellie wanted to scream. She wrung her hands, flexed them, shook them, and wanted to nibble on her fingernails, but she didn't dare because she would be reprimanded by her stepmother.

It was already half past eleven, and Vincent was supposed to pick her up at eleven. Every so often, her stepmother glanced up at the clock perched on the mantel above the fireplace. Irritation grew inside of Ellie. Why didn't that woman appear upset?

Worry settled in Ellie's gut. Had Vincent decided he didn't want to be forced into marriage, so he had skipped town already? Or worse, had he confronted her father without her knowledge, and told the duke that he wouldn't marry her, no matter what scandal it made?

Something inside her stomach lurched. She stopped pacing and placed a hand to her throat. At any moment, she would lose the very little breakfast she had eaten this morning.

When the minute hand on the clock moved ahead one notch, she gritted her teeth and turned toward her stepmother. "I fear he's not coming."

Augusta smiled with her normal fake sweetness. "He will come."

"What makes you so certain?" Ellie moved to her stepmother's chair and squatted in front of her. "Lord Trenton has a reputation of a rogue. He's not going to be easily convinced to marry when he is against the very idea."

Sighing, Augusta placed the sampler on her lap before patting Ellie's shoulder. "My dear, you must have faith in the man. Do you recall last night when Lady Bothwell stated that rakes make the best husbands?"

A laugh bubbled up from Ellie's throat. Was this woman jesting? She must be, because the mere idea was ludicrous. "Of course I remember. But I figured Lady Bothwell didn't know what she was talking about."

"Well, although Lord Trenton is a rogue, I believe he is still a gentleman. He's been left to care for his sisters, and because he didn't desert them, I highly doubt he's going to desert you."

Ellie wanted to argue. He had mentioned that he hadn't accepted her initial offer because he wasn't ready to marry or fall in love. But if she really thought of it, that meant they would make the perfect couple.

Shaking her head, Ellie stood and moved to peek out the window. The sight in front of the manor made her hitch a breath. Her father stood in front of the entryway talking with Vincent. An open carriage waited in the drive as well.

Her heartbeat quickened. He hadn't run off, thank goodness. However, now she had to go on the morning ride with him. What could they possibly discuss? Especially when she had wanted to end their conversation for good last night before her father caught them.

"Is he here?" her stepmother asked.

Ellie had a sneaking suspicion that Augusta had known the whole time that Vincent was outside talking with her father. Why had she made Ellie suffer so?

"Make certain to take Mrs. Jackson with you as your chaperone," Augusta said in an annoying tone. "And don't forget to take your shawl, dear. There is a light wind today."

"I will."

Ellie hurried up to her bedchambers and fetched the shawl and bonnet. As much as she despised wearing a bonnet, she didn't like the way the sun baked her skin if she didn't wear it. Of course, on a perfect day, she loved nothing more than to ride on her horse, letting her hair flap in the wind—as long as nobody noticed.

When she reached the bottom of the stairs, the lady's maid, Mrs. Jackson, waited for her by the door. Vincent had entered the manor, holding his hat. Her father stood nearby watching. Vincent's gaze locked on her, but she couldn't tell if he was happy to see her or not.

What was she thinking? Of course he wasn't happy to see her. He was being forced to marry her.

As she reached his side, he gave her a small smile and slightly bowed. "You are looking lovely this morning, Miss Middleton."

She wanted to snort a laugh but was afraid her father would scold her. However, she could tell Vincent had memorized the comment. Strange how she could tell when he wasn't telling the truth now. Why hadn't she realized that when she made him the offer a week ago?

"I thank you, my lord. And may I return the compliment? You are looking quite dashing today." The words came out of her mouth before she realized that they were true. He had on a beige coat and trousers, and his vest was powder blue. Indeed, he looked quite dapper.

He presented his elbow, and she hooked her arm around it. Without a word to her father, Vincent escorted her outside and to the opened buggy, the maid following behind. Like a gentleman, he assisted her as she climbed inside. Mrs. Jackson sat in the seat behind them, and Vincent hopped in next to Ellie. Still being quiet, he took the reins and urged the horse forward.

The silence between them became awkward. She shifted in her seat, not wanting to sit too close to him. She didn't like bumping against him every time the wheels hit a rock or dipped in the road.

She released a heavy breath and looked at him. His attention was on the road ahead. His expression wasn't pleasant, either. "So, is this how things are going to play out until the wedding?"

He glanced at her. "What do you mean?"

"This awkward silence between us."

"Of course not. We may talk if that is what you wish."

"Then why are you not doing that very thing?"

He shrugged. "Probably because I cannot think of what to say."

"Well, we could start out talking about what happened last night."

"Before or after your father arrived?" He kept his eyes on the road.

She definitely didn't want to talk about what happened before. Then again, if they hadn't shared a passionate kiss, they wouldn't be in this predicament right now. "After."

"There isn't much to talk about."

How she wanted to shake some sense into him. "Are you not in the least upset?"

"Upset is a strong word, I suppose." Clearing his throat, he shifted in the seat. "I try not to express what I feel, mainly because I cannot control the situation."

"Do you blame me for what happened?" she asked softly.

He met her stare for a few seconds. "Why would I do that? After all, I was the one who went after you when I realized you had left the ballroom. And I was the one who stopped you when you tried to leave the grove of trees that first time." He looked back toward the road. "Things happened for a reason last night, and although I'm not quite certain what that reason is, I cannot fight it. I must accept the consequences and continue with my life."

She toyed with the fringe on her shawl and frowned. The tone of his voice told her he wasn't happy about the situation, but thankfully, he wouldn't fight it, either. Mixed emotions filled her again. Did she want him to be happy? At least they could be friends after they were married, couldn't they?

"Wise words." She nodded. "I should also try to accept what has happened." She forced a small laugh. "At least we know each other, instead of strangers being pushed to wed."

"Very true."

"And because we have already talked about this, you know what I expect, just as I know what you expect."

As they neared the park, several couples strolled along the paths or rode in carriages. She took a deep breath and sat straighter. Unease jumped in her stomach. They both needed to act as if they were falling in love.

"Look lively," he said. "Our performance starts now."

This time when she chuckled, it wasn't forced. "Strange that you could read my mind." She smiled at him as he glanced at her. "I was actually thinking that very thing."

He smiled back, but it didn't quite reach his eyes. "I'm glad. It shall make this outing easier."

"Indeed."

"However, I believe you should scoot closer to me on the seat. Perhaps even hook your arm around mine."

"I should?" Her heart picked up speed. She glanced back at the maid, who appeared to be half-asleep, anyway.

"Yes. That would make things appear better," Vincent said.

She must trust his word. Trying not to be too conspicuous, she did as he suggested. Once she had snaked her arm around his,

his body relaxed just a bit, which made her more comfortable. Perhaps this next half-hour wouldn't be so terribly bad after all.

VINCENT REALLY SHOULD change his attitude about everything. After all, he was sitting in a carriage with a very beautiful woman. The yellow and tan day dress with short, ruffled sleeves, and matching bonnet, made her look adorable. Her attire gave her a look of innocence, and being with her like this made him actually want to act more gentlemanly. He was a rogue, but occasionally he retained some gentlemanly qualities.

Last evening he'd stewed about his dire predicament, which kept him awake most of the night. Never had he felt so trapped, and that wasn't a pleasant feeling to have. But this morning, his mindset had shifted. Being her husband gave him the right to kiss her and seduce her. Because of their conversation while alone last night, she now knew that men expected to have heirs. Hopefully, she would eventually want children with him.

He had realized during that time how easily he could talk to her, not to mention how quickly she melted in his arms. Perhaps married life wouldn't be so terrible after all.

He'd also decided that Adam Haddington was dead and buried, and so Vincent should bury the secrets about his friend as well. Since he would never tell Ellie, she would not have any reason to hate him.

This realization had lifted his hopes—until he remembered what she'd said about not giving her heart to anyone. He could probably grow to love her, but only if she returned the emotion. There was no use loving someone unless they loved him back.

Ellie had made it abundantly clear that she could never do that. After the thought lodged in his head, his hopes dropped again. Why was he continuing with this farce anyway?

Yet he knew it was for his sisters. They deserved to have good marriages, even if he couldn't have one.

So far, the plan to *appear* happy together was working. Many people greeted them with nods and waves. Some of their expressions were shocked, while others lit up with delight. Those were probably the duke's friends, happy that someone was finally courting the youngest daughter.

It made no sense why a man hadn't snatched Ellie up by now. Could she have really been so devastated over her soldier's death that she never wanted to marry? It was hard for Vincent to believe that. He had known Adam for years. The man hadn't led an exemplary life. There wasn't anything that special about Vincent's friend. And Candace had confessed that Adam only wanted to marry Ellie because of her dowry.

"Precious," Vincent said, bringing her attention onto him. "Would you like to stroll around the park for a bit? I think it will be refreshing to stretch our legs."

"Yes. I believe that would be nice."

He found a spot to park his buggy, then jumped down and tied the horse to a tree before helping Ellie. The petite woman was so delicate, and he carefully set her on her feet, but not before her body bumped against his. His heart flipped, and he convinced his body that getting excited right now was not an option.

He turned and assisted the maid down before offering his elbow to Ellie. As they began their walk, he glanced her way. She had such a lovely smile. It was the perfect day for a stroll, and the sunlight brightened her face as she greeted people. It was hard not to feel like the luckiest man in England at this precise moment.

They reached a spot in the park that wasn't so congested. Their steps slowed considerably. The maid walked several steps behind.

Out of the corner of his eye, he caught Ellie staring up at him.

"Are you enjoying yourself?" he asked.

"Indeed I am. But the question is…are *you* having a pleasant outing?"

He chuckled. "I am, actually."

"You sound surprised." Her brows lifted. "I wonder why."

"It's nice to be out in the sun, strolling through the park with a lovely lady."

"Oh, Vincent." She tapped his arm playfully. "You don't have to lie and make me believe you've never done this before. I'm quite certain I'm not the first woman you've brought to the park."

"No, you aren't the first, but I can assure you, you are one of the loveliest." He stroked his fingers along her hand. "And for some reason, I feel more comfortable with you."

She laughed. "You do? Why is that?"

"I don't know."

Her eyes narrowed as she studied his face. He rather enjoyed the way her gaze skimmed slowly over his eyes, nose, and mouth, as though she took pleasure in looking at him.

"Perhaps it's because you know you can be yourself around me?" she inquired.

He shrugged. "I believe you are correct."

"Good. Because I want you to always feel that way. I want you to be able to express your thoughts any time you'd like."

"I thank you, Ellie. I shall do that."

After a few more steps in silence, she chuckled. "Vincent, if you haven't realized by now, that was an open invitation to talk to me."

"Now?" He looked at her with wide eyes. "Out here, where everyone could overhear?"

She glanced around before locking her gaze on him. "I don't see many people, Vincent. Mrs. Jackson can't even hear our conversation."

"True."

The scent of roses lifted with the slight breeze, pulling his attention to the right. He recalled her telling him how much she loved roses. Without asking, he steered them off the path and toward the several rosebushes up the slight knoll.

"Vincent, do you mind if I ask you something personal?"

"I suppose that would be fine. How else are we to get to know each other better before we are wed?"

With her free hand, she lifted her dress to her ankles as they slowly climbed the hill. She didn't act as though she was put out by having to walk a little farther on their stroll. He smiled. Ellie was certainly different from the other women he'd seduced. Of course, he'd known that a week ago when she presented him with the most improper—and intriguing—offer.

"What is your question?" he asked.

They reached the rosebushes, and she leaned forward, closing her eyes as she inhaled. Strange to think how pleasing it was just watching her enjoy something as small as smelling roses.

"I was wondering"—she straightened—"if you met with Lady Livingston after the ball last evening, as you told her you'd do." She turned and met his stare. "I'm curious what kind of offer she presented you."

Surprise shook him. It wasn't that Ellie had spoken something shocking as much as it was that he had actually *forgotten* about Candace.

He snorted a laugh. "Lady Livingston? That is what you're curious about?"

"Of course. Why wouldn't I be?"

"Well, to be completely honest, I forgot to meet her after the ball. I haven't talked to her since before we met in the grove of trees."

She tilted her head. "Indeed?"

He nodded. "Yes. I have no clue what she would have offered me."

Ellie's smile stretched wider. "I'm sure you had a suspicion as to what it might be."

He laughed out loud, not caring who heard him. It was quite refreshing being with a woman who spoke her mind, even as improper as the subject matter might be. "Yes, I suspected what she wanted from me."

Ellie hooked her hand around his arm again and started them toward another rosebush instead of back to the path. He didn't mind.

"I've heard gossip," Ellie said, "about Lady Livingston over the years, and the stories I've heard are not good." She peeked up at him as her thick eyelashes fluttered. "Can I ask if you were one of her lovers?"

Shock rooted his feet to the ground as he turned to face her. "Miss Middleton, I'm appalled."

Her eyes widened. "You are? Why, exactly? Are you shocked because I know about you and Lady Livingston, or that I have the courage to ask?"

Sighing heavily, he shook his head. There was one thing for certain…when they married, she would definitely keep him on his toes.

"I'm shocked that you are asking about my relationship with another woman."

Ellie gave him a teasing grin. "Try to compose yourself, Vincent. I've always been a most curious woman."

"Indeed you are." He chuckled.

"So? Are you going to tell me?"

He glanced around them, making sure that their conversation wouldn't be overheard, before he rested his focus on her again. "There is really nothing to tell. We were intimate for a few months, but both of us agreed to move on. She wasn't looking for a husband, and I for sure wasn't looking for a wife."

Slowly, Ellie's grin drooped. "Yes, I suppose that would be a good enough reason to end the relationship."

She stepped away from him toward the rosebush that held the loveliest yellow petals. Bending, she closed her eyes once more as she placed her nose above one of the flowers.

He moved closer to her. "And what about you?" Call him morbid, but he needed to know why she had loved a man who only wanted her for money.

"What about me?" She bent to sniff another flower.

"Will you tell me about your fiancé?"

Ellie snapped to an upright position, and her gaze landed on him. "Adam?"

He shrugged. "Unless you had more than one fiancé."

The muscles in her face relaxed, and she didn't appear to be as frigid. For some reason, the mention of Adam put her in an emotional dither. Perhaps she had truly given her heart to Adam and didn't have anything left to offer another man.

"What do you want to know?" she asked in a tight voice.

"Oh, I don't know." He stepped slowly around the bush. "How did you meet? How long did you know him before he…um, went off to fight one of Napoleon's battles?"

She blew out a breath between her lips, and her shoulders sagged. "Lord Haddington and I met at a ball, similar to the one we attended last evening." A twinkle appeared in her huge brown eyes as the lines in her face softened. "That year I recall being overwhelmed with all the attention gentlemen were giving me. But Adam was different. He wasn't anything like the other overeager suitors. He calmly watched me from afar. I was introduced to him, but not once did he ask me to dance."

"And his actions captured your attention?" Vincent asked, shaking his head. He hated to mention it to her, but *he* had taught Adam that trick with women.

"Yes. I noticed his gaze following me everywhere. He smiled at me, but he didn't make any other gestures." She paused as her smile grew. "It wasn't until the next day, while I was being escorted to the park, that he decided to talk to me." She sighed. "I forgot about the gentleman I was with and gave Adam my full attention."

Vincent chuckled. As he knew, it worked like a charm. "I'm sure your suitor's ego was crushed."

"Yes, I'm sure it was." She stepped to the next rosebush with purple flowers. "I don't recall what it was that attracted me to him so quickly, but I remember thinking how much we had in common. He enjoyed painting and taking leisurely walks in the park. He also enjoyed riding his horse through the countryside. He had one older sister, and of course you remember Justina. But other than that, I believed fate had brought us together."

Vincent wasn't sure why there was an uncomfortable tightening in his chest, but he didn't like seeing her eyes dance when she spoke of Adam. She'd never looked this way when she talked to him, and for some reason, it hurt more than he was prepared for.

He was also upset to learn that Adam had used on Ellie one of the wooing tricks that Vincent had taught his friend. He had told Adam to tell the ladies that their interests were the same. Vincent knew firsthand that Adam didn't like to paint. He had never known his friend to enjoy walks in the park, either.

"Yes, it must have been fate," he quickly answered.

"Adam courted me for one month before asking my father for my hand in marriage. My father was reluctant, and naturally so, since Adam was the second son of a baron. My parents wanted me to be happy, which was why they agreed that I could marry him, but I realized they were worried that Adam wasn't the man I was meant to be with for the rest of my life." She took a deep breath and slowly released it. "I don't know if it was something my father said to Adam, but soon after he asked for my hand, he joined the military to fight Napoleon. Two months later, I received a missive from his sister stating that he was missing. His garrison was in a battle with Napoleon, and several men died. It took several more weeks before he was pronounced dead."

Her voice choked and the light disappeared from her face. Vincent moved closer as he slipped an arm around her waist. "I'm sorry he died."

She nodded as she touched the tip of her finger to the corner of her moist eye. She peered away from him. "Yes, I'm sorry as well."

"Did you attend his funeral?"

"No." A tear trickled from her eye, and she quickly wiped it. "His family lived in France at the time, and I was too distraught to travel."

"Forgive me for making you dredge up bad memories." Vincent picked a flower from the bush and presented it to her. "I know this flower won't replace him, but I'm hoping it will bring some light into your heart."

When she smiled, her lips trembled. "I thank you, Vincent. You are very kind."

"Kind, you say? Already on our outing, I've arrived late, made you upset, and now I've made you cry." He chuckled softly. "I'm sure you are anxiously looking forward to our outing tomorrow."

A laugh bubbled up from her throat. His heart softened. At least he'd made her smile, even if her eyes hadn't brightened because of it.

He offered his elbow again. "Shall we return to our buggy?"

"Yes, I suppose we should."

They walked in silence, but at least she acted captivated by the rose he'd given her. As he helped her into the buggy, the horse became skittish. "Calm down, boy," Vincent soothed the creature as he assisted the maid into the back. As soon as he sat and pulled on the reins, the horse bucked, jolting the vehicle.

"Vincent, what's wrong with the animal?" Ellie asked in a fearful voice.

"I'm not sure. Hold tightly to my arm."

He tried cooing to the animal, but the more the horse moved, the more irritated it became. Within seconds, it bolted. Both Vincent and Ellie were jerked back against the seat. The reins slipped from his hands and dropped to the floor. Reaching down, he tried to grasp them but couldn't. Ellie screamed and clung to his arm.

Panic consumed him. He not only had to keep the horse from trampling people in the park, but he had to make sure Ellie didn't fall out of the buggy in the process.

He wasn't looking forward to the outcome.

CHAPTER SIX

Ellie screamed again. Fear had frozen her limbs, but thankfully, she had enough strength to hang on to Vincent. He struggled keeping her in the seat and trying to reach for the reins that had fallen to their feet. With each step of the out-of-control animal, the reins slipped farther away.

Couples walking through the park scattered in every direction. Ellie wanted to yell at someone to help. Couldn't they see they were in trouble?

Each time Vincent came close to grabbing the reins, the vehicle bounced them on the seat. She didn't want to release Vincent, but she didn't want them both flying out of the buggy, either.

Up ahead, a tree stood in their path. Silently, she prayed that the horse would notice as well. Just before they reached the tree, the animal darted away from the large object. The buggy turned slightly, tipping to one side. Mrs. Jackson let out a cry and flew out, rolling on the ground. Ellie watched her to make certain she was all right. Thankfully, the maid sat up and brushed her hands over her dress.

Closing her eyes, Ellie held tighter to Vincent's arm. Would she be next to fall from the vehicle? He leaned against the turn, which made the buggy settle back on both wheels. She released a sob as she pressed her cheek against his strong arm.

"How is your maid?" Vincent asked in a panicked voice.

"She seems to be all right." Ellie's voice shook.

Determination etched across Vincent's features as he concentrated on the reins. Holding her breath, she said a silent prayer that someone would help. Vincent's mouth tightened, and he lunged for the reins and nearly pulled her from off the seat. This time, his fingers wrapped around the reins. He yanked hard, finally bringing the horse to a stop. The animal continued to buck, fitfully.

Three men rushed up to assist. One took hold of the strap around the horse's head. The second man gripped the front of the buggy, while the third man raised his arms up to Ellie to help her down.

With trembling hands, she reached for the man. Vincent's large, warm hands took hold of her waist and guided her. Within seconds, he jumped down himself.

Ellie's body shook, so she wrapped her arms around her middle. Ladies hurried toward her. One elderly woman slid her arm around Ellie's shoulders, pulling her away from the buggy. Questions exploded all around her, but she couldn't concentrate enough to answer. Her attention stayed on Vincent as he ran a comforting hand over the animal's back, and down each leg, as if searching for what could have made the horse act in such a way.

Vincent pushed his fingers under the blanket lying across the horse's back, and then quickly yanked them out. He muttered something Ellie couldn't understand as the horse jerked again. The other two men tightly held the horse, trying to keep him still. Vincent lifted a side of the blanket to display bunches of sticker weeds.

Ellie gasped. No wonder the horse went wild when Vincent tried to pull the reins. Moving would have caused the animal great pain. She broke away from the crowd of women who had gathered around her, and moved next to Vincent.

"Where did they come from?" she whispered, staring at the burs.

"I was wondering the same thing." He glanced at her over his shoulder. "The only way these would have gotten under the blanket was while we were strolling around the rosebushes. If the burs were there before, the horse would have acted like this before I picked you up."

"I know." She held her breath, not daring to think the thought that suddenly popped into her head.

"In other words," Vincent continued in a soft voice for only her ears, "someone wanted to spoil our outing."

Slowly, she nodded. "But who?"

"I don't know." He smiled teasingly. "Perhaps I made one of your beaus upset that I took you to the park instead of them escorting you."

She chuckled softly. "Aren't you humorous, since we both know I have no beaus."

With the help from the other men, Vincent was able to remove the burs from between the blanket and the horse's back. The women asked questions, but Ellie didn't know how to answer. She tried to reply without worrying them. From up the way, two women were assisting Mrs. Jackson as the maid limped toward Ellie holding her right arm. She broke away from the crowd to help the servant.

"Are you all right?" Ellie asked as she took over for one of the ladies.

"I think my wrist and ankle are twisted, but nothing worse, thank goodness."

They reached the buggy, and Mrs. Jackson sagged against the vehicle. Finally, the crowd trickled away, leaving Ellie with Vincent again. He stroked his palm over the horse's back, murmuring soothing words. Obviously, his touch was magical, because the animal relaxed. It amazed her how quickly Vincent could calm the horse. The deep timbre in Vincent's voice nearly put her under a spell as well.

He turned to the maid. "Here, allow me to help you inside."

Mrs. Jackson nodded and carefully climbed into the vehicle.

Using the reins, Vincent led the horse and buggy back to the main path in the park. Ellie walked beside him, noticing the horse had returned to normal. She breathed a sigh of relief. At least one of them was tranquil. Her nerves continued to jump all over the place.

Her mind replayed their wild ordeal, and it surprised her how well Vincent had handled the situation. It pleased her to know he was worried about her, too.

They reached the road, and he stopped the horse. Turning toward her, he smiled. "Are you ready to climb back in the buggy?"

She really wasn't, but gazing into his warm bluish-gray eyes comforted her in an odd way. A soft smile bracketed his face as he cupped her cheek.

"Are you all right? There isn't much color in your face."

Laughing uncomfortably, she pushed his hand away. "I'm still a little shaken, but I shall be fine."

"The horse won't become wild again, I assure you." He held out his hand for her to take.

As she slid her palm against his, tingles grew inside her belly. She lifted the hem of her dress and climbed inside. Anxiously, she waited for him to join her, and when he did, it took all of her willpower not to snuggle against his arm again.

"I suppose you would like to return home," he said, looking down at her with his caring gaze.

"I would, if you don't mind."

"Not at all. The event has worn me out as well." His smile wasn't full.

He urged the horse into a trot again, and the peaceful ride calmed her considerably. Of course, it was probably more due to Vincent's tender kindness than anything else.

"Do you think," she said after a few moments of silence, "anyone saw what happened? Would they tell you if they noticed someone pushing the burs under the horse's blanket?"

"I can only hope that if they did see, they would tell me." He reached over and grasped her arm, pulling her closer to him on the seat. "You still look frightened. I beg you, hold on to my arm. It will make you feel better."

She nodded and slid her arm around his, cuddling against him. Peace filled her, but she didn't question the strange reaction.

"After I take you home," he said, "I'll return to the park and ask questions. Hopefully, we can catch the irresponsible person who did this."

"That is a wise idea."

During the remainder of the ride, she was satisfied just to use his body to lean against. A smile tugged on the corners of her mouth, and she didn't care who saw her right now. Gossipmongers could start rumors if they wished, but it didn't matter. She was marrying Vincent in seven days anyway. However, she should still guard her feelings. He was only marrying her out of duty.

Frowning, she sighed. At least she knew that although he might not be fully committed to their marriage, he would be kind and tender. That was encouraging, wasn't it?

VINCENT COULDN'T BELIEVE not one person had noticed the sticker weeds being placed under the horse's blanket. Things like this didn't happen by accident. The frustration he had about what happened at the park earlier was that he didn't know if he was the unknown person's target, or if it was Ellie.

He finished dressing for this evening's dinner social at Lord and Lady Berkley's estate. He had received an invitation along with the duke, so riding together made more sense. Vincent had almost called it off, due to yesterday's upset, but Ellie had assured her father that she would be ready.

Before leaving the manor, he grabbed his hat and headed to his horse. He checked to see if there was anything that would upset the animal, and luckily, everything appeared fine. He mounted and rode toward the duke's estate.

Strange to think, but he anxiously waited to see what Ellie would be wearing this evening.

As the servant let him inside the manor, her parents greeted him, but it wasn't them he wanted to converse with. Vincent kept his focus locked on the stairs, even as he answered the duke's questions about what had happened that afternoon in the park.

Finally, the sound he'd been straining to hear echoed on the second floor as the clicking of women's heeled shoes grew louder. When Ellie came into view, he held his breath as he ran his gaze over her gown. No longer did she resemble the young woman of the first day she'd run into him, nor did she look like the innocent beauty whom he escorted to the park. Instead, she had blossomed into an extremely lovely goddess.

The beige gown with a lace overlay enriched not only her square neck bodice, but the high-waisted gown and short sleeves. White ribbons were tied just under her breasts and on the cuffs of her sleeves. She wore white elbow-length gloves, and a string of pearls rested around her delicate throat. Her lovely, dark brown hair was wound in a coil, while wisps of curls hung on her neck and by her ears.

Slowly, Vincent released the air from his lungs as she descended the stairs. She immediately looked at him, and the closer she came, the wider her smile grew. She reached him and curtsied. He bowed but didn't take his eyes off her.

"Miss Middleton, you are a vision of loveliness."

Twin spots of pink darkened her cheeks. "I thank you, my lord, and let me return the compliment. You look rather dashing. I think the deep blue of your waistcoat looks good on you." She rested her hand briefly on the garment before removing her touch.

"I must admit, because of your kind words, it's now my favorite color." He offered his arm. "Shall we go now?"

Behind Vincent, the duke cleared his throat. "Splendid idea."

The strong voice startled Vincent. He'd forgotten about

Ellie's parents being so nearby.

She held his elbow, and he placed his hand over her fingers. Her eyes lifted to his. Heavens, she looked so pretty. Back in his rogue days, if he had seen Ellie like this, he would have targeted her as his next seduction. Strange that the mere mention of *marriage* had him pushing his heels into the ground as fast as he could. As much as he wanted to seduce this woman, he stopped himself for fear of making a fool out of himself.

Vincent and Ellie shared a coach with her parents. He enjoyed the way Ellie's soft arm bumped against him during the ride. At first, she was stiff, but by the time they reached the party, she practically rested against him.

He took pride in walking into the manor with the loveliest woman in England. Many people watched them with wide, curious eyes. A few men threw glares at Vincent, and a handful of women snubbed Ellie. Apparently, they were the talk of the *ton* already.

A familiar face captured his attention. Standing in the back of the room by Lady Berkley was the woman's sister, Lady Livingston. He fisted his hands as his worry escalated. Candace wouldn't cause any problems, would she? He prayed she respected her sibling's house and friends and wouldn't cause a scene. If he had remembered the two ladies were related, Vincent wouldn't have come tonight.

Candace looked directly at him. Lines of confusion pulled at the corners of her eyes and around her mouth, making her appear ten years older. He didn't dare acknowledge her—not yet—so he slid a hand on Ellie's back as they moved into the room. She greeted some ladies, smiling politely and acting genuinely happy to see them.

A butler brought a tray of champagne, which Vincent was eager to taste. Actually, if he could get whiskey, the effect would help him much faster. Unfortunately, he had to accept what was given.

Ellie stood beside him, sipping her champagne as her gaze

combed the people gathered in the room. She would see Candace at any moment, and he didn't know how she would react. Holding his breath, he waited for the moment of recognition.

Ellie's body stiffened, and she stopped the drink nearly at her mouth. He didn't want to say anything, mainly because he didn't know what to say. After a few very uncomfortable seconds, she exhaled slowly and lowered the drink. Her body continued to remain stiff as she lifted her head and met his stare.

She licked her tight lips. "I'm sure you know who is here."

He nodded.

"Were you aware that she would be here?"

"No. If I had known, I wouldn't have come."

She kept her gaze on him, although malice lit her eyes. "Are you going to leave my side to go talk to her tonight?"

He arched an eyebrow. "I hadn't planned on it, but after all, we are at a party, so I expect both of us will mingle."

Ellie's shoulders sagged. "Vincent, how many people in this room know about your affair with that woman?" she whispered.

He wanted to laugh, but he didn't dare. Was Ellie jealous, or was she just being controlling? He prayed it wasn't the latter. He abhorred women who wanted to run his life. "How would I know? Do you wish me to go ask all of the guests?"

"Of course not." Her nostrils flared and her lips thinned.

He gently caressed her arm. "My precious," he said softly, "please don't worry. I promise not to do anything that will embarrass either of us tonight."

She lowered her gaze and turned from him. The silence between them bothered him, but so did the thoughts running through his head. Was this how she would act once they were married? Was it her intention to keep him from speaking to *any* lovely woman, or just his former mistresses?

Slowly, anger built inside him. He didn't want to hold bitter feelings toward Ellie after they were married, but if she planned on turning into a shrew, he wouldn't handle it well.

Ellie's parents took her away to introduce her to some other people, leaving Vincent by himself. He shouldn't have come tonight. And he shouldn't have agreed to marry Ellie. Yet he wasn't given a choice.

He lifted the glass to his mouth, only to realize it was empty. He searched for a waiter, and then placed his empty glass on the tray before taking a full glass of champagne. For certain, this drink wouldn't dull his senses as he wished. Tonight would be torture.

New arrivals entered the room. Vincent recognized a man he hadn't seen since he was in school. A woman hung on the man's arm. By their dour expressions, neither of them appeared too happy. Vincent rolled his eyes. He was willing to bet they were married.

Inwardly, he groaned. Would this be him and Ellie in a few years?

A throb began pounding in Vincent's forehead, so he rubbed the spot, hoping to relieve the pain. Truth be told, one of the main reasons he had never wanted to marry was because since he was a lad, he'd watched married couples slowly fall out of love. Happily married couples rarely existed. He didn't ever want to be in that situation. If he fell out of love with a woman, he would just move on to another one. That had been his way of life for several years.

Leaning his shoulder against the wall, he watched Ellie interact with the others. She was shy with some people, and with others she wasn't. Her actions made him curious, but he hesitated to say anything to her about it. Perhaps she wasn't aware of what she was doing.

Just then, a man walked up to Ellie's father and greeted him. Lord Calvin Drake was a name Vincent had heard whispered in gossip circles. The tall, broad-shouldered, robust man was on most eligible women's dream list. He'd been single for many years, but lately there was talk of him looking for a wife. Not only did Lord Calvin have charm, but the marquess' youngest son was wealthy to boot. Both of the man's parents came from *old money*.

As the introductions were being made, Ellie's eyes lit up like stars and her smile widened. Vincent's gut twisted. Why hadn't she looked at *him* in such a way? Worse, why did he even care?

"I'm assuming the rumors are true."

The deep, sensual voice next to Vincent snapped him out of his thoughts, and he jumped. He jerked his head in her direction, and his heart dropped. *Lady Livingston!*

His first reaction was to see if Ellie had noticed whom he was talking with, but he quickly ushered away that response. He wasn't committing a crime because he was with his former mistress. As long as they were in public, everything would be fine.

"Lady Livingston," he said, and bowed.

"Lord Trenton." She curtsied. "I saw you standing all alone, and I just knew I had to come over." She presented him the famous pout that she gave to men when she wanted something. "Why didn't you meet me after the ball?"

He wanted so badly to peek over his shoulder to see if Ellie was watching, but he fought the urge. What was wrong with him? "I had to get my sisters back to the manor. I didn't have time to meet you, as I'd thought."

Frowning, Candace shook her head. "Why don't I believe you?"

He gave her a nonchalant shrug. "I suppose you will believe what you want, but it's the truth." Well, perhaps not *all* of the truth.

"Why didn't you tell me you were courting Miss Middleton when we chatted at the ball?"

"Because I have only just started to court her."

She arched an eyebrow. "Truly, Vincent. Tell me what is really going on. Courting a duke's daughter is not something you would do."

He chuckled before taking another taste of his drink. "Lady Livingston, it's really nothing to worry about."

"Are you in love with her?"

He kept himself from laughing out loud. Candace didn't need

to know everything in his life. "So, my lady, since we didn't get a chance to talk after the ball," he said, quickly changing the subject, "why don't you tell me now what your *proposal* is? I'll admit, I'm intrigued to know what is going through your head."

Her eyes narrowed on him suspiciously. "I'd rather talk in private."

"But, my lady, we might never get that chance again."

Her expression fell. "Why? Are you going to marry Miss Middleton?"

Vincent couldn't lie about this. Candace would find out eventually. In less than a week, to be exact.

"Indeed. I'm going to marry her."

Anger burned in her gaze as her face tightened. "But Vincent," she said very quietly, "I was going to ask you to marry *me*."

CHAPTER SEVEN

ELLIE'S HEART RACED as she studied Lord Calvin Drake's handsome face. The resemblance between him and his cousin, Adam Haddington, was remarkable. There were moments during their introduction when she thought she was peering into the eyes of her dead fiancé. Both men had the same dark blond hair. Both men had the same color eyes. But Lord Calvin held himself a little taller, and certainly smiled more. He also sported facial hair, which wasn't very popular with gentlemen. However, it looked amazing on Lord Calvin. Meeting him had brought back so many memories of Adam, and it took all of her willpower not to cry.

"I'm very glad I have finally met my cousin's fiancée. I had heard so much about you," Lord Calvin said.

She nodded as a lump of emotion swelled in her throat. "And I'm happy to finally meet you, as well."

He had the most remarkable green eyes. She dared not stare into them for too long for fear her mind would accept this man as her fiancé who'd returned from the dead to take over his cousin's body. Silently, she laughed at the strange thought. She really needed to stop living in her dreams and enter the real world.

"Is it permissible to call upon you tomorrow afternoon?" he asked.

Her heart leaped and the words *yes please* were ready to

spring from out of her mouth, but she quickly quashed them. She couldn't possibly have him call upon her for two reasons. The first one was probably most important—that she needed to forget about Adam Haddington. She couldn't waste her life on a man who was dead. And the second reason, of course, being that she was soon to marry Vincent.

She looked at her father. He gave her that all-too-familiar arched eyebrow. The duke was probably expecting her to jump at the chance to be with one of Adam's relatives, and he would *not* approve.

Sighing, she looked into Lord Calvin's dreamy eyes again. "I fear, my lord, that I must decline. My father will be signing my betrothal papers any day now."

The handsome man's countenance drooped. Even the light in his eyes disappeared. "I'm sorry to hear that, but I'm sure your future husband will be one lucky man."

She wanted to laugh again. She doubted Vincent was thinking that now.

Lord Calvin bowed to her father, and then to her, before turning and leaving. She wanted so much to stop him. The urge to ask him about Adam's life was strong, but she mustn't give in. Adam was in her past, and Vincent was her future.

And speaking of the little devil…

She skimmed the crowd, searching for her almost-fiancé. Immediately, she recognized the charming seducer who stood way too close to Lady Livingston, and whose smile was much too wide. Ellie's heart twisted as irritation rose within her. He'd broken his promise already? Although he had worded it that he wouldn't do anything to *embarrass* either one of them. He didn't actually say he would never speak to Lady Livingston ever again.

Taking in deep breaths, Ellie prepared what she was going to say to him, but just then, Lady Berkley announced that they could go into the dining room for the meal. Ellie headed toward Vincent and his former mistress, eager to break up their quaint discussion. However, before she reached his side, the other woman turned and sashayed away.

Ellie slowed her steps and tried to conceal the anger rumbling inside of her. Vincent turned just as she reached him. His eyes widened, and a flash of guilt etched across his face. But within seconds, he smiled and took Ellie's hand, hooking it over his elbow as if nothing had happened.

"Did you have a nice visit with your new friend?" he asked, leading her toward the dining room. "I'm surprised he would dare wear facial hair. It isn't the fashion, you know."

"My new friend? To whom are you referring, Lord Trenton?"

He gave her a skeptical glance. "You know perfectly well, my precious. I'm speaking of your little visit with Lord Calvin."

Her heartbeat quickened. *Vincent saw me?* "Uh, yes. I was happy to meet Adam Haddington's cousin."

Vincent's eyebrows lifted. "His cousin?"

She nodded. "Yes, they are related, even though I haven't met him until tonight. Was it a crime to talk to him?"

Vincent scowled. "Of course not."

"And what about you?" she asked, trying to keep her voice calm, as they were nearly to the table. "How was your visit with Lady Livingston? Did you enjoy yourself?"

"As much as I dared," he said in a low voice as they stood behind their chairs, waiting for the host and hostess to sit first.

They didn't continue the conversation, only because the host and hostess sat, and they started the meal, beginning with soup.

Ellie peeked at Vincent beside her, and his head was bent as he ate his soup. Taking small spoonfuls, she slowly consumed hers, since she had suddenly lost her appetite. Why did she always argue with Vincent? This wasn't the way she wanted to start a marriage.

Quickly, she brought her mind to a halt. What was she thinking? She knew this marriage wasn't going to be happy. She needed to remember that although it wouldn't be perfect, at least she wasn't marrying Augusta's obstinate nephew.

As Ellie took another sip of her soup, she moved her gaze

around the table...and stopped on the man who was watching her. Although Lord Calvin was eating, he still had his eyes on her. The speculative expression on his face made her cautious. Could he be trying to see if she was truly happy without Adam? Then again, she didn't know why he cared. She gave him a polite smile before lowering her attention back to her bowl.

Soon, several conversations grew around the table. She didn't know which one to be part of. She sat by her father, and he discussed politics with his friends. Vincent entered into a conversation with the gentlemen sitting nearest to him about horse racing. Neither conversation roused her interest. However, watching Vincent was quite entertaining.

Stars sparkled in his eyes as he talked about horses, and his whole expression grew bright with excitement. His voice lifted, but it wasn't loud. Instead, the energy he displayed on the topic soothed her. She loved horses, too, and it was thrilling to know they had at least one thing in common.

The meal passed quickly, and soon the women were moving into the drawing room to work on their embroidery while the men stayed in the dining room to smoke cigars and drink port. Ellie wasn't in the mood to embroider. She was very uncomfortable being in the same room with Lady Livingston. Vincent's mistress sat much closer to her than before, and because of the glares the woman threw her way, her chest tightened and made it harder to breathe.

Finally, she could take no more. Ellie leaned closer to her stepmother and whispered, "It's quite stuffy in here. I'm going to step outside to get some fresh air."

Augusta's curious eyes met Ellie's. "Make certain you take one of Lady Berkley's maids."

"I will."

The room was abuzz with gossip, and Ellie prayed nobody would really notice her leaving, especially Lady Livingston. On soft feet, she stepped into the corridor, closing the door behind her. She glanced around the spacious hall, but no servants were about. That was all right. She would go no farther than the front porch, so she didn't need a chaperone.

She hurried outside. The night's cool breeze blew against her moist skin. Smiling, she closed her eyes and lifted her face toward the moonlight streaming upon the porch. No longer did she feel suffocated. The refreshing air around her calmed her slightly.

There were still a few more hours before they would return home. Lady Berkley had entertainment planned for her guests, and Ellie hoped she would be able to make it through the evening.

"You are absolutely breathtaking."

Vincent's voice startled her, and she jumped. Snapping her eyes open and focusing on the man beside her, she placed a hand to her chest, feeling her wild heartbeat beneath her palm. "Wh-what are you doing out here? You are supposed to be inside with the other men."

He stepped closer, leaned against one of the many thick white columns on the porch, and folded his arms. "I should ask you the same. Weren't you enjoying yourself with the other women?"

Vincent's teasing expression made her smile. She liked the way one side of his mouth lifted higher than the other, and the way his eyes were partially squinted.

"I'm certain you know the answer to that, my lord."

"Indeed I do." He shrugged. "I was bored with cigars and port, and I needed some fresh air."

Inhaling deeply, she nodded and walked to the edge of the porch. "It's a very lovely evening to enjoy the crispness of the air."

"I agree—however, I believe the woman I'm with is much lovelier than the cool night's breeze."

Her cheeks warmed, and she couldn't stop from gazing into his warm eyes. "You are full of compliments tonight. It makes me curious as to why."

Vincent moved away from the column and stood mere inches away from her. He stroked his knuckles along her cheek. "The words come naturally when I'm admiring pure beauty."

"I wonder why you're talking to me this way, especially because our words to each other were very brusque right before we took our meal."

"They were."

"Why the sudden change?"

He sighed and dropped his fingers from her face. "I had hoped your attitude had changed toward me. After all, you couldn't take your eyes off me during the meal."

Ellie's face grew hotter. "I, um… Well, it's because I was very interested in the topic of horses. I was pleased to see you enjoy horses just as much as I do."

One of his eyebrows lifted. "You do?"

She nodded.

"That's good to know. We should go riding one morning."

"I would love that."

His smile relaxed. "I hope to own my own horse-breeding farm one day. I have always wanted one."

"That does sound enthralling." She moved closer and grasped his hands. "We could have all different breeds, could we not? I would help you out by exercising them daily."

Chuckling, he brought her hands up to his mouth and kissed her gloved knuckles. "Yes, I would love that."

Her heartbeat quickened, and once more, she felt as though she couldn't breathe. Yet this was much different from when she had sat in the stuffy drawing room with the other women. She really should pull away from him, but she became lost in his smoldering eyes.

"Promise me," she said softly, "that we will do that after we're married."

His head bobbed up and down, but his gaze dropped to her mouth. "I promise."

Ellie couldn't believe how much she wanted him to kiss her. Everything that had happened since they arrived at the Berkleys' manor seemed to disappear. Now, out here alone, her silly jealousy didn't matter. All she wanted was to be held in his comforting arms and experience the thrill of his lips merging with hers.

Silence stretched between them as her anticipation grew. Was he going to kiss her? Or did he want her to make the first move? Her patience thinned rapidly, and if it took her to press her mouth against his first, so be it.

Readying herself, she licked her dry lips. Just as she moved toward him, he slid his arms around her waist and pressed his body next to hers. Immediately, their lips met. Hungrily. Passionately.

A heady sigh of delight flew from her throat, but she didn't care. She flung her arms around his neck and met his mouth as it slanted back and forth over hers. She caressed her tongue against his, which made him tighten his hold around her.

She couldn't get enough. Was it wrong to want more? Yet they stood on the porch of their hosts' manor, instead of being totally alone. This was highly improper. If caught, they would surely cause a scandal, regardless of whether or not they were going to marry soon.

"Vincent," she said breathlessly, "we should stop."

"Why?" His hands roamed over her back as quickly as his mouth moved across hers.

"Because…if we don't, I'll never want to stop."

A deep groan rattled through his chest as his lips trailed from her mouth to her neck. "What if I don't want to stop, either?"

His words nearly had her melting to the ground. If neither of them could stop, they were in a lot of trouble.

Laughter rang from inside the house and startled her. Vincent must have heard too, because he stepped away from her. She leaned back against the nearest column, mainly to help her stand as she tried to catch her breath. Vincent's chest rose and fell as quickly as hers.

He smiled at her, and she returned the gesture. It delighted her to know he enjoyed the moment they shared as much as she had.

"I should let you go inside first," he said. "We cannot be seen going in together."

"I agree, but I'm supposed to have a maid with me as a chaperone."

He held up a finger. "Then allow me to go inside first, and I'll find a maid for you."

She smiled wider. "I thank you, Vincent."

He hurried inside. Taking deep breaths, she tried to regulate her erratic heartbeat. She rubbed her lips, wondering if they appeared as swollen as they felt. Most likely. And her face... She placed both palms on her cheeks. Would her pleasurable expression let everyone know what she'd been doing out on the porch?

Soon, the front door opened, and a maid stepped out. "Miss Middleton? Were you looking for me?"

"I was. Would you take a quick stroll with me through the flower garden?"

The older woman nodded as she walked with Ellie. So much was spinning through her head that she didn't want to converse with the servant.

This growing attraction she had for Vincent was exhilarating. Yet part of her heart wouldn't let go of Adam's memory. Guilt for betraying the cherished memories they had shared tried to override the passionate moment with Vincent. Which emotion should she accept? However, if she pushed Adam from her mind, she would feel more complete with Vincent, which, undoubtedly, made for a better marriage. Well...as long as he returned the feelings.

It was hard for her to admit how jealous she'd become while Vincent and Lady Livingston were together earlier. Vincent was a naturally charming man, but Lady Livingston...

Ellie bunched her hands into fists. She just couldn't tolerate another woman—a former mistress, no less—gazing upon Vincent as if she wanted to devour him body and soul.

She had never liked that woman. They had never formally met, but she recalled Adam's mentioning her in a passing conversation one time. Apparently, he knew her. Ellie arched an eyebrow. Hmm… Exactly how *well* had he known Lady Livingston? Why hadn't Ellie wondered about it while he was alive?

It didn't matter now, but hopefully, Vincent would give up his mistresses after they were married. Although originally Ellie had told him he could keep them, she now pictured herself being happy with him. She could see them having children together. And she even felt as though she could fall in love…

"Ellie?"

Augusta's high-pitched voice jerked Ellie out of her daydreams. The duchess stood on the porch, waving her arm to get Ellie's attention.

She glanced at the maid and shrugged. "I suppose we should go inside now."

"Yes, Miss Middleton." The servant rubbed her palms up and down her arms, shivering.

Strange to think, but Ellie hadn't been cold. Probably because thoughts of Vincent kept her very heated.

She hurried out of the flower garden and up the stairs to her stepmother. "Forgive me for taking so long. It's such a pleasant evening—"

"It's not pleasant at all," Augusta interrupted. "The wind is quite nippy." She moved toward the front door. "Come. We must hurry. Lady Berkley has something special arranged tonight. Miss Dorothea James will sing for us."

"Who is that?" Ellie asked as her stepmother hooked her arm around hers as they entered the manor.

"She is a well-respected opera singer."

"How lovely." She smiled, hoping she'd enjoy it. Before Adam had died, he'd taken her to an opera, and she had found it entertaining.

They walked into the ballroom, which had chairs set up for

the guests, and a mini stage at one end of the room. The guests were finding their seats or chatting with others. Ellie searched through the throng of people to find the most handsome man at the party—the man with the perfect lips. Her gaze rested on him, but it was the woman next to him that brought Ellie's happiness to a halt. The red-headed woman wore a daringly low-cut red gown, and practically flaunted her full bosom underneath Vincent's nose. Didn't Lady Livingston have any decorum?

Ellie's heart wrenched. Vincent couldn't possibly have chosen to sit beside his former mistress, could he? He'd promised he wouldn't embarrass her, and for certain, this would embarrass Ellie *and* her father. But it was more than that. She felt betrayed. They had just shared a very passionate kiss, but he'd left her side to find Lady Livingston.

"There's your father over there," Augusta said, pointing to a corner of the room.

"Augusta? I suddenly don't feel very well." Ellie rubbed her belly. "Do you think our driver could take me home?"

The duchess frowned, which added lines around her mouth. "Absolutely not. Someone will have to accompany you, and I would like to stay and listen to Miss Dorothea James. And I know your father wants to hear her as well." She shook her full head of auburn hair. "My dear, you shall just have to get over your stomach ailment. I'm sure Lord Trenton would like to enjoy the rest of the evening with you, too."

Ellie's attention was riveted to Vincent and his mistress. "No. I think you're wrong."

"Not to worry." Her stepmother patted Ellie's hand. "I shall have your father fetch him to come sit with us. The farther away Lord Trenton gets from *that woman*, the better off he'll be."

It was good to know Augusta had heard the rumors of Lady Livingston, too.

As Ellie made her way toward her father, she kept her attention on Vincent. Surprisingly, he ended the conversation with his former mistress and stood. The slightly older woman placed a bold hand on Vincent's arm. It appeared she was begging him to stay, but he shook his head and moved away.

Ellie's hopes lifted, and she sighed. At least her father wouldn't have to make a scene by dragging Vincent to sit by them.

Once she and her stepmother had found their seats and sat, Ellie frowned, staring at her lap. The daydreams she'd had right after the passionate kiss were slowly fading. Clearly, she'd made the mistake by thinking there was something more between her and Vincent. Perhaps this particular rogue would never reform. If that happened, then falling in love with him was certainly out of the question.

Vincent's masculine scent of spice stirred her senses mere moments before he sat next to her. She couldn't look at him. It was too soon. If she had to look into his face now, she might snap at him for talking to *that woman* and sitting next to her. Could Ellie, as his almost-fiancée, ask him to stop talking to his former mistress? Would he resent her if she did?

"My precious," Vincent whispered, leaning close to her ear. "I would rather look upon your radiant smile than sit beside Lady Livingston."

Ellie sucked in a breath. He knew what she'd been thinking?

Slowly, she raised her gaze to his. His amazing blue eyes pleaded with her, and his smile warmed her injured heart. "You would?"

"Any day of the week, and on weekends."

She chuckled softly. "Why does she keep bothering you?"

"I shall tell you later. In public is not the place to discuss something so personal."

Her heart flipped and happiness swelled within her. He was actually going to be honest with her instead of hiding secrets. "I thank you, my lord."

"Now, will you smile and enjoy the rest of the evening?"

She nodded. Relief settled over her as she relaxed into her seat.

The party passed quickly, thankfully. Miss Dorothea James turned out a splendid performance, which was the topic on the ride back home. It surprised Ellie to see her father and stepmother so excited about one singer. Then again, the diva did have a superb voice.

They reached the manor, and her father and stepmother exited the coach first before the footman helped Vincent down. He turned and offered his hand to Ellie. She slid her palm against his, and immediately, her body warmed. These reactions were happening more often, and she was tired of fighting them.

It would be better if she just allowed herself to fall in love with him. She felt that she was nearly to that point already.

They walked side by side toward the house. It relieved her that Augusta and the duke had left them alone, although Ellie feared it wouldn't be too much longer before her father or a maid poked their head outside and called for her.

"I had a lovely time tonight," she said after a few minutes of silence.

Vincent met her gaze and nodded. "I did, as well."

"I apologize that the evening started out rocky, but I'm happy it ended wonderfully."

"I suppose I'm to blame for that." He sighed and stopped. "I honestly didn't know Lady Livingston would be there, and it was very insensitive of me to talk to her."

"But didn't you tell me that she came to you?"

"Yes."

"Well, it would have been rude to shun her."

"True, but I would rather her be upset with me than you." He took hold of Ellie's hands and gently rubbed her knuckles.

"Will you tell me what she was so persistent about?"

He inhaled deeply and released it slowly. The smile faded from his face. Immediately, she braced herself, fearing that she wouldn't be happy with the outcome.

"The reason she wanted to speak with me after the ball last night was because she wanted to propose to me."

Ellie gasped. "Propose, as in ask you to marry her?"

"Yes."

Anger rose inside of her, but so did humor, and she laughed. "But didn't you tell me she has many lovers?"

"She does indeed."

"Then why would she want to marry?"

He shrugged. "She told me she was tired of all of the men in her life, and she wanted just one. Because we had parted friends, she chose to ask me." He hooked her hand around his elbow, pulling her closer as they slowly moved toward the manor. "She'd heard of my situation and that I was low on funds, and so her proposal was similar to yours." He smiled at Ellie. "It shocked her when I told her that I couldn't possibly marry her because I was going to marry you."

Ellie hadn't realized she'd been holding her breath until she released the air in one big gush between her teeth. Happiness danced in her chest. "You did?"

"Yes. After all, in a few days it won't be a secret any longer. Correct?"

"My father will make the announcement soon." She stopped and rested her hands on his chest. "Vincent, tell me why you have had a sudden change of mind about me."

His eyes widened. "Why would you think that? You know I enjoy spending time with you."

"True, but I also know you were not looking forward to our wedding."

"Have *you* had a change of mind about our wedding?" He stroked her cheek. "Because a woman who kisses so passionately, and doesn't want to stop, tells me that she's eager for more intimacy."

Heat flamed inside her, and she lightly chuckled. "If I admit it, will you?"

He took her hands and brought them to his mouth as he brushed his lips over her knuckles. "You *do* want to marry me, don't you? And not because you don't want your father to betroth you to Edgar Stone."

She laughed loudly. "Well, Augusta's nephew was certainly my main motivation, but I'll admit that after kissing you a few times, I'm looking forward to life as your wife."

His smile relaxed, and he placed his lips on her hand, keeping them there longer than before. "And I'm looking forward to sharing many passionate nights with you."

Oh heavens! He had planted the thought inside her head, and now she was going to think about that until they were wed. This man, who always had seduction on his mind, knew exactly what he was saying, and he probably knew exactly what kind of reaction she would have.

Their wedding couldn't get here soon enough.

CHAPTER EIGHT

VINCENT LAY IN bed on his back with his arms crossed behind his head, as he stared up at the ceiling. He'd had this ridiculous smile on his face ever since kissing Ellie at the Berkleys' dinner social. He hadn't been able to get her off his mind. Sleep wasn't his companion of late. Instead, images of Ellie that filled his head, keeping him in an alternate dream world.

Strange that he would feel this way, especially since her actions before the meal had served to upset him. But afterward...

He grinned. If he had to put a name to the way she'd acted before the meal, he'd say it was jealousy. Yet why would she be jealous of Candace? He was marrying *her*, not his former mistress.

Sighing deeply, he shook his head. He shouldn't be feeling this way. Eventually, she would discover his involvement with Adam, which would end drastically for them. He couldn't allow his heart to get involved with that woman. But could he stop it now?

Memories resurfaced about those days before Adam Haddington had left to join the other soldiers in battle. Adam's family wasn't well off, not like some titled families, but they weren't poor, either. After Adam had asked the duke for Ellie's hand in marriage, he talked to Vincent. For some reason, the duke had made him feel as though he would never earn enough money to support his daughter. Adam was feeling desolate about his finances, and Vincent had convinced his friend to join the military. Never did he think Adam would be killed in battle.

Vincent frowned and sat up in bed, running his fingers through his messy hair. If he hadn't convinced Adam to join the military, he'd still be alive and married to Ellie. And Vincent wouldn't have to carry the burden of guilt of sending his friend to his death—or of marrying the woman Adam had been engaged to.

Other voices echoed in his head, confusing him. Last night, Candace had mentioned that Adam only wanted to marry Ellie because she was wealthy. If that were the case, then why had Adam joined the military after Vincent suggested it? For that matter, why had Adam felt disappointed that he wasn't making enough to marry Ellie?

Whose story should he believe?

The clamoring of voices in the hall brought Vincent out of his jumbled thoughts. Something was wrong. Why else would people be hurrying in the hall?

He jumped out of bed and shrugged on his robe just as someone pounded loudly on his door.

"Vincent, wake up," Laura said frantically.

He quickly opened the door. His sister's face was pale, and she held a large rock with a note tied to it. Behind her stood Lilly, whose appearance resembled that of a ghost as well.

"Vincent, someone just threw a rock through the dining room window." She reached out her shaky hand, holding the rock toward him.

"They *threw* it at our window?"

"Yes."

"Did you see who it was?"

"No." Both his sisters shook their head.

He yanked off the string securing the note to the rock, then unfolded the paper. He skimmed the few sentences, and his heart sank. *Stay away from Ellie Middleton. This is your second warning. Remember the sticker weeds?*

"What does it say?" both sisters chimed together.

He shook his head. "It's nothing to worry about. I shall deal with this personally."

As he turned back into his room, anger quickly grew inside him. Who would be foolish enough to do this?

"Vincent?" Lilly whined. "What about the broken window?"

"I said I'll handle it," Vincent snapped, and kicked the door closed with his heel.

Whom could he ask about this? It wasn't like they had a houseful of servants. The only person he could think that might not want him marrying Ellie would be Adam, but Vincent didn't believe in ghosts.

As he dressed, his mind scrambled to think of others who might not want to see him married to her. The only other person would be Lady Livingston. But she wasn't underhanded enough to do something this vindictive. She would just move on to another man. Vincent hadn't been *that* important in her life.

By the time he was dressed, his head throbbed with uncertainty. Should he make the duke aware of this? Perhaps Ellie's father might know something. Vincent didn't know what else to do. He could inform the authorities, but even they wouldn't be able to find the culprit.

Skipping breakfast, Vincent wandered outside and searched around the area where the rock would have been thrown in the window. He didn't see any boot marks in the dirt. However, there were horse's hooves.

He grumbled and marched back inside the manor and into the dining room. His sisters must have cleaned up the glass, because he didn't see any shards on the wooden floor. He would have to replace the window, and pray it didn't cost too much.

Vincent scratched his head as he stared out the broken window. What if this person wasn't someone he knew? What if this person only knew Ellie? Yet if they knew the young woman, they'd *want* to see her married, wouldn't they? Unless she had an admirer who hadn't made his intentions known yet. But would they go as far as throwing a rock through the window? That was quite immature. So, was the perpetrator someone in their youth?

Gritting his teeth, he rubbed the back of his neck. There was no way he'd do as the note instructed. But if he didn't follow their directions, would there be a third warning? As mentioned in the note, this unknown person had placed the sticker weeds under the horse's blanket. Obviously, they were quite serious.

Vincent would love nothing better than to get his hands on this person. He'd show them that Vincent Wallace, Earl of Trenton, would *not* succumb to threats. They needed to talk to him face to face. But even then, he wasn't going to stop seeing Ellie. After all, it was her father who was pushing the wedding. Vincent really didn't have any other choice.

He turned, rushed out of the room, and left the house. The only thing he could think to do was to talk to the duke. Something must be done, and quickly. Vincent prayed that Ellie wasn't in danger. But she had been with him when the horse bucked out of control. So yes, she was in danger.

He saddled his horse before mounting and riding as fast as he could toward Ellie's estate. Hopefully, Dominic would assist in this search to find the fool responsible for all of this. Vincent's wedding grew closer. He couldn't risk having another episode.

ELLIE WALKED ON clouds this morning. For the first time in three years, she hadn't dreamed about Adam, and hadn't awoken with tears on her face. And surprisingly enough, she didn't feel guilty for betraying him by looking forward to having more passionate moments with Vincent.

Humming, she floated down the stairs and to the music room at the end of the hall. She hadn't touched the pianoforte since before Adam died, and she suddenly felt like playing again. She sat on the bench and placed her fingers on the ivory keys.

Immediately a tune popped into her head. She had played this with her mother when she was a little girl. The memory made her smile. Although she missed her parent terribly, thinking of her always brought happiness to Ellie's heart. For the longest time after her mother's passing, Ellie believed her mother was her guardian angel. She had *felt* her mother's presence, especially after Adam died.

Voices from outside the music room window interrupted her thoughts. Sighing, she pulled her fingers off the pianoforte's keys and glanced toward the window. The male voice didn't sound familiar, but the female voice sounded like Augusta. Was the woman reprimanding another servant?

Ellie scowled. She didn't like the way her stepmother had taken over the household. The way her father didn't notice—or acted like he didn't care—was unnerving. And why Ellie couldn't trust Augusta, she didn't know. She wondered if her guardian angel was trying to warn her.

She moved away from the musical instrument and headed toward the window. Just as she reached it, the male voice said her name. Ellie froze, and dared to eavesdrop on their conversation, thankful that they couldn't see her.

"You don't have need to worry, my dear Edgar. Leave Ellie to me. I'll sway her attitude toward thinking you will be the better husband."

Bile rose in Ellie's throat, and she placed a hand over her mouth. When had Augusta's nephew arrived? And why wasn't Ellie informed? If she'd known the imbecile was coming, she would have gone to stay with Aunt Sylvia in London.

"Honestly, *Auntie*, I don't see how you can accomplish such a feat. Didn't you see the way they looked at each other yesterday?"

Edgar's whiney voice had Ellie rolling her eyes. He sounded like a boy instead of a grown man of thirty. In the little time she had known Edgar, he had proven what a spoiled, selfish, violent man he could be. She didn't want anything to do with him.

"Be that as it may," Augusta remarked in a haughty voice,

"there are ways to sway her father. After all, the duke hasn't signed the betrothal agreement yet."

Inwardly, Ellie snickered. Apparently, the woman didn't know the duke had already approved of the wedding and just waited for the right moment to sign the papers. After all, he was the reason she and Vincent were marrying in the first place.

"Then let me suggest you do something quickly," Edgar snapped. "We are running out of time."

Ellie frowned. What was that supposed to mean?

"Leave it to me," Augusta said. "I can persuade the duke. But I cannot do this alone. If you want to impress Ellie, now is the time."

"I have something planned." Edgar chuckled. "I'm sure Ellie will love it."

Ellie's stomach lurched, and she moved away from the window, not wanting to hear more. Her father needed to know about this. Certainly, he wouldn't allow Augusta to get away with this trickery.

Hurrying out of the room, determination guided her steps. From room to room, she searched for her father, but to no avail. Not even the butler knew where the duke was this time of the morning.

She stopped at the side door near her father's study. Looking outside, she scanned the west yard carefully. The sweet fragrance from her mother's prized flower garden carried through the light breeze. Thankfully, Ellie still had something on the estate to remind her of Mother.

Rubbing her forehead, she tried to focus back on her father, and what his schedule might be today. The frantic pounding in her head made it impossible to think clearly. As far as she recalled, their family didn't have any pressing engagements until this evening, when they would attend another ball.

A horse's neigh from off in the distance snapped her out of her thoughts. Perhaps her father was riding this morning.

Without another thought, she rushed outside and down

toward the stable. Oliver, their main stable man, stood in front of the double doors, brushing down her father's horse.

"Oliver," she said, out of breath.

His gaze snapped up to her before he bowed. "Yes, Miss Middleton."

"Have...you seen my father." She tried to catch her breath, but it was difficult.

"Not since he went riding this morning."

She blew out an exasperated breath, moved to the outside wall of the stable, and leaned against it. Her headache throbbed harder, and she rubbed her forehead as she closed her eyes. This was ridiculous. Where would he have gone?

"Miss Middleton?" Oliver asked sheepishly. "Did something happen to your horse, Pegasus?"

"Not that I'm aware of." She peeked at the servant beneath her lashes. "Why?"

"Because Pegasus is missing."

Headache forgotten, Ellie jumped away from the wall and turned to enter the structure. She scanned inside, searching for her beautiful white and gray Gypsy Vanner horse. The stall was empty.

"Oliver," she shrieked as she ran out to the servant. "Where is Pegasus?"

"I don't know." He shrugged. "When I awoke this morning, your horse was gone."

Panic filled her, squeezing her heart and bringing tears to her eyes. "We must find her. I've raised her since I was ten years old."

"Yes, Miss Middleton." He nodded. "I shall alert the other stable hands, and we'll search the area."

Oliver led her father's horse inside the stable as he shouted instructions to the other servants.

She dashed, unladylike, across the yard, heading toward the glade. Pegasus liked to graze nearby the glade, and she prayed this was where she had wandered.

From a distance, her name was called. She stopped and

looked toward the rider coming toward her, waving a hand. When she recognized Vincent, she released a sob and covered her mouth, waiting for him to reach her. Concern etched his expression as he stopped his horse and jumped off.

"Ellie, what's wrong?" he asked, taking large strides toward her.

"Oh, Vincent." She ran to him. His strong arms wrapped around her shoulders as she pressed her head against his muscular chest. "Pegasus is gone."

"Your horse?" He stroked her unbound hair that she hadn't had styled yet.

"Yes." She lifted her head. "Vincent, Pegasus never wanders off."

"Shh…" He brushed away the tears from her cheek with the pads of this thumbs. "I'll find her."

She grasped the lapels of his overcoat. "Let me come with you."

His gaze roamed over her long hair hanging over her shoulders, and then to her face. "I'm quite certain your father wouldn't approve." He ran his palm over her hair again. "You need to ready yourself first, my precious."

She scowled. "I don't care what my appearance is. I need to find my horse. So are you taking me or not?"

Slowly, he nodded and cupped her face. "Calm yourself. I shall take you."

Sighing, she leaned against him. "I thank you, Vincent. I shall have Oliver find my father and inform him of my whereabouts."

Vincent turned them toward his horse and lifted her on top before mounting behind her. A warm, comforting feeling surrounded her as she relaxed against his chest. One strong arm circled her waist as he used his other hand to grip the reins. His hot breath blew against her cheek, making her feel more secure in his arms.

He guided his horse back toward the stable, where he instructed the stable man to find her father and let him know where

Ellie was. The servant nodded and dashed toward the house.

Without another word, Vincent urged his horse into a fast gallop. She searched as far as her vision could go, but she didn't spot Pegasus. Dread filled her more the longer they rode around the estate.

"Where is she?" Ellie sobbed.

Vincent rode to the end of her father's property and stopped the horse. She covered her face with her hands as the tears fell freely. They couldn't give up now.

"Ellie, my precious." Vincent kissed the back of her head. "We need to locate your father. I believe he can help us."

"There's no time." She shook her head, keeping her hands over her face.

"But we must. I believe there is more to this than just a missing horse."

Dropping her hands, she looked at him over her shoulder. "What do you mean?"

"I received a threat this morning. In the note, they mentioned there might be another incident if I didn't do what they instructed."

She blinked, trying to clear her teary vision as she focused on his handsome face. "What did they instruct you to do?"

Vincent was silent for a few moments before he licked his lips. "They want me to stay away from you."

Fear rushed through her, and she sucked in her breath. "Oh, please, tell me you're teasing."

He shook his head. "They threw a rock in the dining room window. They also took responsibility for the sticker weeds under the horse's saddle blanket. Sadly, this is not a joke."

A tremor passed through her. She clutched his arm. "Do you know who *they* are?"

"Not yet."

"Do you think they took Pegasus?"

He shrugged one shoulder. "At this point, I will accuse them of anything that goes wrong." He leaned forward and kissed her forehead. "Now do you understand why I think we should find your father first?"

Nodding, she withdrew just enough to peer into his blue-gray eyes. "Yes."

She faced forward and cuddled against his chest as he guided the horse back toward the manor. Her mind swam with unanswered questions, confusing her more. Someone wanted him to stay away from her? What utter nonsense! Why would anyone—

Her memory played back the conversation she had eavesdropped on between Augusta and Edgar. Could it be them? She wouldn't put it past Edgar to be so underhanded. And it wouldn't surprise her to know that Augusta was in on it with her nephew. But *why*? What was their reasoning for wanting Ellie and Edgar to marry?

For certain, she would make her father aware of what she'd heard. She just prayed he believed her, as when she had brought her concerns to him about Augusta before, he just pushed them under the rug as if they were not important. Well, this time they were very important, and with Vincent by her side, she would make her father see what was going on.

They reached the house. Vincent jumped off his horse first, and then lifted her down. Their gazes locked, and she enjoyed how gentle he was with her, as if she were a porcelain dish.

He took her hand as they turned toward the porch steps, but just then, Dominic flew from the house. When he noticed them, he stopped sharply. Deep lines were around his eyes and mouth. His attention shifted between Ellie and Vincent.

"What's wrong?" Dominic asked.

"I should ask you the same thing." She released Vincent's hand, walked up the stairs, and touched her brother's arm.

Dominic sighed heavily. "Father has gone missing."

CHAPTER NINE

THE NEXT TWO hours crept by. Vincent paced in the duke's drawing room, along with Dominic and Ellie. The Metropolitan Police had arrived and asked everyone questions. Their inspectors scoped out the property, but neither the duke nor Ellie's horse were located.

Many times, Vincent wanted to hold Ellie and comfort her, but that wouldn't be proper until their wedding announcement was made...and he now wondered if that would ever happen. Indeed, there were games afoot, and none of them were worth playing.

Ellie eyed her stepmother warily. As misfortune had touched the duke's household, it appeared to bring Edgar Stone with it. There were many reasons why she didn't like that man. One of them being that Ellie's parents had wanted her to marry the terrible fellow. But over the years, the imbecile had also given Vincent several reasons not to like him. Stone was a poor gambler, and a worse loser. He was a violent drunk, which was why he struck women until they were bruised and bleeding.

Vincent poured some of the duke's finest port in a glass and tossed it down. Helplessness swept over him. There must be something he could do to assist in the matter. Ellie, her brother, and even her stepmother appeared desolate. If Vincent had only known the duke better, perhaps he'd be able to help the police with the investigation.

He looked back at Ellie. A maid had fixed her hair into a coil at the back of her head, but Vincent imagined it the way it had been this morning. Although she wore a day dress, she appeared as though she'd just awoken from a long night's rest. Her long hair had waved down her arms and back in a very seductive fashion. Usually, he didn't see a woman's hair like that unless he was bidding them farewell the next morning after an eventful evening of passion.

From across the room, her gaze rested on him. The police inspector who'd been asking her questions finally left. Vincent walked toward her. The poor woman's eyes were red and puffy from her crying. An overwhelming urge to enfold her in his arms came over him, stronger than before. If they were the only two people in the room, he'd gladly take her in his arms and comfort her.

"Walk outside with me?" he asked when he reached her.

"Yes. I do need some fresh air."

She hooked her hand around his elbow, and he led her out of the drawing room and outside. The sun disappeared behind a dark cloud, and the wind picked up. But Ellie acted as though she didn't mind the slight chill in the air. Vincent enjoyed the refreshing temperature, but especially the open space. If he had stayed inside that room one more minute, he would have screamed.

Ellie stopped, closed her eyes, and tilted her face upward. Her bosom rose and fell from her deep breaths. He could stare at her like this for hours without getting bored. She was simply adorable.

"Oh, Vincent. What are we to do?" She looked at him. "What if Father isn't found?"

He took her hands into his loosely. "Try not to think that way."

"How can I not? You received a threatening note, and now this." She paused, glancing toward the stable. "I believe it's all connected some way."

"It certainly seems planned."

She turned back to him. "Did you tell the police about it?"

"I did, and they seemed rather put off that I hadn't reported it earlier."

"Why hadn't you?"

"Because I wanted to speak to your father first." He squeezed her hands. "I knew he would know what we could do about it. That is why I came this morning, when I found you by the stable."

Sighing, she stepped closer to him and rested her head on his chest. "I told the police about the suspicions I have over Edgar Stone and my stepmother."

Curiosity rose inside of him. "What suspicions?"

Her body stiffened before she looked up. "I didn't tell you?"

"No."

"I overheard Augusta speaking with her nephew. The whiney little bugger still wants to marry me, and Augusta promised she could *sway* my father's thinking. Augusta told Edgar to do something that would impress me." She huffed. "I don't think the man is intelligent, but would he take my horse and father as a way of impressing me? I don't think so."

Anger pulsed inside Vincent. How dare those two try to complicate Ellie's life? "I pray the police take what you told them seriously. Like you, I don't think Edgar is smart enough to think of a plan like this, but the duchess may be that vindictive."

"I'm quite certain Augusta is very intelligent and calculating. I've always felt that she manipulated herself into my father's life."

"Then I suggest you keep a close watch on her." Vincent caressed Ellie's cheek with his knuckles. "And I'll keep an eye on Stone as much as I can."

"Actually, I believe he's staying with us, so I may be able to spy on them." She sighed again and cuddled against his palm. "We need to find my father. I don't want my life to be a Cinderella tale with the mean stepmother."

He chuckled. "But didn't Cinderella marry her prince at the end of the story?"

"She did."

"Then if your life turns out like that, you will have something to look forward to."

She arched an eyebrow. "Vincent, you aren't being very humorous, you know."

"I know. I'm just trying to make you smile, if even just a little."

The corners of her mouth lifted gently, and her eyes didn't appear so sad. "Thank you for being with me now, during this turmoil. You don't know how much it relieves me to have you here."

"I wouldn't have it any other way."

Her gaze dropped to his mouth. Cotton dryness grew in his throat, and he tried to swallow it. His breathing quickened, and the urge to kiss her became strong. Yet was it proper? Especially now, when she'd been through so much today?

"Vincent?" she said in a whisper. "Have I told you how wonderful you are?"

The words slammed into his heart. He had never had a woman say such words and genuinely mean them. He suddenly didn't care if anyone was watching. He was going to show Ellie exactly how much those tender words meant to him.

In one swift movement, he pulled her into his arms and lowered his mouth. The second his lips touched hers, she inhaled sharply, and followed it with a heady sigh. Her soft body melted against him as she wound her arms around his neck.

Passion took over, inflaming his whole body. He really should take her someplace private for what he wanted to do right now, but he couldn't stop kissing her long enough. Never had he wanted a woman so much it made him weak in every way possible. And heaven might send down a lightning bolt right now, because he just couldn't wait until the wedding to make love to her.

"Precious," he whispered against her lips.

"Yes?"

He moved his hands over her back, pulling her against him closer. "Where can we go…to have some privacy?"

She released a low moan. "How about my bedchambers?"

Excitement built inside of him—she wanted this as much as he did. "Will anyone see us going there?"

"I don't…know," she said in between kisses. "But if they do…then we'll have a speedy marriage."

Inwardly, he chuckled. He liked the way her mind worked.

Off in the distance, voices lifted in excitement. Vincent didn't want to break their passionate kiss to see what was going on, but when the voices grew louder, both he and Ellie pulled away at the same time.

Toward the front of the house, a lone rider galloped toward the manor. Dominic, Augusta, and some servants ran toward the horse.

"*Father!*"

Ellie's cry startled Vincent. She darted toward her father, holding her dress up to help her run faster.

Breathing deeply and slowly, Vincent tried to tame the desire still flowing through him like turbulent waters. There was no way he could greet the duke like this. Vincent only hoped that Ellie's excitement for her father's homecoming would override the passion that had been written on her face only moments ago.

ELLIE SAT CLOSELY beside her father on the sofa as he answered the police's questions. It pleased her to know he had noticed her horse missing after his morning ride, and that he'd gone after the animal. He hadn't taken his favorite horse only because he'd just put the animal through a vigorous ride. He didn't have any excuse as to why he hadn't alerted Oliver to what he was doing, only that he was concerned about Ellie's missing horse.

Sadly, he hadn't found Pegasus.

Her heart ached for the animal who'd been her companion since she was in her tenth year. With any luck, the mare would eventually find its way back home.

She glanced around the room. Vincent had gone home, and his absence was greatly noticed. At least by her. He had wanted to talk to her father about the threatening note, but for some reason, he decided now wasn't the best time. She, too, wanted to find the person—or persons—responsible for trying to control their lives so that her father could put a stop to it.

Ellie did as she promised Vincent—she kept an eye on Augusta. The woman appeared to have been very distraught over the duke's absence. Could she have been acting this whole time? Ellie wouldn't doubt it.

And Edgar had mysteriously disappeared once the duke returned home. Didn't Augusta want her husband to know the idiotic nephew was staying with them? Well, Ellie couldn't wait to be the first one to tell her father of their uninvited guest.

The midday meal had come and gone, and wearily, Ellie climbed the stairs as she headed for her bedchamber. A small nap was required if she hoped to be able to make it through tonight's events. She wasn't exactly looking forward to dancing and trying to converse with other men. She wanted to be with Vincent, and him alone, in private, and continue what they had started minutes before her father returned home.

Although what she and Vincent wanted to do was wrong on so many levels, at least it would speed up the marriage. And right now, that was all she wanted. She hated this process of courting just to keep everyone in society from gossiping. The *ton* were going to spread rumors no matter what happened. Things between her and Vincent were already settled, so why couldn't they just get it over with quickly?

She climbed to the second level of the manor, and as she turned the corner, she came face to face with her worst nightmare. Edgar was in no way handsome, and he definitely wasn't muscular. He *thought* he had charm, but lacked it greatly. Perhaps that was why he required his *auntie* to help him secure a wife. Most women would be able to see right through Edgar's character and know that he wasn't the man they wanted in their lives.

Immediately, she fisted her hands and gritted her teeth as she silently wished him to disappear from her life forever.

"Miss Middleton. You are the very person I was coming to find." He pushed his fingers through his patch of wavy red hair.

"Well, I hope you're not too disappointed that I'm on my way to my bedchamber to take a nap."

"Actually, what I have to say will only take a moment. I shall walk with you to your room."

She held up her hand, stopping him. "I'd rather you didn't."

The imbecile must have seen it as some kind of intimate gesture, because he took her hand in his, stroking her arm gently. Irritation flowed through her, and she yanked her hand away, slapping him in the process. How dare he take such liberties.

"Lord Stone! Contain yourself," she hissed.

He shifted from one foot to the other. Edgar wasn't a tall man, not like Vincent, but he was a couple inches taller than her.

"Forgive me, Miss Middleton. My excuse is that your nearness does that to me, and I yearn to touch you."

She rolled her eyes. "Then might I suggest that you stay far away from me, starting this very moment. Then perhaps your *urge* will go away."

As she tried to step around him, he chuckled and grasped her elbow, stopping her.

"Oh, Miss Middleton. You are most humorous today." His wide smile made the freckles stand out on his pale face.

"Humorous? I assure you, I'm far from that. I've had a trying morning with my father being gone, and my horse missing. Now I would very much like to rest in my room. So if you'll please let me pass...?" She glared at him.

He frowned. "Ellie, I know we got off to a bad start after we were first introduced—"

"Beg pardon, my lord, but I did *not* give you permission to use my name so personally, and I will never give that permission to you."

His bushy eyebrows lifted. "But we are practically family."

"Actually, we aren't, and we are never going to be, so I pray you get that notion out of your head quickly." She folded her arms across her chest. "Lord Stone, I don't like you, and there is nothing you or your aunt can do to change it. Please understand that now, because I don't want to waste my breath explaining it again."

Ellie rushed passed him before he could stop her again. Hopefully, she was rude enough to him that he would get the hint. She didn't have patience for him.

She entered her room and quickly slammed the door shut. Leaning against the thick piece of wood, she breathed slowly, trying to calm her temper. If that man didn't leave her alone, she would scream. Would her father understand her worries and dismiss Edgar from their home? Then again, Ellie had heard Augusta tell Edgar that she could *sway* the duke to do anything.

"Augh!" Ellie marched to her bed and threw herself on the mattress. She feared sleep would be impossible now.

She rolled to her side and stared out the window. A slight wind blew, disturbing the leaves on the large oak tree beside her window. The tree beckoned her to escape, just as it had done when she was a young girl. She had not always been the most obedient daughter, and there were many times in her youth when she climbed out the window, saddled Pegasus, and rode her mare at night. Riding was the only thing that calmed her spirit and relaxed her.

Frowning, she pulled a pillow against her chest. But she couldn't climb out onto the tree and escape to the stable to fetch her horse now. And where would she go? She definitely couldn't stay here. Would Vincent mind her coming to visit his sisters again? The idea tempted her, but she knew she'd not be in good spirits. Not with the upsetting day she'd had.

She sighed and closed her eyes as her mind returned to that very passionate moment with Vincent earlier today. Would she have done anything differently? Maybe she should have taken him up to her room right then. No, that wouldn't have been wise, since her father chose that moment to make his grand appearance.

A hard knock shook the door and snapped Ellie out of her memory. She turned her head toward the door but didn't move from her bed. "Who is it?"

"It's Augusta, my dear."

Ellie rolled her eyes. She didn't want to see that woman just as much as she hadn't wanted to see her nephew earlier. "What do you want?"

"I would like to talk."

"Augusta," Ellie answered, hoping she didn't sound as irritated as she felt, "I'm lying down. I'm tired."

"Please, dear. Your father urged me to come talk to you."

Ellie hesitated. Dare she believe the woman? Augusta had used the excuse before, and it had worked. Now Ellie wondered if she should deny her stepmother's request. Unfortunately, it boiled down to one thing; did she have the patience to argue with the older woman?

Grumbling under her breath, Ellie scooted off the bed so she could answer the door. She opened it before turning back toward her bed and flinging herself on the mattress. "Make it quick. I'm really tired, and I need to get rested before tonight's events."

"Oh, my poor dear." Augusta rushed to the bed and stroked Ellie's back. "Do you wish us to cancel our evening? I'm certain your father would rather stay home, as well. Lord Trenton would understand, too."

Not see Vincent until tomorrow? That was not an option. He was the only person who could calm her ire. He was the only person who understood the turmoil boiling through her. And he was the only one whom she felt safe with.

"No, Augusta." She tried not to glare at the other woman. "I don't want to cancel. I just want to sleep for an hour, mayhap two. I'll feel rested after that."

Augusta sighed heavily before sitting on the edge of Ellie's bed. She swept an auburn lock of hair away from her forehead, patting it as though trying to keep it with her coiled hair.

It had always been difficult for Ellie to think of this woman as her parent. She was so much younger than Ellie's father—much too young to know anything about parenting. Even Dominic didn't think of Augusta as his mother. The woman was much too self-centered.

"My dear, your father and I are worried about you. We both feel the stress of finding a husband has made you extremely irritable."

Ellie held in a surprised gasp. Was she jesting? The burden of finding a husband was making Ellie hard to live with, but whose fault was that?

"Indeed?" She arched an eyebrow. "What made you come to this conclusion?"

Augusta nodded toward the hall. "I overheard the way you spoke to Edgar a few moments ago, and I must say, I'm very displeased that you are not more polite. He has taken a liking to you, and he has treated you with nothing but kindness. You could at least show him a little bit of respect in return."

It was difficult for Ellie not to roll her eyes. Could the woman be that obtuse? "The truth is, Augusta," she said between clenched teeth, "I don't want that man in my home."

A flash of anger crossed the older woman's expression and darkened her eyes. "But it's my home, too."

"It's been mine longer."

Whether it was the stress of finding a husband, or the strain of everything that had happened today, Ellie was exhausted from having to hold her tongue around a woman she couldn't trust.

Augusta gasped and placed a hand to her bosom. "I say, Ellie, that was just uncalled for."

"Actually, it's not." Ellie shook her head as she moved off the bed and stood. "I have tried to tolerate you since you married my father, but I cannot do it any longer, especially since you have brought your nephew to *my home* to torment me. If you want me to return to my normal self, then I beg of you, send Edgar back where he came from. He is *not* wanted here."

Augusta released another loud gasp and stood. Her brow was creased, and lines of anger appeared around her mouth and the corner of her eyes. "I will not stand for this kind of talk about my nephew."

Ellie pointed toward the door. "Then leave. Nothing is stopping you."

Huffing, Augusta folded her arms across her bosom and stomped out of the room. Ellie followed so that she could close the door.

Her hands shook as fury built inside her. Tears pricked her eyes, and she didn't know whether to cry or shout at the top of her voice. She couldn't be in this house another moment with *that woman.*

There was only one thing to do. Ellie needed to convince Vincent to cause a scandal that would force them to wed sooner. Then again, perhaps she didn't have to say anything to him. What if she just started the scandal herself and let the consequences fall where they may?

After all, Vincent *was* a rogue.

Ellie smiled. For Vincent, tonight would just be a normal evening. He might enjoy it. And for her, it would be a way out of this house. It would also fulfill her curiosity about the marriage bed. But she was quite certain she would enjoy herself immensely and never regret it.

CHAPTER TEN

VINCENT WAS PROUD of Ellie for being so strong. Most women would have called off all activities for the week because of what had happened to her father, but thankfully, it wasn't Ellie who bowed out of the ball. The duchess was the one who had complained about a headache, which made the duke cancel last night's event. However, tonight was a different function, and Vincent was thrilled to see that Ellie was here and alert. And once more, she was the loveliest woman at the ball.

Ellie was a cross between an angel and a seductress. The bulk of her silky, dark brown hair was wrapped loosely on her head, with tendrils by her ears and on her neck. Wisps of baby's-breath flowers gently decorated her hair. Hanging from her ears were pearl-drop earbobs, and a matching necklace circled her slender throat. She was an angel.

But it was the square-neck bodice of the deep purple sensation she wore, with bell-shaped sleeves and elbow-length black gloves, that gave her the appearance of a seductress. The gown's train was slightly longer than she'd worn before, and the black lace overlay on the skirt parted down the front.

Vincent was certain she would entice more men than just him at the ball tonight. There would be many who left the ball with their hearts shattered upon realizing Miss Middleton only had eyes for Lord Trenton.

Surprisingly enough, he only had eyes for her, as well.

Over the course of the last few days, Vincent had slowly felt his rakehell life slipping away. What shocked him more was realizing that he didn't mind the change. The thought of only having one woman for the rest of his life pleased him, as long as it was Ellie Middleton.

He enjoyed the way his body tingled whenever she touched him. He took pleasure in hearing her little sighs of delight when he held her in his arms. He cherished the way his body burned while they shared a passionate kiss. And he looked forward to making her his wife in all senses of the word.

Vincent stood beside Ellie as they chatted with her parents and some of their friends. Vincent didn't have much to contribute to the conversation, only because Ellie's beauty had left his brain numb, as well as his tongue. All he could do was smile and nod, and stare at Ellie as though he'd never seen anything so lovely in his life. The flowery fragrance surrounding her made him want to bury his face in her neck and inhale deeply until he was intoxicated by her scent.

Finally, the music started up, announcing that the ball had begun. Vincent immediately offered his arm to Ellie, who accepted with a bright smile. He didn't say anything as he escorted her out on the floor, but the minute her eyes locked with his, she chuckled.

"Lord Trenton," she said softly, "you are acting very strangely this evening."

"Am I, my precious? I wonder why."

"Yes, I wonder that as well. Are you all right?"

"No, not exactly." He grinned.

One of her eyebrows lifted. "My lord, I'm not quite sure what you're hinting at."

Tilting back his head, he laughed heartily. He wasn't about to confess his inner thoughts. Not yet. "Oh, my precious Ellie. You are such a delight. Don't you realize that you have turned me into a different person?"

"How extraordinary. I didn't think I could accomplish such a feat."

They traded partners, but he kept his gaze on the prettiest woman at the ball. He enjoyed the way she hesitantly threw glances his way as she tried to pay attention to her dance partner. Her face relaxed, and her eyes darkened as if she believed him to be the most handsome man, too. If only the orchestra could play the waltz, the scandalous dance from Germany that would keep her in his arms for the whole tune.

Finally, the country dance had him pairing with Ellie again.

"I fear, my lord, that I've never seen you so out of sorts."

"Out of sorts? What do you mean?"

She cocked her head. "You nearly stepped on Miss Hampton's foot, and you certainly didn't look at her. Have you nothing to do but stare at me all evening?"

"Oh, I assure you, staring at you all evening is very pleasurable."

She chuckled. "And what about speaking to others? Don't you want to do that tonight?"

"Although I have much on my mind, I would rather not talk to someone I hardly know, especially if they enjoy spreading gossip."

She nodded. "I definitely understand your reluctance now."

They had to trade partners again, and just as before, Vincent couldn't take his stare off Ellie. It delighted him when she stared at him the whole time as well. Once she was back at his side, he squeezed her hand gently.

"However," he added as he lowered his voice, "I look forward with great anticipation to when we can talk to our hearts' content. Just the two of us, with nobody around to overhear."

Her face turned red, and she laughed. "Oh, Lord Trenton, you can most certainly count on it tonight."

He sucked in a breath. Was she serious? Did she even know what he was talking about? But she did. She wasn't a dimwit like other ladies.

"Tonight?" he questioned, hesitantly.

Her smile widened as her eyes narrowed and held a hint of desire. "Yes, tonight. I cannot wait any longer."

Warmth spread through him the longer he thought about what they could accomplish—alone in some place very private. Now he prayed that time passed quickly, because the wait would surely kill him.

The dance ended, and she was swept away by another man. The promise in her eyes gave him hope, making him anxious. Would it be immediately after the ball? Of course. During the ball would be scandalous. He wanted details, but he couldn't interrupt her just to talk more about their tryst. Not yet, anyway. He would dance with her again soon, so he must be patient.

Inwardly, he chuckled. Patient? How could he be that when excitement was rushing through him as he stood against the wall, imagining how their evening would turn out?

An hour later, he watched as she danced with yet another man. This time, Vincent wasn't worried about others trying to charm her. There was no need to find fault with the gentlemen, which, thankfully, made Vincent's job easier.

Sighing, he forced himself to scope out the other guests at the ball. He knew Lady Livingston wasn't attending this function, mainly because she hadn't accosted him yet. Knowing that she wasn't there made him more relaxed. Although he loved to see Ellie's jealousy flare up, he didn't want to exhaust himself trying to keep away from his former mistress.

Out of the corner of his eye, he noticed a familiar man watching Ellie with a wary eye, and Vincent's guard lifted a notch. Lord Calvin Drake appeared quite dapper this evening in his gray suit jacket and trousers with black waistcoat. Several women standing nearby made dove eyes at him, which seemed to go unnoticed by the lord. Vincent didn't approve of the way Drake watched Ellie with a forlorn expression.

He scratched his neck. Hadn't Drake just been introduced to Ellie? If so, why did the man have a yearning sense about him as he studied the duke's daughter? His goatee still bothered Vincent, but that was neither here nor there. Something about the man troubled him. Drake was Adam's cousin, so then why was he suddenly showing interest in Ellie? Of course, she would want to get to know Drake, mainly because of Adam's connection. Would Drake use that as an opportunity to turn on his charm? Vincent couldn't allow that to happen.

Once the dance was over, Lord Calvin moved toward Ellie. Vincent's chest tightened. He couldn't have that man dancing with her. But stopping Lord Calvin would only make a scene. He couldn't do that to her or her family.

When Drake reached Ellie and she looked up at his face, Vincent held his breath. *Turn him down!* But the sparkle in her eyes and her widening smile let Vincent know she would be dancing with Drake tonight.

When the couple walked out on the floor, Vincent fisted his hands by his sides. Why jealousy had crept inside of him, he didn't know. *He* was the one she was going to marry. And *he* was the one she would meet tonight in private. So why should he worry about Lord Calvin?

His heart squeezed. Naturally, she'd think of Adam while chatting with Lord Calvin. And why wouldn't she? The two men were cousins. But Vincent wanted Adam out of Ellie's heart. *He* wanted to be the one to remove his former friend from her mind so that her thoughts would turn to him.

Ellie laughed at something Drake said, and it felt as though someone had jabbed a knife into Vincent's heart. He hated this emotion, and he wished it to disappear. His mind tried to re-create images of Ellie in his arms, kissing him as though there was no tomorrow. But he couldn't close his eyes long enough to conjure up the memory.

At long last, the dance ended. Vincent pulled himself away from the wall and hurried toward Ellie. He would claim the next dance, even if he had to start rumors just to do it. He wanted her to gaze at him with stars in her eyes, and laugh at something he said with her deep, sultry voice.

Just as he arrived by her side, Lord Drake turned to leave. Vincent made eye contact with the other man. Drake gave him a small bow and walked away. Annoyance ran through Vincent. The man could have at least greeted him in some way besides the nod.

Vincent looked into Ellie's eyes, and the tightness in his chest relaxed. He sighed, allowing the worry over the other man to leave him. He took her hand in his and rubbed her fingers gently. "Dance with me."

Her expression seemed to soften. Smiling, she nodded.

Thankfully, this was a much slower song, which didn't require changing partners. "Are you enjoying yourself, my precious?"

She nodded. "I am. How about you? I've only seen you dance with one other person tonight, and she was as old as my father."

He chuckled as his heart flipped in his chest. It appeared that she had been keeping an eye on him, as well. "Truth be told, I wish the hours would pass quickly. I'm very eager to take you someplace private."

Her eyelids lowered. "As am I."

If he could only take her right now. "Do you think people would question it if we leave now?"

Laughing, she nodded. "I'm quite certain of it, my lord."

He scowled playfully. "I suppose convincing your father that you suddenly have a stomach ailment is out of the question."

She arched an eyebrow. "Actually, that suggestion does have merit."

Her response took him by surprise, and he shook his head. He couldn't possibly have heard correctly. "Are you serious?"

"Are *you*?"

All humor left him as desire took over, growing quickly inside him. He pulled her closer and gazed deep into her amazing brown eyes, which turned darker by the second. "Let us leave, and I'll show you how serious I am."

She licked her lips and nodded. "After the dance, I'll talk to my father."

"Good." He smiled mischievously.

"Where will we meet? I'm certain my father will want to take me home."

Vincent shrugged. "Not unless you convince him that I should take you home. After all, I drove my own vehicle this time."

"But the wedding announcement hasn't been made yet, so we shouldn't be seen leaving together."

"True, but in your father's mind, our wedding will take place in a few days anyway."

She grinned out of the side of her mouth. "You have really been thinking about this, haven't you?"

"Ever since our last kiss," he said softly as he lowered his focus to her mouth. "I cannot stop thinking about it."

Her throat jumped. "That pleases me to know. I was hoping you'd say that."

"I was hoping that you were hoping I'd say that."

She laughed, and her eyes twinkled. His heart leaped. Finally, she'd given him that look she had bestowed on Lord Calvin Drake. But it was different. She appeared more genuine with him.

Why was he allowing this woman to twist his heart? He didn't want to analyze his feelings right now, but he hoped she never stopped making him smile.

ELLIE'S NERVES JITTERED inside of her. Dare she convince her father to have Vincent take her home? Never had she been so bold. But then again, this was the first time in her life she'd put herself in this predicament. After what had happened with her stepmother yesterday, she knew this had to be done. Marriage to Vincent was the only way away from Augusta and Edgar Stone.

Inside Ellie's gloves, the palms of her hands moistened as she walked toward her father. Thankfully, Augusta was on the dance floor with some gentleman, and the duke was hobnobbing with one of his friends while sipping a flute of champagne.

She took a deep breath for confidence, and silently told herself that everything would work out fine.

As she came closer to her father, she placed her hand on her belly and tried to appear as though she was sick to her stomach. When her father saw her, he frowned and quickly excused himself from his friends. He took hold of her shoulders and peered into her eyes.

"What's wrong?" he asked.

"Father, I don't feel too well." She groaned to add emphasis.

"But you were feeling fine not too long ago."

"Not really. Slowly, over the course of this evening, my stomach has grown worse. While dancing with Lord Trenton, I nearly swooned. He bade me to come inform you." She swallowed hard. "I really feel the need to go home and lie down."

Her father cupped her cheek and then placed his hand on her forehead. "You do feel warm, and your cheeks are redder than normal."

Ellie held back a laugh. She *was* warm and her cheeks were red. Vincent made her feel things she never thought she'd experience.

She nodded. "Lord Trenton did say I looked under the weather."

Her father stretched his neck as he gazed over the crowd. "Let's find Augusta, and we'll leave—"

"No, Father. I don't want to ruin yours and Augusta's evening. She is having so much fun that I would never forgive myself for ruining it." The lie came easy enough. "What if...Lord Trenton took me home?"

Her father met her stare and arched an eyebrow. "Vincent? With no chaperone?"

She rubbed her forehead and squinted as though she had a

terrible headache. "There's nothing to fret over, Father. We will be engaged any day now."

"That doesn't matter," he snapped. "If someone saw—"

"Then we will make it so that nobody sees. You can walk me out to the coach, and Vincent can sneak out and meet us there."

He shook his head. "I would feel better if someone else went with you."

Inwardly, she groaned. "Fine, then ask our host if we can borrow one of his maids."

"Yes. That might actually work." He grasped her arm and pulled her over to a chair. She sat, still acting as though she was sick. "Stay right there and I'll locate a servant for you."

"As you wish, Father." She closed her eyes, but as soon as she heard his boot steps growing lighter, she peeked from underneath her lashes. He was out of her vision, so she opened her eyes and scanned the room for Vincent. He stood nearby, and she motioned him over.

He reached her and held her hand. "What did he say?"

"He wants us to take one of the maids here as a chaperone." He scowled, and she quickly shook her head. "But she can ride atop the coach with the driver and footman."

A smile stretched across Vincent's face. "Yes, that is the perfect spot for her to sit."

It didn't take long before a maid was located, and Ellie's wrap was brought to her. Vincent walked beside her father as they headed out to the coach.

"I trust you will be a gentleman," the duke said to Vincent.

His cheeks darkened, and he nodded. "But of course. Haven't I been that to your daughter this whole time?"

"Uh, yes…except the time when I caught you sharing a kiss at our last ball."

Vincent forced a laugh. She cringed, hoping he didn't overdo it in front of her father.

"Well, since then, of course," Vincent added.

"I'm still reluctant."

Ellie didn't like her father's answer, but she didn't argue. She still held a hand to her stomach and the other to her head, walking as if she barely could stand. "Father, don't be ridiculous. Lord Trenton wouldn't take advantage of me in this condition."

Her father threw Vincent a glare. "He'd better not."

She didn't want to let her father know that within two minutes of leaving the party, she wouldn't be in *this condition* any longer.

Once she was settled into the coach with Vincent sitting across from her, the footman closed the door. Her heart beat erratically, but she dared not move. She didn't want to say anything for fear she would bring bad luck to their plans.

The vehicle jerked into motion, and she breathed a sigh of relief. She'd been meeting Vincent's gaze, and he, too, expelled a gust of air. After a few minutes, he chuckled, and she joined him. Of course they made certain they didn't laugh too loud. She was sure her father had paid the driver or footman to bring him a report.

Vincent moved from his seat and scooted beside her. Taking her hand in his, he lifted it to his mouth and brushed his lips over her knuckles.

"Why do I feel like a boy in my youth again? Do you know how long it's been since I fooled my parents like that?"

Nodding, she grinned. "Probably as long since I have done it."

"You gave a great performance." He winked.

"And you, my lord, lied to my father." She bumped him with her shoulder.

"So did you." He bumped her back.

"I know, and I'm sure I'll feel guilty about it later, but right now I'm going to bask in the knowledge that he fell for our story."

He relaxed against the seat. "Do you think the servants will listen to us?"

"I know they will. My father will expect them to."

The coach only had a small lamp inside, and it was turned up bright. Her father was more than likely the culprit. But at least she could stare into Vincent's adorable, blue, smoldering eyes.

Slowly, the humor on his face disappeared as seriousness took over. He slipped his arm around her shoulders and gently tugged her back to rest against him. She adjusted herself so that she could continue to gaze into his eyes without breaking her neck.

Her breathing quickened, and he hadn't really done anything. She hadn't really lied about her stomach jumping, because right now it felt as if butterflies were whirling around inside her. She trembled, but with anticipation.

He brought up a hand and stroked her cheek. "I don't think I told you tonight, but you're a vision of loveliness. When I saw you walk into the ballroom, I nearly lost my breath."

Ellie narrowed her eyes, studying him closely. "Vincent, if I'm not mistaken, I believe you are telling the truth this time."

"I have always told the truth when complimenting you." His fingers slowly slid down her neck. "I couldn't take my eyes off you tonight."

Her cheeks warmed, hotter than her body was right now. "I know. I saw you."

"Was it uncomfortable for you to have me watching your every move?"

"No," she whispered as she caressed his chin. "I have never felt so adored than upon seeing your expression of desire."

His breathing quickened, as did hers.

"My precious, before another minute goes by, I must ask you something."

She held her breath for a moment. Was it bad? But the look on his face didn't indicate anything negative. "What is it?"

"When you first presented me with the marriage bargain, you mentioned you wanted it to be in name only." He licked his lips. "Over the past few days, I've realized how attracted I am to you, and, well...I don't want our marriage to be in name only."

Her heart leaped. She leaned closer, keeping her gaze locked with his. "Neither do I. Your sultry kisses have convinced me otherwise."

Vincent released a groan and pulled her into his arms as his mouth covered hers. As before when they'd kissed, her body heated quickly. Knowing what they both wanted this evening made her nervous and excited at the same time. She just prayed nothing would ruin their pleasurable evening.

CHAPTER ELEVEN

VINCENT'S HEART RACED so fast he almost couldn't breathe. He'd never felt so much excitement when seducing a woman. With Ellie, it felt like the first time. It was as though he'd never touched skin so silky smooth or kissed the tender lips of such a passionate woman. At this moment, there was nothing he wanted more than to watch her face when he touched her, just to see her enjoyment.

As he devoured her kisses, he traced his fingers down her throat, not believing how he trembled from feeling such softness. Her bosom rose and fell quickly. She quivered from his touch.

She pressed closer to him as a deep sigh rattled from her throat. Gradually, she slid a hand up his arms, but then quickly pulled away as if she was hesitant to touch him. He broke the kiss so that he could take hold of her hand. When had she removed her gloves? It didn't matter now. This was much better.

"It's all right to touch me," he muttered as he kissed the palm of her hand before laying it on his chest. Before she could verbally answer, he placed his mouth over hers again.

Hesitantly, her hand glided over his chest. What he'd give to have better access to her in a more comfortable location. But that would come later. The fact that she wasn't afraid to be intimate filled him with great joy. She was innocent, but he looked forward to giving her lessons, and he anticipated her learning.

Vincent broke the kiss again and trailed his lips down her neck. Her breaths were fast and heavy as she tilted her head back, allowing him access. Her flowery scent was as intoxicating as he remembered.

"Ohhh, Vincent," she sighed.

"Yes, my precious?"

"Why had I never felt this way before?"

He smiled. Apparently, her first fiancé didn't know how to make a woman melt. But at this moment, Vincent was thrilled that his friend hadn't, and that he would be her first. "Not to worry, sweet Ellie. It will be my goal to make you feel like this all the time."

"*All* the time?" She hiccupped a deep laugh. "Perhaps I shouldn't be like this when other people are around."

He raised his head slightly to peer into her beautiful eyes that were dark with passion. "Very true. I shall only do this when we're alone."

A soft smile bracketed her face as she stroked his cheek. "How did I get so fortunate to find a man as perfect as you?"

His heart swelled. Lately, she was saying words such as this— words no other woman had said before.

"My sweet Ellie." He resumed kissing her neck as he trailed his mouth toward her bosom. "You are the one who has made me this way."

She threaded her fingers through his hair, holding his head to her chest. Instead of words, she told him how much she enjoyed what he was doing with the little moans she released. Of course, this only made him more anxious. Perhaps starting their intimate evening in a coach wasn't the best idea he'd ever had.

Her scent buzzed through his head, making him dizzy with passion. But there was another smell that lingered, growing stronger by the second. Before he could pinpoint it, raised voices from the servants sitting on top of the coach ripped through the silence. Ellie's body stiffened. Soon, the odor he'd detected became noticeable. *Smoke.* Then the servants' words became clear. *Fire!*

"Fire?" Ellie asked in a voice lower than normal as she struggled to straighten in the seat.

He turned to peer out of the small window beside him, but through the darkness, he didn't see anything. Ellie scooted toward the window on her side and drew back the covering. She gasped.

Vincent moved closer to her to get a better look. Off in the distance, flames reached for the sky. Curious, he knelt on the floor and cracked the door open. He wasn't certain where they were, but when the surroundings became familiar, his gut twisted.

The fire was on his property!

He cursed. "Take us there," he shouted at his driver.

"Yes, my lord."

The coach turned toward the fire, and Vincent held on to the door, keeping his eye on the fire. Worry clawed its way through him like an out-of-control animal. Was the fire at the house? Thankfully, Lilly and Laura were attending a ball with their cousins tonight and wouldn't be home.

"What's wrong?" Ellie clutched his arm, pulling him back inside.

"Something is on fire on my property."

She gasped. "No. That cannot be right."

Suddenly, the threat he'd received yesterday resurfaced. He hadn't stayed away from Ellie. He would *never* stay away from her.

"Vincent, do you think it was the person who threatened you before?"

He met her panicked gaze and nodded. "Yes. I'm sure of it."

The coach rounded another bend as they drew closer to his estate. He held his breath until the manor came into view. Relief poured over him, and he sighed. The fire wasn't there. But where…?

Then the stable came into view, all lit up with orange and red flames. Black smoke drifted through the air.

"Vincent! Your horses," Ellie screamed, jerking on his arm.

A knot formed in his throat and his eyes stung with unshed tears. He'd had four horses—four that would be used to start his stud farm.

The coach slowed, and he pushed open the door and jumped out. He ran as fast as he could toward the burning structure, but his heart already told him that his horses had not escaped.

When the heat from the fire became too much to bear, he stopped. "Noooo," he screamed. Whoever had done this act of revenge was merciless. Vincent wouldn't rest until the person was caught.

In silence, he watched as the fire consumed the stable, burning each board, each wall, each beam, until it crumbled apart. It was as if he watched his life dissipate before him. The life he'd tried so hard to establish these past few months had vanished with one destructive spark.

"Oh, Vincent." Ellie sobbed beside him as she took his arm and pressed her cheek against him. "I'm so sorry this happened to you."

His heart hurt too much for words to form in his mouth. He couldn't tear his stare away from the burning structure. However, to acknowledge Ellie, he placed his hand over hers resting on his arm. She entwined her fingers with his.

The few servants he had—and those on the coach—had run up to the stable, and threw dirt on the fire, trying to put it out. Ellie tore away from him to assist them. Pulling himself out of his melancholy, he joined in. Thankfully, there weren't any close trees to make the fire spread.

Vincent tried not to think about all that he'd lost in this senseless act, instead, focusing on dousing the fire. It didn't take long before other people joined in, throwing dirt on the fire. The servants from neighboring estates stood with them. Thankfully, there were some kind-hearted people in this township.

It seemed like it took forever, but finally the fire was extinguished. He shook hands with those servants who had assisted as they wearily returned to their homes. Poor Ellie was covered in dirt, and her lovely hair fell out of the coil to hang down around her shoulders. Smudges of dirt marked her beautiful face, but he'd never felt so strongly about her as he did at this moment. Being a duke's daughter, she shouldn't have helped, but her unselfish act of kindness had proven to Vincent that she cared for him.

One of his servants had fetched water from the well and brought him and Ellie a cup to drink. Vincent hadn't realized how thirsty he was until this moment. He and Ellie locked gazes as they drank. Exhaustion pulled on her expression, especially in her weary eyes. His heart twisted. He should have begged her to leave instead of staying and helping. But it made his heart light to know she cared enough to stay, regardless of the labor.

Lowering the cup, he sighed and gave her a weak smile. "Well, Lady Ellie." Slowly, he moved to her side. "I suppose I should get you home quickly now."

She nodded with a frown. "Yes, I suppose that is the logical thing to do."

"It would be." He took her dirty hand in his. "As much as being alone together sounds better, I have much to do tonight."

"I know."

He glanced at his coach. "I'll have my driver take you home."

"Please keep me informed to what you will do tomorrow."

He nodded. "Of course I will."

"And my father would be more than happy to assist you."

"Yes, I know." He lifted her hand and kissed her knuckles. "Forgive me for such a tragic end to our wonderful evening."

"It's not your fault."

"I know, but we were looking forward to doing other things."

She released a weak laugh. "Fate had other plans."

He glanced back at the burned structure and frowned. "Obviously."

Vincent released Ellie as he walked with her back to the

coach. His limbs felt as if he dragged heavy objects along with him. He glanced down at his legs, to make certain he wasn't pulling something. They reached the coach and stopped.

"I shall see you on the morrow," he said.

"Yes. Try to get some rest."

"And you must do the same."

"I fear," she said, chuckling softly, "that as soon as I hit my pillow, I will fall asleep quickly."

He looked up at the driver. "Please take her home, and if her father is there, explain to him what happened."

"Yes, my lord."

The footman held out his hand to help Ellie inside, but just as she placed her hand in his, she stopped. Her head whipped to the right of them to the grove of trees. Curious, Vincent peered in that direction. His heartbeat quickened as anger rushed through him. Was the culprit who'd burned his stable still here and hiding?

A shadow moved…and then another. Vincent jumped into a run, ready to tackle the person responsible. Just before he reached the trees, Ellie let out a squeal and darted in that direction as well.

Vincent's heart dropped. He hoped he could stop her in time.

JOY SOARED INSIDE Ellie as she darted toward the trees. The four shadows changed into shapes, and she couldn't believe her eyes. They weren't people, but…Vincent's horses!

"Oh Vincent. Look." She clapped her hands eagerly. "The horses didn't die in the fire after all."

Vincent stared wide-eyed into the trees, his mouth hanging open. It only took a second before he snapped out of his daze and darted toward the animals. Ellie reached the closest and stopped. She didn't want to frighten the horse, so she cooed soft words and gently stroked his mane.

Across from her, Vincent had his arms around the neck of another horse, pressing his forehead against the animal's hair. Even through the shadows, she recognized the strong love he held for them. She couldn't hear what he was saying, but his voice was tight with emotion.

Tears pricked her eyes as happiness enveloped her. She smiled with quivering lips. It made her heart melt to see how much he cared for his horses.

He lifted his head and patted the horse, before moving to the last animal. Vincent treated each animal the same, showing them gentleness and love.

Then something struck her, leaving her breathless. If Vincent acted this way around horses, he would treat a woman with the same kind of love and caring emotion. In a few days, she would be his wife. *She* would be the one whom he showered his love upon. But did he love her? For that matter, did she love him?

He'd only been courting her for a few days, and overall, he'd been very kind and extremely tender with her. When they were in the coach earlier, he didn't paw at her or make demands as some men, but he kissed her and touched her with such kindness that she never wanted to leave his arms.

Was she already half in love with this amazing man? And what about the love she had for Adam? Could her feelings have possibly vanished within a few days? She didn't see that as a possibility, and she hadn't truly mourned over losing her first love since meeting Vincent.

He came to the horse she stood beside to show the same respect as he had the other three animals. But this time, he met her stare and didn't break it as he stroked the mane. A knot formed in her throat, and she wanted to throw her arms around Vincent's neck and blurt out her feelings. Yet she didn't dare. She wanted to be sure she loved him beyond a shadow of a doubt before actually saying the words.

Vincent exhaled slowly. "It appears, my precious, that we will still be able to start our stud farm after we're married."

Her heart flipped. "It does, my lord."

He stepped closer and placed his hand over hers as it rested against the horse's neck. "Do you know how much I want to kiss you right now?"

Tingles buzzed through her body, making her weak in the knees. "What is stopping you?"

One side of his grin lifted higher than the other. "The servants. They are watching."

Inwardly, she groaned. She didn't need to peek at them—she trusted Vincent's word. "Then know that I want to kiss you right now as well."

Closing his eyes, he breathed faster as though fighting against his urges. "My precious," he whispered as he opened his eyes, "will we ever get that moment? Every time we try to steal some time for passion, we are always interrupted."

She chuckled. "Yes, it does seem there is something trying to stop us."

He lifted her dirty hand and kissed her knuckles. "We shall try this again tomorrow."

"Yes." Her mind scrambled to remember what plans they had. When she recalled, she hitched a breath. "Vincent, tomorrow my parents are having a dinner social."

"That's correct, they are."

"You leave the party early, and then I shall complain of a headache and retire to my room."

"Do you wish me to sneak into your room?" he asked quietly.

"No. I shall come to your house."

He shook his head. "I'm not certain that is the best—"

"Yes, it is. That's what I shall do. It will work this time, I assure you."

Vincent was quiet for a few seconds before he nodded. "My sisters are visiting their cousins. They won't be back for two more days."

"See?" She grinned wide. "My plan will work perfectly."

"I believe you are correct."

He kissed her knuckles one more time before turning her away from the horses and leading her back to the servants who waited by the coach. Hope sprang back into her chest and gave her the energy to move.

Vincent helped her inside and gave her one last smile. She winked. As he closed the door, she tried to stop the giddiness from letting loose. Within twenty-four hours, she and Vincent would seal their wedding vows...before they were married.

During the short ride home, she mapped out in her mind how things would happen. She'd find an old pair of breeches and a man's shirt. She'd stuff her hair in a servant's cap to make herself look like a boy. Then she'd take one of her father's horses and ride to Vincent's estate. Night's shadows would be on her side, because nobody would notice her gone.

Ellie's smile widened as she relaxed back against the seat. Her mind kept going...

Once she had reached his manor, he'd take her gently by the hand and pull her inside. Vincent would wear only his shirt and trousers. She would see his bare, muscular chest, and it would be sprinkled with light brown hair. Even his feet would be bare. Looking into each other's eyes, they wouldn't be able to contain their passion any longer. They would fall into each other's arms immediately, fusing their mouths together.

Sighing, Ellie closed her eyes as her daydream continued.

Vincent wouldn't be able to contain himself, and he'd lift her in his strong arms and carry her upstairs to his bedchambers. His long legs would take the stairs two at a time. His room would be dark, only a few candles lit. The blankets on his bed would hold his scent of pine and leather. He'd lay her on the bed first, and then loom over her...

The coach jerked to a stop and brought her out of her dream. Sadly, she would have to continue this dream tomorrow when it really happened. She would do everything in her power to make certain it occurred with no interruptions this time.

The footman opened the door and helped her down. She

thanked him, and had taken her first step toward the house when a horse's neigh stopped her. She swung toward the sound. In the full moon's light, she saw Pegasus trotting toward her, and a man holding the reins. At first, she didn't recognize the man, but as he walked closer, his identity struck her like a hand across her face.

What was Edgar Stone doing with her horse?

CHAPTER TWELVE

ELLIE STARED DUMBFOUNDED at Edgar as he brought her horse closer. The man's happy smile churned her stomach. He acted as though he was bringing her a trunk full of gold and treasure. True, she loved her horse completely, but she didn't want to give Edgar any thanks. Not yet, anyway.

"Good evening, Miss Middleton." When his gaze skimmed over her dirty hair, gown, and hands, he stopped short, his eyes widening. "What in the blazes happened to you?"

"You found Pegasus." She ignored his question and hurried to her horse, taking the reins from Edgar's hand. She stroked the animal's neck and hugged him. "Oh, my baby. Where did you go?"

Edgar cleared his throat. "I found him near the Hamptons' estate."

She gasped and glanced at Edgar. "That far?"

"Yes. When I noticed him, I knew right away he was yours."

Warily, she cocked her head and narrowed her eyes on him. His red freckles weren't as prominent in the dark, but his red, bushy hair still glowed like a lantern in a fog. "Pray, how did you know Pegasus was mine? I don't believe you have ever seen me ride her."

His face brightened with a blush. "But Miss Middleton, I *have* seen you riding—when I visit my aunt."

Either the man was lying, or he had spied on her while staying in *her* home. Her stomach twisted again. Just the thought of him watching her ride made her nauseated. "Well, then, I'm happy you found my horse and brought him back."

He stepped closer and grasped her hand. "Miss Middleton? Won't you give me another chance? As you can see, I care very deeply for you."

Ellie gritted her teeth. She wanted to tell him how much she loathed men who treated women like last week's sewer. She rummaged through her mind for something nice to say, but she couldn't think of anything. "My lord, I cannot give you a second chance. I do not like you, and I never will. Please, don't press the issue any further. Bothering me about this matter will only cause me to hate you more."

He sucked in a breath and shook his head. "No, that's not possible."

Ellie shrugged. "Actually, it is *very* possible. I have seen the way you treat other women, and I would rather not be one of them." She turned Pegasus toward the stable. "Now, if you'll excuse me, I'm going to take my horse and get him ready for the night."

"Here, Miss Middleton." Vincent's footman jumped to her side, taking the reins. "Allow me to do that. You've been through so much tonight. I fear your father will want you to go to bed straightway."

She smiled. "Yes, you're correct. And I thank you for all the help you've given this evening."

She glanced at Edgar, who stood staring at her with a flabbergasted expression on his face. The conversation she'd overheard between him and Augusta returned to her thoughts. No wonder Edgar was so stunned. *Auntie* Augusta had promised him she'd take care of things. Ellie was relieved to know that her stepmother hadn't made good on her promise.

She climbed the porch stairs and, as she glanced back over her shoulder, noticed that Edgar was still standing in the same spot, staring at her. Instead of the puppy-dog look he'd been giving her lately, he glared at her with evil eyes.

Chills ran up her arms and down her back. Never had she felt more fearful. Quickening her step, she hurried inside the house and closed the door behind her. No doubt he was still staying in her home, even though she'd instructed her stepmother to send him packing. How could she get any rest now? And what, pray tell, would the vile man do next?

VINCENT HID A yawn behind his hand, trying not to let anyone at the duke's party see how exhausted he was. Bright and early this morning, he had contacted the constable, who had some police inspectors drop by the burned stable and ask Vincent questions. They questioned the few servants he had, but nobody saw anyone sneaking around in the dark that could have started the fire.

This was definitely not an accident. Someone vicious, with a cold, calculating heart, had done this.

Once the police inspectors left, Vincent rode to Ellie's house to speak to the duke. Sadly enough, Ellie was still in bed, and so Vincent wasn't able to see her.

The duke's concern heightened Vincent's worry. They couldn't let another so-called accident happen. How could they stop it? The duke promised that he would announce Vincent and Ellie's engagement at tonight's dinner party. He prayed they would be able to find some clue as to who the person who wanted to wreck their lives might be.

As Vincent greeted people at the party, his gaze was mostly on Ellie. Tonight she looked stunning. Of course, she could wear boys' breeches and he'd think she was beautiful. But this evening, she wore a powder-blue gown, similar to the one she wore last night. The square neckline didn't seem as bold as the other one, but it still emphasized a generous bosom. The sleeves were shorter on this gown, and small beads of fringe hung off the edges. She wore her hair the way he liked it—loose, with tendrils around her ears.

He didn't dare take up too much of Ellie's attention, but it seemed the guests at tonight's party swarmed around her constantly. Vincent couldn't find a moment to speak with her privately. They still needed to go over their plans for this evening's main event once they left the party.

"My good man. Aren't you the lucky chap?"

Vincent's attention was pulled away from Ellie when her brother approached him. Vincent gave his friend a quizzical stare with an arched eyebrow.

"Lucky? Pray, how do you figure that, when only last evening my stable was burned to the ground?"

Dominic slapped Vincent's shoulder and shook his head. "There are two reasons that make you the most fortunate man at tonight's social." He swept a gaze around the room. "Look at how many people have offered to assist you in rebuilding your stable."

Vincent nodded. His friend was correct. It surprised him how many people had given him money or offered up their servants to help rebuild the stable. This was certainly a kind township. "Yes, I suppose I should be grateful that most people have such giving hearts."

"You should." Dominic folded his arms across his chest. "And the second reason you are the luckiest man in this room is because you are about to become very rich."

Startled by the comment, Vincent tilted back his head and laughed heartily. Dominic had picked a poor time to say such nonsense, but it was good for a chuckle. "You are very humorous, my friend, but I fear your timing is bad for such a teasing remark."

Dominic shook his head. "I'm very serious, Trenton. Don't you recall asking me to invest some of your money?"

Vincent paused in thought and held his breath. "Yes, but that was only a week ago. Results don't show so quickly."

Dominic shrugged. "Exactly, but for one of the speculations, the results are in." He playfully slapped Vincent's shoulder again. "My good man, the investment came through. Not many people believed in this speculation, which makes the odds very good. And you will soon be a very wealthy man."

The news was so unbelievable that Vincent didn't dare become too excited. Slowly, he shook his head. "Dominic, if you're lying about this—"

"I assure you. This is the truth." Dominic held up his right hand as his grin widened. "I invested a small amount of money, which means I'll get a profit as well."

Vincent's life lately had been shaky, and he hesitated to believe this. But Dominic had never led him astray before, and after everything that had happened to Vincent these past few months, he didn't think his friend would be so cold-hearted as to lie.

Gradually, excitement grew inside Vincent's chest. Immediately, he knew he had to tell Ellie. He searched the room again, and found her standing next to Augusta and some of her friends. The strained expression on Ellie's face told him she needed rescuing…and quickly.

"Dominic, if you'll excuse me," Vincent said, "I need to share the good news with my soon-to-be wife."

Dominic grinned and nodded. "Indeed, this is a joyous occasion."

Vincent tried not to rush to Ellie's side, but he found himself taking larger strides than normal. When she finally noticed him, her face lit up with happiness. His heart melted. *He* was the one who could make her react this way.

He reached the circle of women, and their chatter stopped. He bowed. "Pardon my intrusion, but could I borrow Miss Middleton for a few minutes?"

The duchess's haughty glare made him pause. What had he done to upset her? But quickly enough, he forgot about the woman and focused back on Ellie.

"Indeed you shall," she said as she stepped toward him.

He offered his arm, and she hooked her hand around his elbow. Two steps away from the other ladies, he finally covered her hand with his palm and smiled.

"Your brother has just delivered some happy news."

"What is it?" she asked, her eyes twinkling like stars.

"That first day at your house when you ran into me, I went riding with your brother and asked him to invest some money for me. Dominic just informed me that everything went exceedingly well, and I will soon be a very wealthy man."

She gasped. "Are you jesting?"

He chuckled. "I asked your brother that same thing, but apparently, he is serious." Vincent gently squeezed her hand. "My precious, we are going to be rich."

Her expression grew softer. "Oh, Vincent. Being wealthy doesn't matter to me. I want to marry you no matter what."

His heart flipped. "Money doesn't matter to you because you have it. But I have been without it, and I assure you, it is a necessity."

"Forgive me. I didn't mean to sound ungrateful."

"No, precious. I know you didn't mean it like that."

Her smile grew. "But I am very happy to see you so happy."

"Good." He nodded. "Because I'm ecstatic."

They stopped near a corner of the room, and she faced him. "I spoke with my father this morning after you left. I begged him not to tell Augusta about the wedding announcement." She glanced around them. "If anyone here is responsible for the fire, we will be able to tell by their expression after the announcement is made tonight." She met Vincent's gaze. "Don't you agree?"

"Yes. I'll certainly watch if anyone acts suspicious."

"I'll be keeping my eye on Augusta's vile nephew." She cringed. "The evil man was waiting for me last night when I returned home."

"What?" Vincent gasped, his voice louder than it probably

should have been.

"Apparently," she whispered, "he found my horse grazing by Lord Hampton's estate."

"But…that is miles away."

"I know." She cocked her head. "I suspect Edgar Stone of taking Pegasus in the first place, and then returning it to make him appear as if he is my rescuer." She shook her head. "I just don't believe his story."

"I don't believe a word out of his mouth." Vincent rolled his eyes. "He has never been one who could tell the truth."

The clinking of a glass and a man clearing his throat brought the chatter around the room to a halt. The duke stood with a champagne glass in his hand and smiled at the guests while servants passed trays of the drink around to everyone.

"Forgive me for interrupting, but I have an announcement to make."

"This is it," Ellie whispered, leaning toward Vincent.

Swallowing hard, he hoped he'd be able to see if any of the guests could be added to the suspects list.

"I'll be watching Edgar Stone," she said.

"Yes, I would bet money that he did it."

A servant passed them with the tray of champagne. Vincent took a flute and handed it to Ellie before taking one for himself.

"First," the duke began, "I want to thank you—my good friends—for coming tonight. I'm very happy that you are all here to share in this joyous occasion."

Some of the guests appeared baffled as they whispered to each other, shaking their heads and shrugging.

"I would like to announce," the duke continued, "the engagement of my daughter and Lord Trenton."

Gasps bounced off the walls as all eyes turned to Vincent and Ellie. Smiling, he glanced from face to face, trying to see if anyone appeared guilty. Most everyone looked shocked and bewildered. But nobody appeared angered.

"I will post the banns very soon," the duke said. "So, let us raise our glasses and toast to my daughter and her soon-to-be husband."

Murmurs of congratulations rose in the room as everyone lifted their glasses and took a sip. It irritated Vincent that he still couldn't figure out who was the one threatening him. Perhaps the person wasn't in the room. That certainly narrowed down the list a little.

Within moments, a swarm of people came up to Ellie and Vincent. Some of their expressions looked genuine, but others were fake. Unfortunately, that didn't make them suspects.

Vincent tried to be as polite as he could. After all, some of these people had given him money to help rebuild his stable, or offered their servants to help build it. But more than anything, he wanted answers about who was threatening him. And would they strike again now that the wedding announcement had been made?

Once Vincent and Ellie were by themselves again, she looked up at him and frowned. The spark in her eyes had diminished. Even the way she breathed was slower. She appeared as exhausted as he felt.

"Unfortunately, I could not tell if anyone was guilty," she said.

"I couldn't, either. What about Stone?"

"Believe it or not, he wasn't here during the announcement. I saw him earlier, but then he disappeared."

Suspicion rose within Vincent, and he stiffened. "That's good to know, especially if I return home to find something else has happened to my property. I'll know where to point the police inspectors."

She nodded. "I never thought of that, but you are correct. He would be the perfect suspect."

He turned to peer back across the crowd and sighed. "Is it wrong of me to want this party to end early?" he asked softly.

"Not at all. I'm also anticipating the end of this party, especially when I feign a headache and leave to go to my room."

A grin tugged at the corners of his mouth when he looked back at her. "Which means I had better figure out an excuse to leave as well."

"Actually, you already have an excuse. You are very tired because you stayed up most of the night putting out the fire and trying to find your horses."

"Which is exactly what happened." He took her hand in his and squeezed it softly. "Dinner has passed, and your stepmother is getting the room ready for card playing. I suppose now is the perfect time to bow out. Your father will understand."

"Of course he will," she said in a lower voice.

"When shall I expect you?"

"I shall arrive approximately two hours after you leave here."

He ran a finger along her hand. "That will be perfect."

A hush fell across the room as Augusta tried to get everyone's attention. She explained what she had planned and what game tables were set up.

Vincent gave Ellie a wink. "It's time to play our part."

Her cheeks reddened. "It is."

Once the crowd started moving toward Augusta, Vincent made his way toward the duke. Two other lords stood by Ellie's father, so Vincent patiently waited until he could get a private moment with the duke.

Vincent's heart raced, and he wondered if tonight's planned event between him and Ellie would really happen. Lately, they had been interrupted, which made his anticipation that much greater. At the same time, he worried that the threat looming over him would be his downfall. He couldn't allow this unknown person to dictate what Vincent could or could not do, especially with Ellie.

"Ah, there is my soon-to-be son-in-law." The duke clapped a hand on Vincent's shoulder. The older man looked around them quickly before meeting Vincent's gaze. "Do you have anything to report? Did you notice anyone acting differently during my announcement?"

Vincent shook his head. "Both Ellie and I were watching, but unfortunately, we could not see anyone."

The duke scratched his head. "I had hoped for better news."

"As did I, Your Grace." Vincent swallowed hard. "However, I fear the excitement of the day, and the unsettling events of last night, have taken their toll on my nerves. I hope you'll forgive me if I bow out of the remainder of the evening and return home to sleep."

Nodding, the duke crossed his arms over his large chest. "Of course you can leave. I'm surprised you had the energy to come to the dinner party."

Vincent chuckled wearily. "How could I miss your big announcement?"

"So true." The duke laughed and motioned toward the door. "Now return home and rest. These next few days will keep you and Ellie hopping with invitations, I'm sure."

"I'm certain they will." Vincent bowed to the duke and started his walk toward the door. He glanced at Ellie, and she smiled at him. His heart melted. By the excitement dancing in her eyes, he knew she was looking forward to this night just as much as he.

An hour later, he paced the hall in his house. Ellie hadn't told him if she was going to enter through the back way or come through the front door. It pleased him to know that when he finally reached his house, everything would be in order. His sisters were still at their cousins, and the house was quiet.

Vincent had stripped off his waistcoat and cravat, and even kicked off his shoes. Beyond a doubt, he'd be extremely eager to see Ellie when she arrived, and he would probably be very impatient to make love to her. He worried that he'd be too impatient.

No, he mustn't. She had never been with a man. He must take things slow and not rush anything. She needed to experience every detail. As did he.

A rattle from one of the side doors disturbed the silence. Excitement leaped in his chest. He spun around and rushed toward the sound. At long last, Ellie had come.

The hall was dark, so he quickly grabbed a lit candlestick from the main hall and brought it with him. The image of a woman appeared in the shadows. His heartbeat skipped.

A strong scent of perfume enveloped his senses before he saw her face, slowing his steps considerably. Ellie didn't smell like that.

And then the woman's face appeared. Shock—and then fear—rushed through him. Immediately, anger took over, bringing his temper to a burning rage.

What was Lady Livingston doing here?

CHAPTER THIRTEEN

V INCENT PANICKED. HE needed to get Candace out of the house. Quickly! In his mind, he pictured Ellie showing up while Candace was still here. That would *not* go over well. He feared Ellie just wouldn't understand and forgive him this time.

He must stop the situation before it worsened. Ellie didn't need to know about Candace, and Candace definitely didn't need to know about Ellie.

"There you are," she purred as she slithered toward him like a snake ready to sink its teeth into his neck. "I wanted to surprise you." She held up her hands. "Are you surprised?"

Even through the shadows, he could see she'd worn one of her seductive gowns. For certain, she was here to entice him. He wouldn't let her.

He arched an eyebrow. "If a building fell over on me now, I wouldn't be more surprised."

A deep, throaty laugh rattled through her. "You are so humorous. I miss that."

"What are you doing here?" he asked in a gruff voice.

"Come now, Vincent. Do not act so upset. You used to love it when I showed up unannounced for seduction."

"That was before." He shook his head. "I'm a different man now."

She laughed and dragged her finger along his chest. "I'm

certain you *want* to think that, since you'll be marrying the duke's daughter, but I assure you, deep down inside this wonderful man, you will always be the same irresistible rogue I've always wanted."

Vincent had never turned a woman down, not like *that*, and so Candace would be his first. He wasn't sure what to say—never had he purposely been rude to a woman, either. Candace would be the exception.

Whatever he did, it needed to be done quickly. There was no time to waste. Ellie could *not* walk in on this.

"I'm happy that you think so highly of me"—he grasped her hand to remove her touch—"but I must insist that I'm a changed man. I am looking forward to my upcoming nuptials. Miss Middleton will make me deliriously happy."

"You cannot be serious." Candace tilted back her head and laughed, sounding sultrier than the last time. "My dear Vincent. What has happened to you?" She pressed her bosom against his chest. "Where is the man I used to know? He would have never allowed a woman inside his heart, not to mention one that could trap him into marriage."

"She didn't trap me," he snapped. "I was the one who pursued Miss Middleton."

"Oh, please." She shook her head. "You cannot lie to me. I know you too well."

Panic rose higher within him. This wasn't working. He needed to get her out of the house immediately.

"Candace, what would it take for me to convince you to leave? Tonight is *not* a good night for this."

"But it is. Your sisters are gone. It's just you and me." She leaned up and kissed his chin.

His irritation grew. "How did you know my sisters were not here?"

"Vincent, Vincent…" She sighed and rested her head on his chest. "How many times must I remind you that I'm a woman who gets what she wants? I want you, therefore, I'm going to pay someone to keep watch over your manor and know personal details about your life." She tilted her head back to look into his eyes. "How else will I be able to make a bargain with you, otherwise?"

"Candace, I told you before that I wasn't interested." He tried to push her away, but the insistent woman wouldn't budge. "Know this now…I'm marrying Ellie, not you, and there is nothing you can do to change it. I'm eagerly awaiting our wedding day."

"But, my passionate man, I can give you so much more. Not only do I have lots of money, but I can assure you that your nights will be filled with cravings you've never experienced before."

Arrogant woman! "I will only tell you one more time before I physically pick you up and throw you out. Candace, my answer is no. My answer will never change. Leave my house. I don't want you. Not now, not ever."

She pouted. "Give me a chance to change your mind. I'm sure you won't regret it." She slid her hands up his arms, hooking them around his neck. "If anything, let's get together for old times' sake."

The moment she placed her mouth over his, he knew it was wrong. He had no feelings for this woman. Well, except for anger and frustration, but nothing of desire. Ellie was the woman he wanted. His roughish days were gone forever now, and he looked forward to his life married to her.

Turning his head, he broke the kiss. "It's not going to work, Candace. I'm in love with Ellie." After the words had left his mouth, his heart raced with happiness, confirming the truth behind the statement.

"Love?" She cackled loudly. "Vincent, my dear, you cannot be serious. How could you be in love with your best friend's fiancée? Why…it's just not done."

He rolled his eyes, gritting his teeth. "Adam is dead. It doesn't matter now."

"But it will always matter in your heart. Do you honestly think you could live with Miss Middleton knowing that she was in love with Adam Haddington first? I think not. You are the man that needs a woman to love him first. Don't you think she will be comparing you to her deceased fiancé the whole time you are together?"

His head argued with his heart. Candace was wrong. It didn't matter if Ellie had loved Adam first. However, deep down in the recesses of his conscience, he knew he'd always feel guilty for sending his friend off to battle.

"Let me love you," she whispered as her lips hovered near his. "You will never have to feel guilty being with me."

ELLIE COULDN'T BELIEVE how smoothly things were working out for her. It was as if the stars and the moon had aligned just right to make everything happen just the way she wanted.

A half-hour after Vincent had left, she complained of a headache to her father, and, just as she figured, he excused her to go to her room. Her maid helped her into her nightgown, and Ellie released her for the night. The minute the door was closed, Ellie sprang into action, dressing as quickly as she could in the boy's breeches and man's shirt that she'd taken from one of the servants' rooms.

Her body trembled with excitement as she carefully walked down the servants' stairs. Thankfully, the staff was still kept busy with the party. Augusta would have every single servant on hand just in case she needed something, knowing her.

Ellie reached the kitchen and paused again. Peeking inside the room, she prayed nobody would see her. So far, everything she and Vincent tried to do had failed miserably. She could *not* allow this special night to be ruined as well.

Voices echoed from the hall outside the kitchen, but none of the servants occupied the kitchen at this moment. She darted across the room, taking large steps, until she reached another door. This door led to yet another hall, but thankfully, it was only used by the servants.

Cautiously, she slipped out of the kitchen and into the corridor before rushing to the nearest door. No voices were heard from this section of the house, which made her breathe a little easier.

Outside, the bright moon lit her way toward the stables. She stuffed her long hair up into the boy's cap on her head. Her hands shook as she hastily saddled her horse and mounted. She urged Pegasus slowly out of the structure until she was far enough away before gently digging her heels into the animal's belly to push Pegasus into a run. Finally, she was on her way toward Vincent's estate.

Images danced in her head, which she wanted to keep in order to fantasize what tonight might be like. This *was* going to happen between her and Vincent. It would go exactly as she'd dreamed about the night before…plus more. It was those other things she'd only heard about from lovers that had her heart pounding with anticipation.

The moon was high in a cloudless sky this evening, and the gentle wind on her face was refreshing. Several times, the cap tried to fly off her head, but she quickly adjusted it. Nobody could know she was a woman—the duke's daughter, no less. If anyone discovered who she was, that would cause a scandal quicker than what she and Vincent planned on doing tonight.

As she rode closer to his manor, she saw the place was dark. But as she stopped her horse and hopped down, she could see through the front windows. A few flickering candles lit the way. She hooked the reins around a post and, on unsteady legs, walked slowly up the front porch. Her heart hammered against her chest so forcefully that she feared she may swoon before even seeing him. Although she was nervous, she wasn't scared. She trusted Vincent to be gentle and understanding.

She stood at the front door, wringing her hands. Should she knock? Or had he unlocked the front door? Ellie shrugged and reached for the knob. The door opened soundlessly, and she breathed a sigh of relief. As she stepped into the entrance hall, voices drifted from a different direction.

Ellie inhaled sharply. *We are not alone!*

She licked her dry lips and took quiet steps farther into the house. Immediately, she detected Vincent's voice...and a woman's. Her throat tightened. Were his sisters here when he hadn't planned on them being home? Oh dear. If they saw Ellie—

At that moment, a woman's laugh danced through the air. Ice stiffened Ellie's limbs, and she froze. This was *not* Vincent's sisters. The husky tone was too mature. Too sultry.

Fear gripped her stomach and twisted. *No!* She wouldn't believe Vincent had another woman here—not when he was expecting her. Then again, Ellie was earlier than she'd told him. When they'd talked about this evening, she told him two hours after he left. So, she was a good hour early.

Her head pounded with uncertainty, and she couldn't stop her feet from moving her toward the voices. At first, she couldn't decipher the words because they bounced against the walls in an echo. Finally, silhouettes of two people in each other's arms materialized through the shadows.

Vincent's hands rested on the woman's shoulders while her arms were hooked around his waist. The woman's voluptuous body was pressed intimately against Vincent.

The woman laughed again as she twisted a lock of Vincent's hair around her finger. "Now, Vincent...you cannot tell me that slip of a girl will make you happy. But you *know* I'll be able to accomplish that on a daily—and nightly—basis."

"Candace, I beg you, please—"

"No need to beg yet, my dear, sensual man. Wait until we get to the bedroom."

Disgust lurched in Ellie's throat, and she slapped a hand over her mouth to keep from retching. They hadn't heard—or seen—

her yet, and she'd make sure they didn't.

Carefully, she stepped back away from the intimate scene. Tears filled her eyes as her heart crumbled. The pain throbbing in her head kept her from hearing any more. The only sound now was the breaking of her heart and her soul dying.

Her vision blurred, but she found the door and left, closing it softly. It wasn't until she reached her horse that she released the sobs building up in her throat. Thankfully, Pegasus knew the way home, because she couldn't lead the animal in the right direction if her life depended on it.

Something deep within her argued with her decision to flee. Her conscience told her to turn the horse around and return to the manor. She needed to call Vincent out for his deceit. But her pride wouldn't allow it, winning the argument. She would look like a blubbering fool if she faced Vincent now, and she didn't want to appear so weak-minded in front of him.

Why had she believed him? She'd trusted him. His eyes had told her he'd wanted tonight with her. Unless that was all a lie, too. If he didn't care for her, why had he led her on? But then, she'd forgotten that he was a rogue. He knew how to twist women's hearts into his web of deceit in order to get what he wanted.

She wiped the tears pouring from her eyes. Apparently, now that he was wealthy, he didn't need her money…which meant he didn't need *her*. Unfortunately, her father would still force them to wed, and especially now because of the announcement he'd made earlier. If she didn't marry Vincent now, *she* would be ruined.

The horse made it to the stable, and she jumped down. She didn't have time to remove the saddle or brush him, and she prayed one of the servants would see to it sometime tonight. It was a struggle to lift each leg as she walked out of the stable and headed for the servants' door.

Ripping the boy's cap off her head, she let her hair tumble down around her shoulders and back. Her appearance didn't matter now. Everything she'd done tonight was all for naught.

"Eleanor? Is that you?"

The man's question startled her, and she jumped. Fear of a different kind rushed through her body. *I'm caught!*

A man walked out of the shadow of the towering oak tree. At first, she couldn't see him through the tears blurring her vision, but his voice seemed oddly familiar. She cleared her throat, hoping it didn't sound as if she'd been crying. "What are you doing out here? Why are you not inside at the party?"

As the man walked closer toward her, his appearance began to take on a form, and she recognized Lord Calvin Drake—Adam's cousin. Thinking of her dead fiancé made her want to bawl all over again, but she refrained. She blinked quickly, hoping it would dry the tears still swimming inside her eyes.

"I wasn't invited to the party," he said, stopping in front of her.

She prayed the shadows would keep him from seeing her face. "Forgive me. I didn't see you very well, Lord Calvin."

He leaned forward as if studying her face. *Blast it all!* He could see her tears.

"Eleanor, have you been crying?"

Forcing a laugh, she swiped under her eyes and cheeks, trying to remove the evidence. She hadn't given him permission to use her given name, but she didn't have the energy to correct him now. "Please don't worry yourself. It's nothing."

"Why are you dressed this way?" He smiled. "Are you sneaking out of the house at night to ride your horse again?"

His question jarred inside her head. What in the blazes was he talking about? How did *he* know she used to do that? "Pardon me? Why would you ask such a thing, Lord Calvin? We barely know each other."

Sighing, he scrubbed his hand over his facial hair and shook his head. A memory popped into her head. When Adam was alive, he had done this gesture as well. Then again, she was certain most men did it. She'd seen Vincent do it a time or two.

Yet when Lord Calvin did it, memories of Adam resurfaced, making her ache that much more.

Why had Lord Calvin come into her life, especially now? Perhaps she was cursed to remain loveless all of her life, because the man she'd given her heart to three years ago would never be with her. And now, the man she thought she'd come to love didn't want her.

"Forgive me, Eleanor. I'm certain this is all confusing for you, but I know I have to speak what's on my mind."

Her thoughts drifted away from his words again. Adam used to call her Eleanor, even though she preferred Ellie. But when Adam said it, she heard the tenderness in his voice. It was probably her fault for thinking about the dead man. After what she'd witnessed between Vincent and his former mistress, was it any wonder Ellie wasn't thinking clearly?

"No, Lord Calvin. I fear I don't understand any of this. I've had a terrible upset tonight, and I need to retire to my bedchambers."

"Please, Eleanor." He closed the space between them and touched her arm. "If I don't say this while I have the courage, I might never be able to say anything again."

Her heart sank lower. Was he like Edgar? She wouldn't be able to stand hearing another man declare his love and devotion to her when she knew they were lying. Why would any man want her? She was irritable, and she hated socializing. All she wanted to do was paint and ride her horse.

Lowering her gaze to the ground, she sighed and rubbed the throbbing in her forehead. "I just don't think this is the perfect time for that. I have an awful headache and I just don't want to think at all tonight. Please understand, Lord Calvin."

She turned to leave, but his soft chuckle had her raising her gaze to him as he stroked his facial hair.

"Now see, that's the problem right there. I'm not really Lord Calvin."

Ellie blinked, wondering if her vision was playing tricks on her. After all, her mind was pretty much gone by now. "Beg pardon? If you're not Lord Calvin, then pray, who are you and why are you here?"

He sighed and licked his lips. "Eleanor, it's me. Adam."

CHAPTER FOURTEEN

ELLIE STOOD DUMBFOUNDED. Either that, or her brain—and ears—had ceased to function properly. Her head swirled with confusion, making her dizzy. She couldn't possibly have heard what she thought. If Lord Calvin was trying to play with her emotions, she'd punch him in the face.

Her vision became narrowed, as though he was standing farther away. She blinked, feeling the world turn around her.

"Wh—what did you say?" she asked hesitantly as she stumbled.

Lord Calvin leaped forward and took her in his arms before she fell to the ground. Taking deep breaths, she regained her balance and pushed him away. He took her hand in his and caressed it softly.

"I'm Adam. I'm alive."

Alive? Impossible!

Her mind rushed back to the moment she'd received the letter from his sister, alerting Ellie of his death—killed in battle. She'd never felt so desolate. Her whole heart had broken into a million pieces. She hadn't wanted to leave her bed for days, even weeks. She couldn't bear the thought of living this life without him.

In the letter, his sister had mentioned a graveside service. Ellie was too heartbroken to attend. But she was certain his family had gone. So, if he wasn't dead, wouldn't Ellie have heard from his sister by now?

"No." Slowly, she shook her head. "Adam was killed in battle."

"Yes, that was the story I told everyone."

Her chest tightened, and suddenly, she couldn't breathe. She swayed again, and this time when he held her in his arms, he wouldn't allow her to pull away.

"Let's move you to somewhere you can sit."

His words seemed muffled in her ears, but she nodded and allowed him to lead her back into the stable and onto a stool. She sat and leaned against the wall behind her. Ellie studied his face the best she could with unclear eyes and dim lighting in the stable. He did resemble Adam. But this man seemed to have more muscles—and, of course, facial hair. She recalled that Adam had a dimple on his right cheek. Unfortunately, she couldn't see it on this man because Lord Calvin's beard covered that spot.

"Ellie, please forgive me for springing the news on you this way. I didn't know how else to say it." He patted her hand gently.

"No...no. I cannot believe this—any of this." She jerked her hand away. "Adam Haddington is dead. If he were alive, he would have contacted me sooner. But it's been three years." She paused and scowled. "Three very long and miserable years. Do you understand that? The kind and considerate and *loving* man I was in love with would have not trampled on my emotions in such a way."

A frown claimed Lord Calvin's expression. "I know it was wrong to keep this a secret, but the truth is I couldn't say anything. I couldn't even tell my family until about six months ago."

Breathing deeply and steadily helped the dizziness in her head disappear faster. Finally, Ellie regained her strength. With it came a spout of anger. She shoved her palms against the man's chest, moving him away from her so she could stand. He fell back on his bottom, looking up at her with wide eyes.

"You are really Adam Haddington?"

"Yes."

"Prove it."

He rose to his feet, brushing the hay and dirt off his trousers. "How should I prove it? Was it not enough that I remembered that you enjoyed sneaking out of the house at night and riding Pegasus, or that I called you Eleanor?"

"No!" Tears stung her eyes, but she refused to shed them. "I need more. This is too unbelievable. And I've been so naïve lately, I'm afraid to trust my own heart anymore."

"I understand."

His stare stayed on her during the next few silent moments. Her heart beat differently this time. So much had wrecked her life lately. Could she possibly have another disaster happen to her so soon? She wouldn't be able to handle any more. This was probably all just a bad dream, brought on by what she had witnessed between Vincent and Lady Livingston. Hopefully, she would awaken from this nightmare very soon.

"Before I left for battle," he said softly, "you gave me your favorite locket. It was something your grandmother gave you before she died. You told me that you would wait for me to come home so we could be married."

Her heart twisted. *The locket!* She had forgotten about that necklace. The memory resurfaced, and she recalled giving him the locket and crying in his arms. He was dressed in his military uniform. He looked so handsome in the red coat and white trousers. He'd kissed her one last time, and she vowed she'd treasure that moment forever.

The tears she'd tried to stop rushed forth and blurred her vision. Although he'd given her the proof, it was so hard to believe. Who would believe something like this, anyway? Perhaps she was still dreaming…

"Eleanor"—his voice broke—"you didn't wait for me as you promised."

"Are you jesting?" She found the strength in her voice to

shout at him. "You were dead!" She pushed past him, suddenly having the energy to pace the stable. "I mourned three long years for you. I didn't want to marry anyone else, just to keep your memory in my heart forever."

"But you are engaged."

She rolled her eyes and glared at him. "Only because my father forced my hand."

Adam's face brightened, and he moved toward her. He grasped her hands and held them to his chest. "You don't love Lord Trenton?"

Memories of what she had heard and seen earlier this evening rushed back into her mind. Vincent and Lady Livingston in each other's arms. Just as before, she experienced the crushing blow to her heart, feeling as though it was slowly being ripped from her chest. She didn't know which pain was worse— finding out her soldier fiancé was killed in battle, or that the man who'd swept her off her feet had betrayed her.

She huffed and folded her arms. "What an insensitive question to ask."

"Forgive me."

She tried to push the image of Vincent and his mistress out of her head and focus on the conversation she was having with a dead man. "So, Adam, tell me why you had to lie to everyone? Why did you have to pretend that Adam Haddington was killed?"

His shoulders sagged as he ran his fingers through his dark hair. "Napoleon had spies everywhere. I never knew whom to trust. But one night while I was in camp, I stumbled across some information that was essential to stop Napoleon. One of the men in my camp had been a traitor. I knew it was up to me to turn him in. Misfortune was with me from day one, and I nearly died before getting this information to my superior. Most people believed I had died. That was when I decided it was better for me to stay dead and sneak the missive to the prince regent as someone else, than to see if fate would allow me to live a second time." He walked to one of the stalls. "Around this time, my cousin, Lord Calvin Drake, was ill. The physicians didn't know what was slowly killing him. I came back just in time to see my cousin leave this world to meet his maker. That's when I decided to take over his role and leave Adam Haddington buried in the ground." He turned and looked at her. "When I spoke to the prince regent himself, he also instructed me not to tell anyone that I was still alive. As Lord Calvin Drake, I could be a spy for the prince."

The pain in her skull increased. All of this was just too strange. Distrust took over her feelings, and she wanted to scream at him for lying to her. But doing so would only make her headache worse, and she couldn't take it. She couldn't think any more tonight. She couldn't *feel*, either.

"Adam, this is too much information for me to absorb to-night. Please, allow me to retire to my bedchambers and think this over. I honestly need to be alone now."

Sadness was in his eyes as he walked to her. "Yes, I'll leave you. I don't want to hurt you any longer, my love."

My love? Did he know that those words made her want to cry all over again? What was love, anyway? Was it hurting people? Lying to them? Apparently, both Vincent and Adam thought that was what love meant, because they hadn't hesitated to do these things to her and toy with her emotions.

"Goodnight, Adam." She turned to leave, but again, he grasped her hand, stopping her.

"Remember, Adam is dead. I'm Lord Calvin Drake now."

At this moment, she just didn't have the strength to care. "Fine."

As she convinced her weary legs to move back into the man-or and up the servants' steps, she prayed her mind would allow her to sleep tonight. How else could she figure out this mess she'd made of her life?

She feared she would never be the same after tonight. No wonder married women were so cynical.

ANOTHER PLAN HAD failed.

Vincent yawned and stretched as he sat up in bed. Again, another night had passed without much sleep. He blamed Candace for it this time. It had taken him longer than necessary before he finally tossed the woman out of his house. He worried that maybe Ellie had stumbled upon Lady Livingston and left, but he made certain his former mistress was out of his house before Ellie was scheduled to arrive.

As each minute ticked away and the night crept by, he wondered if something had stopped her while she was trying to sneak out of her house. It appeared fate was not working with them, and they would have to wait until *after* the wedding before they could fulfill their fantasies.

By the time the sun reached high in the sky, his stomach twisted with worry. The overpowering urge to see Ellie became stronger than before, and he feared the worst. What if she had arrived earlier and seen Lady Livingston? His stomach twisted. Would he be able to smooth things over with Ellie? Just the thought of her loathing him left a hollow ache in his chest.

As much as he wanted to talk to Ellie, he didn't dare be at her place first thing in the morning. It was considered bad manners to arrive unannounced so early in the day. Instead, he took his time dressing before walking out to the charred wood of what used to be his stable. With his boot, he moved the ashes around. The cleanup would be tiresome and probably take a few days, especially if he did it by himself. Although he wanted to get started on building a new stable, perhaps it was best if he waited for his money to come in so he could pay people to help him. Hopefully, it would be soon. He needed some place to keep his soon-to-be-wife's horse, Pegasus.

"Good day, milord."

Vincent turned to see his servant, Dalton, walking toward

him from the servants' cottages down the lane. "Good morning. How are you?"

The middle-aged man nodded and grinned, displaying his crooked brown teeth. "I'm good. Thank you, milord. I saw you out here and wondered if you were planning on cleaning this up."

"I had thought about it." Vincent scratched his chin as he glanced back at the mess. "But I just don't have the ambition to get on it yet."

"I will help you."

Vincent smiled at his servant. "I know, and I thank you. If we can round up a few more men, the task will be easier."

"Do you wish me to do that, milord?"

"Yes, if you don't mind."

"Not at all." Dalton turned to leave, but then stopped suddenly and spun around. "Before I go, I must say that I was happy to see you got rid of Lady Livingston last night."

Vincent sucked in a breath. His servant knew? Then again, servants knew a lot about the people they worked for. "Yes, I didn't want her in my house."

"I hope she is out of your life for good. I heard from my cousin who works for the Berkleys that Lady Livingston is with child. She's desperately trying to find a man to marry before her pregnancy becomes noticeable."

Shock passed through Vincent yet again. "She is pregnant?"

Dalton nodded. "The true father is one of the Berkleys' stable hands."

A laugh bubbled up in Vincent's throat, and he just couldn't hold it back. "Well, I must say, I'm very glad the woman finally got what she deserves."

"I agree." Dalton grinned. "Oh, and I must apologize for not stopping that lad who entered the manor last night when you had...um, company."

Startled, Vincent blinked quickly as his heart raced. "What lad?"

"An hour or so after you returned home from your party, a

lad rode up on a horse and walked right in your front door without knocking. I hurried to catch the scamp, but within minutes, the lad left and rode off. I feared he might have stolen something, but nothing was in his hands. That happened before you tossed Lady Livingston out of the house, of course."

Vincent's blood froze—and his breath caught in his throat. "Do you remember what kind of horse this person was riding?"

"Of course, milord. It was a lovely animal. White and gray."

Pegasus! His chest tightened and he couldn't breathe. Ellie *had* been here.

Vincent swore and raked his fingers through his hair. "Dalton, I have to leave for a few hours. I'll be back afterward, and we can work on cleaning up the ashes."

He didn't wait for a reply from the servant, and flew back into the house to quickly change his clothes. He couldn't present himself to Ellie wearing these old rags.

Frantically, he rushed through everything as his mind scrambled to think of a way to convince Ellie nothing had happened between him and Candace. But how could he do that when she hadn't stayed to watch him usher Candace out—and quite roughly, in fact?

The more he tried to think of the words, the more dread washed over him. Would she call off the wedding? Was that even an option since the duke had found them in a compromising situation? Vincent prayed the duke would still force his daughter to marry. Yet...he didn't want to push Ellie to do anything she didn't want to do. This must be her decision. Not her father's.

Vincent dressed in a black coat and trousers with a gray vest over a pristine white shirt and cravat. He thought about taking his hat, but at the last minute decided against it. He didn't want to have to worry about how to hold his hat when his main purpose was to use his hands—and lips, of course—when he begged Ellie to forgive him for not kicking Candace out of the house sooner.

The ride to the duke's estate was tedious. He imagined the worst...and his heart couldn't take it. He prayed she would give him the chance to explain what had really happened.

Just as he'd thought, the house was still. The windows still had drapes covering them, and none of the servants were out in the yard. When he took his horse to their stables, nobody greeted him.

Vincent dismounted and tied the reins of his horse around a post before taking long strides toward the manor. His first thought was to sneak in through one of the back doors, but he worried about being caught, so he made his way to the front door instead.

First, he tested the doorknob, but it was locked. Taking a deep breath for strength, he knocked. Several seconds turned into minutes, and he heard nothing from inside. Apparently, he'd come too early.

Grumbling, he walked away from the house to peer up at the windows again. Which one belonged to Ellie? If he had to scale a wall just to see her, he would.

A shadow crossed by one of the windows. Stepping closer, he studied that section of the manor. The drapes were open slightly, and as he watched, a woman's form moved from inside. His heart skipped a beat. *Ellie!*

He counted the windows from the west side of the house before darting toward one of the side doors. Good fortune was on his side now, because it opened. Cautiously, he stepped inside the house and listened. The inside was just as silent as outside.

Vincent took soft steps toward the servants' stairs and climbed up to the second level. If the servants were awake, he didn't see them, thankfully. He counted doors until he reached the one that was Ellie's room. Softly, he knocked.

From inside, footsteps padded on the floor, growing louder as they came toward the door. His heartbeat quickened. Vincent prayed he'd gotten the right room. He didn't know how he would explain this to her stepmother if she happened to open the door instead.

CHAPTER FIFTEEN

E LLIE'S EYES WERE raw from crying, and although she hadn't peered into a mirror lately, she would bet good money that they were also very red. She couldn't sleep, but she didn't want to stay awake, either. Her mind was full, and her soul had been shredded to pieces. All of this was too much to handle, but she didn't have any other choice.

Once she'd reached her bedchambers last night—and after crying more—she thought about talking to her father. She didn't know what to do. But she hesitated, because she didn't know if Adam—Lord Calvin—wanted others to know his secret. Was he still a spy for the Crown? But she needed to tell *someone*, if only just to get it off her chest.

The knock at her door startled her. She'd been pacing most of the night, and nobody had come to check on her. Who could be coming to her room now? After last night's party had continued until the wee hours of the morning, who could possibly be awake besides her? If it was her stepmother—which Ellie highly doubted—she wouldn't allow her entrance into the room. That was a face she didn't want to see, especially since Ellie was out of sorts.

She walked to the door and opened it slowly, wanting to see who was standing on the other side before she could open it fully. After all, she was still in her nightdress.

Vincent's handsome, but deceitful, face came into her vision. Not believing she was seeing correctly, she blinked. His face had been in her mind most of the night, and apparently, it hadn't left as she had wanted.

Inhaling sharply, she shook her head. Now was not the time—or the place—to speak with Vincent. "No—"

Panic sparked in his eyes, and he quickly pushed the door open and stepped inside. Anger replaced her sadness.

"How dare you?" she snapped.

"Shh…" He closed the door with his foot. "Ellie, I know I shouldn't be here, but I had to come see you. This is an urgent matter. Forgive me for not waiting."

"No, Vincent." She swung away from him and folded her arms across her bosom. "I don't want to talk right now."

He rested a gentle hand on her shoulder. "My precious, please talk to me. There has been a misunderstanding, and we need to discuss it."

"Misunderstanding?" she shrieked, and spun around, facing him. She wanted to pummel his chest but refrained. "What is there to misunderstand? I saw you with Lady Livingston last night—the same night, let me remind you, that *we* planned to be together. The same night we had planned to give ourselves to each other. Or had you forgotten about that?"

"Ellie, listen to me." He grasped her arms, but she yanked them away. "Yes, Lady Livingston was there—uninvited—but if you had only stayed a few moments longer, you would have seen me toss her out of my house. I didn't want her there. I wanted *you.*"

Huffing, Ellie rolled her eyes. "If you didn't want her there, then what was she doing in your arms?"

Vincent sighed and folded his arms over his wide chest. "Tell me, Ellie, what exactly did you see?"

"Didn't you hear me? The woman was in your arms, you imbecile."

"Yes, I heard you," he answered calmly. "But bear with me

on this. I want you to tell me exactly what you saw."

This was easy for her to answer, since the silhouette of him and that dreadful woman had been branded in her memory. And no matter how many times she tried to forget, the recollection wouldn't disappear.

"Your hands were holding her shoulders, and her arms were wrapped around your waist as she pressed herself against you." She swallowed the lump of emotion rising in her throat. "She was telling you that I wouldn't make you happy, but she would be able to accomplish that day *and* night. She also said something about your begging her once you two were in your bed."

Tears grew in Ellie's eyes, even though she fought them. Reliving this heartbreaking moment was more than she could handle.

Determination flashed across his face, and in two steps, he closed the space between them, pulling her up against him as he wrapped his arms around her. Immediately, she stiffened.

"Like this?" he asked in a deep voice as he stared down into her face. "Was this what you saw?"

The intimate way he held her made her suck in a breath. She wanted to kick his leg, slap him, or something…if not for the warmth rushing through her limbs right now. "No," she answered.

"Because when I hold a woman I'm very attracted to, I like my arms to surround them completely as if she is in a cocoon. When I invite a woman into my embrace, I hold her in this manner, and drop my face so close to hers as I prepare for the inevitable kiss we both want."

Confusion spread through her. This was nothing like the stance she'd witnessed between him and Lady Livingston. The woman had seemed the aggressor, not Vincent.

"So tell me," he continued, "was this what you saw? Was I holding her like this?"

"No."

"I begged her to stop," Vincent explained with sadness in his voice. "I kept telling her that I was going to marry you…that I *wanted* to marry you. Not her. I told her that only *you* could make me happy." He took a deep breath and released it slowly as his arms relaxed slightly. "Not long after that, my temper finally snapped, and I shoved her out of my house. She wouldn't accept no for an answer, and I wouldn't allow her to convince me otherwise. I'm not a violent man, but I would have been with her if she hadn't left."

Part of Ellie's broken heart wanted to believe and trust him. But it was difficult. She honestly didn't know him that well. She didn't know if he lied to women just to seduce them. She couldn't forget that he'd been a rogue before inheriting the title.

"Why was she there?" she asked with a shaky voice.

He stroked the long hair hanging down her back. "She had mentioned that she had someone watching me. That's why she knew my sisters were gone and that I'd just returned from the duke and duchess's party. Lady Livingston still wanted to marry me, which is something that will *never* happen."

He lifted a hand and brushed the tears trailing down her face. "When you saw us in each other's arms," he continued, "I was trying to shove her away, which was why my hands were on her shoulders. If only you had stayed to watch a few more minutes, you would have seen me yell at her and tell her I didn't want to have anything to do with her ever again. My servant, Dalton, witnessed it. If you don't believe me, then I pray, ask him."

As she stared into his beautiful blue-gray eyes, her heart twisted with confusion. He was telling her the truth. She knew it. Did it matter now? Adam was back in her life. Hadn't she given her love to her soldier and promised to love him always?

Burying her face against his shirt, she released a fresh batch of tears. Her body shook uncontrollably. "Oh, Vincent. Forgive me for doubting you. I was such a jealous fool."

Strong, but gentle, hands moved soothingly over her back. She breathed in his intoxicating scent of pine and leather, and it touched her everywhere. This, too, would always be branded in her memory.

"Oh, Ellie, my precious," he said with a tight voice as he kissed the top of her head. "It's all right. The truth is out in the open now. You need not fear any longer."

His statement was quite comical, especially now. He didn't know about Adam, and although she wanted to tell him, she hesitated. Adam hadn't said anything about his life being a secret *now*. Did he want others to know? After all, he had finally told her the truth.

"Actually, no." She lowered her hands and raised her gaze to his. "Vincent, there is more that you don't know about."

His forehead creased. "More? With Lady Livingston?"

"No, not her. It's…Adam."

A sympathetic expression crossed Vincent's handsome features, and he cupped the side of her face. "You can tell me anything, my precious. We will soon be husband and wife, and I want our marriage to be one of honesty."

Once more, pain twisted inside her. "Then there is something I need to tell you. I just learned about this last night when I returned from seeing you and Lady Livingston…you know." She gulped.

"What is it?"

"Adam…isn't dead."

VINCENT PEERED INTO Ellie's serious, watery brown eyes. Had he heard correctly? No, there had to be some mistake.

"What?" He shook his head. "What do you mean Adam isn't dead?"

She blew out a heavy breath. "Do you remember meeting Lord Calvin Drake, Adam's cousin?"

"Yes." He gritted his teeth, knowing he wasn't going to like what she was about to say.

"Well, Lord Calvin is really Adam."

His mind skidded to a halt. He hadn't expected her to say *that*! "Wh-what?"

She nodded. "Apparently, Adam was a spy for the prince regent. When Adam was in battle, he almost died, but it was because someone was trying to kill him for the information he discovered. The prince told him to let his identity as Adam die, and that was when he took over his cousin's identity as Lord Calvin."

Vincent was speechless, and his mind was empty, which rarely happened. However, pain tightened his throat, more severely than when he had realized that Ellie saw him with Lady Livingston.

If what she said was true, then... It became difficult to breathe. Ellie would want to marry Lord Calvin, since she had given her heart to him first. She'd told Vincent the first time she offered him that ridiculous proposal that it would be in name only because she could never love another man.

Slowly, he lowered his arms and withdrew his touch by taking a step back. Sorrow seeped into his soul. Ellie appeared genuinely upset over this. Why wasn't she rejoicing? But perhaps she was upset because she had come to care for him after all. Perhaps she would miss him when he withdrew his proposal and allowed her to be with the man she truly loved.

Not many times in Vincent's life had he wanted to cry, but the longer he stared at Ellie, the more everything became hopeless. Tears would build in his eyes at any moment, he was certain.

He cleared his throat. "What a remarkable tale. I'm sure Adam has had the adventure he always wanted."

"Yes, I suppose."

"So, he returned to live out the rest of his life as an earl?"

"Yes. That is how I understand it."

Vincent opened his mouth to ask if Adam wanted her back, but he quickly closed it before the words exited. Of course the man wanted Ellie back in his life. What sane man would refuse such a passionate beauty?

"Have…um, have you told your father?"

She shook her head.

"I wonder how he will be able to deal with this. After all, just last night he made the announcement about our engagement, and now he needs to rescind it." He licked his dry lips. "Is that even possible?"

More tears fell from her eyes. "This, I don't know."

Anger, disappointment, and regret mixed together, spreading through his hollow heart. He exhaled roughly and dragged his fingers through his hair, turning away from her to pace the floor. "Perhaps this was why fate couldn't bring us together as we wanted."

"Yes, perhaps," she replied softly.

"I must say, I'm truly disheartened over this turn of events. But I suppose all is for the best. After all, Adam is getting the woman he wanted, and you are marrying the man who holds your heart." He stopped and looked at her, wanting her to correct him, but knowing she wouldn't.

Her gaze lowered to the floor as she nodded quietly.

Emotionally destitute, he realized if he didn't leave soon that he'd fall on his knees and beg for her love. He couldn't do that for his own peace of mind. He couldn't make such an utter fool of himself, either.

"Then I suggest you speak with your father today about the issue, and send me a missive to let me know what to expect. I'll act any way your father wishes me to act in front of Society. I only want your happiness."

Tears stung his eyes, so he quickly hurried out of the room before she noticed. As much as he wanted her to run after him and confess her undying love, he knew that would never happen. He wasn't her first love. And he would never be.

CHAPTER SIXTEEN

ELLIE PEELED HER eyelids open the best she could. They felt like dead weights. Exhaustion from crying and worrying about the situation between her and Vincent—and Adam—had finally taken its toll and put her to sleep.

Her drapes were drawn, and a tray of food sat on her small table. Wearily, she pulled herself out of bed and walked to the food. She nibbled on the dry bread and salty cheese, and plopped two grapes in her mouth, but that was all she could eat.

She wandered to the window, pushed back the drapes ever so slightly, and peeked outside. The sun was setting on the horizon. *I've been asleep all day?* Perhaps it was best. She was tired of crying…tired of wanting her life to change. She was exhausted with trying to reach for something she would never have. Fate hadn't been very kind to her, and she didn't know why.

Ellie hurried to the water basin and splashed her face. She was sure her eyes were still puffy and red, but she needed to talk to her father. He would know what to do. She hoped.

She threw on her dressing gown and pushed her bare feet into slippers before leaving her room. As she moved down the stairs, she listened for voices. Augusta's voice came from the drawing room. Knowing her stepmother, she probably had some visitors, which usually meant that the duke was in his study with a bottle of brandy and a cigar.

Bypassing the drawing room so that no guests would see her in her night clothes, Ellie scooted down the next corridor. As she neared the study, her father's cigar scent lingered in the hall. She couldn't detect voices, so he was probably alone. Lately, Dominic hadn't been staying home much. Ellie suspected he might be trying to find a woman to marry, since their father was hounding him, as well.

She stopped in front of the door. Staring at the hardwood, she breathed deeply, trying to gain courage. Would her father help her? Since Ellie's mother died, he'd not been the same man. He'd been distant, and she wanted the other father back in her life—the one who took the time to listen to her problems or her heartaches.

Would he ever become that father again?

She knocked softly.

"Enter." His deep voice rang from the room.

She turned the doorknob and walked inside. The cigar scent was stronger in the air, almost overbearing. She waved a hand in front of her face. "Goodness, Father. How can you breathe in this stuffy room?"

"Forgive me. I didn't think I was going to have company." He motioned to the window. "Open the window and let in some fresh air."

Needing to breathe, she quickly did as he requested. When the evening's cool air caressed her face, she closed her eyes and inhaled the fresh scent.

"Why are you in your night clothes?" he asked.

Ellie turned toward him, but leaned back against the wall nearest to the window. "I've actually not changed my clothes since last evening. I've been in my room all day. Have you not noticed?"

"No. Forgive me, my dear. I fear I haven't been very attentive of late."

Her heart twisted from the forlorn hum gripping her father's voice. The duke stared at his empty glass, wearing a frown.

"Father…" She sighed and moved to his side, patting his shoulder. "What is amiss? Will you please talk to me like you used to?"

He lifted his troubled gaze to her and nodded. "I try to be strong, especially in front of my children, but deep inside"—he placed a hand on his chest—"I cannot stop wishing your mother was still alive."

Ellie smiled as tears collected in her eyes again. "I wish that all the time. But I know she is in heaven, and she is my guardian angel. You must believe that, too. It's the only thing that helps me deal with the pain of losing a parent." She bent and kissed her father's cheek. "But I don't want to lose another one."

"No, my dear. You won't lose me." He cupped her cheek.

"But Father, I already have. You don't talk to me like you used to. And I'm quite certain you are just as distant with Dominic."

His eyes grew moist with emotion. "Yes, I have become rather distant, haven't I?"

She grasped both of his hands and squeezed. "Then we shall deal with our loss together, and we shall overcome."

"What would I do without you?" He smiled weakly.

"I hope you never have to know that answer." She bent and kissed his cheek again before straightening. "Father, I need to talk to you now, if you don't mind. Something has happened, and I need your advice. I need to know how to handle this unexpected problem."

Nodding, he cleared his throat and sat up straight in his chair. "I shall try my best to help."

She moved to the nearest chair and sat, wringing her hands in her lap. "Father, last night I had a visitor—"

"Last night? Before or after the party?"

"It was after I had retired for bed."

His eyebrows pulled together. "Someone came to your room?"

Oh dear. She must arrange her words so that she didn't say something unnecessary. "I couldn't sleep, so I went out to the stable to saddle Pegasus. That's when I had the visitor. They saw me and came to speak with me."

Leaning back in his chair, he linked his fingers across his middle. "Who was it?"

She forced a small laugh. "You will not believe it. The truth is too strange."

"Explain yourself." One eyebrow lifted higher than the other.

She proceeded to tell him about seeing Lord Calvin Drake, and the confession he had thrown at her. She studied her father for his reaction, and thankfully, it was the same as she'd had. Disbelief was on his face, so she continued to tell him *why* Adam had lied to everyone.

Her father released a growl and stood from his chair. He marched back and forth across the floor, shaking his head.

"I don't believe it," he muttered before glancing at her. "What if this is just another man after your fortune?"

"No, Father. It's really Adam."

"How did he make you believe?"

"I gave Adam my locket—the one that my dear mother gave me before she died. Adam told me he still had that locket." She shrugged. "Only Adam knew I had given that to him, since it was done in private, right before he left."

Her father pushed his fingers through his thinning brown hair. "I've never heard of such a thing. I still doubt it."

She chuckled. "Yes, well, it's the truth."

His head snapped up. "Does he still want to marry you?"

"Yes." After she said the words, she thought back on their strange conversation. Had he actually *said* he wanted to be her husband? In all of the shock and heartbreak of seeing Vincent and Lady Livingston, Ellie couldn't trust her memory anymore. Not today, anyway.

"And what are your feelings?" her father asked in a soft, understanding voice.

Tears stung her eyes again. Hadn't she shed all her tears by now? "I…don't know. I loved Adam and hadn't wanted to let go of his memory. But after meeting Lord Trenton, I thought I had found a man who would be able to replace my memories."

Confusion filled her, tugging painfully at her heart. Did she still love Adam, even though he was now Lord Calvin Drake? Or did she really love Vincent?

"But what will Society think? Will they expect me to marry the soldier I pined away for all those years? Or will they be unforgiving if I marry Vincent? I just don't know—Vincent or Adam?"

"Ellie, you told me he goes by Lord Calvin now. They won't know he was Adam Haddington."

"I know." She covered her face with her hands. "But I will know the truth."

"My dear." He sat beside her and wrapped comforting arms around her shoulders. "Please don't fret. There is always a solution to every problem."

Sniffing, she lowered her hands and looked at him. "What is the solution, Father?"

"What does your heart tell you?"

"I…I don't know yet. It's been crushed so many times in the past twenty-four hours, I cannot trust it any longer."

"Then that is something you will have to decide. We shall postpone the wedding with Lord Trenton until you realize who holds your heart."

"But what about Society? I'm the daughter of a duke. I have to follow rules, and not cause a scandal—"

"Shh…" He touched a finger to her mouth. "Don't you worry about them. Let me worry about it."

She struggled to smile. "I suppose I don't need to make a decision now."

"No, not yet. Give your heart time to adjust, and then see which man truly makes you happy. Only you can decide which man will be your friend for the rest of your life, just as your mother was my friend before she died."

Ease settled over her. He was right. She didn't need to decide anything now, which was a good thing, because she feared she would make the wrong decision. She would continue to see Vincent, and she'd also allow Adam—Lord Calvin—to visit her. She prayed her heart would tell her which one to choose. She didn't trust her own mind yet.

"I thank you, Father." She threw her arms around him and rested her head on his shoulder. "I'm happy that you have returned. Please don't ever go away again."

Chuckling, he kissed her forehead. "Now that I realize what I'm doing to my children, I vow I shall not let it happen again."

She pulled back and met his gaze. "Father? Do you really love Augusta?"

Sadness altered his expression. "No. I met Augusta when I was still mourning your mother. I was lonely, and I thought she could replace my dear Martha." He shook his head. "Augusta cannot. I believe she tricked me into marrying her, because she changed into a controlling shrew once we were wed."

"Oh, Father." Ellie clutched his hands. "She is running this household as if she is the queen herself. Neither Dominic nor I want her here. Would it be so terrible for you to divorce her?"

"Trust me, I have thought about that many times. Unfortunately, unless she has committed adultery, I cannot divorce her."

"Dominic and I don't trust her. She's…sneaky." Ellie frowned. "I cannot put my finger on it, but she's calculating in an odd sort of way."

"Yes, I see it now. For weeks, she has been trying to push me into allowing Lord Stone to marry you. I was weak and went along with her plans." He stroked her cheek. "Will you forgive me, my dear?"

"I will, but please instruct Lord Stone to leave the house posthaste. Augusta has him living here. Did you know that?"

"Yes. I'm sorry for that, but I promise, that will be the first thing on my agenda tomorrow."

Relief swept over her, and she sighed. "That's the best news

I've heard all day."

He stood and pulled Ellie to her feet. "Go back upstairs to your room and sleep. You need to look your best tomorrow. I'm sure you'll have two men vying for your heart."

She tilted her head. "Do you really think Vincent would vie for my heart? After all, you practically pushed us together."

Her father laughed heartily. "I think Vincent will come around and show his true colors. I've seen the way he looks at you, and he's smitten."

"We shall see, won't we?"

As she left the study and headed back toward her room, she pondered the strange emotions fluttering in her chest. Did she want Vincent to *show his true colors*? Or was she really and truly in love with Adam?

Hopefully, her heart would hurry up and decide. She was weary of this constant headache.

Then again, now that Vincent had money, would he want to marry her at all? At first, the bargain was to wed so that he would have her money.

She rubbed her pounding forehead. Negative thinking like this was not good for her health.

VINCENT SPENT THE next two days building his stable from sun up to sun down. When he paused to take a break, he drank brandy, hoping that the strong drink and the hot sun would warp his mind, and perhaps erase some of his memories.

Dalton had gathered more men to assist in building the stable. Vincent didn't talk much, but the other men conversed amongst themselves. As much as he tried to release the hold Ellie had over him, he couldn't break it. There was no way he could compete with the man who *held her heart*, as she had once told him. So why was he even trying?

Inwardly laughing, he wondered how he'd allowed a woman to take control of his feelings in the first place. What was it about her that kept him coming back for more? Perhaps it was the way she laughed, or the way she smiled. He had certainly enjoyed seeing the twinkle in her eyes lately. And he especially liked seeing the yearning on her face whenever she wanted to be alone with him.

In just a little time, she had him imagining things a rogue like himself shouldn't even be thinking. Vincent had visualized himself settling down and raising children with her. Why had he done that? Now he'd always be a lost man.

Swiping his gloved hand across his sweaty brow, he looked upon the newly built stable. All it needed was to be painted. He'd do that tomorrow. At least it gave him something to do. Unfortunately, he had nothing to do this evening. He wasn't tired from all the physical work he'd done these past two days as he tried to stop thinking about Ellie. He had even fixed things up around the manor.

Before Lord Calvin Drake had entered Ellie's life, this evening's event might have been his wedding night. It was difficult not to think about being with Ellie, holding her all night, and kissing her whenever his heart desired.

Vincent shook his head, pushing aside the improper thoughts. Thinking in this manner was torture, and certainly not healthy. What he needed to do was return to the man he'd been before Ellie entered his life. Unfortunately, Society still considered him engaged. He would have to wait until the duke announced that they were withdrawing the wedding plans so that she could marry the love of her life, Drake.

Vincent didn't want to be around when that happened. He'd get roaring drunk for an entire week after that. Mayhap longer.

And living only a mile away from her would be hard enough. If she married Lord Calvin, at least they'd live farther away.

Vincent's heart clenched again. He didn't know how he could handle her marrying that man. Although Adam was his friend at one time, things were so much different now. No longer would Vincent feel guilty for sending his friend into battle.

He stretched his arms above his head as he moved away from the stable. The helpers had long since gone home. Vincent needed a bath. And to sleep. And a bottle of brandy…not necessarily in that order, either.

He turned back toward the manor. In the distance, someone on horseback rode toward him. Although he wanted it to be Ellie coming back to tell him she wanted *him* and not the other man, the closer the rider came, the more he could see it wasn't a woman.

Within moments, Vincent recognized the rider. He gritted his teeth, waiting for the man to stop and dismount.

Adam Haddington—also known as Calvin Drake—jumped off his horse so perfectly that Vincent wondered how the man had achieved the move. When Adam had left to join the battle, he could barely mount, let alone dismount without stumbling. Had he really gotten that good in three years? Vincent supposed it was possible.

"Good day," Adam greeted Vincent as he approached. "I see you have erected the stable. It looks amazing, my good man."

"Yes. I had some help, thankfully," Vincent grumbled.

He studied the other man, trying to see Adam in the person standing before him now. The hair color was the same, maybe slightly darker, as was his eye color. But Lord Drake wasn't the thin man who had left three years ago. This person in front of him had muscles. Was this *really* Adam?

"I hope you don't mind that I dropped by unannounced," the earl said, "but I really needed to talk to you."

"Yes, we do have a lot of catching up to do." Vincent nodded. "After all, I thought you were dead for three years."

Lord Calvin's eyes grew wide. "You know?"

"Ellie told me." Anger rose inside of Vincent, growing hotter by the second. It was hard to face the man who would win her heart.

"Oh. I'm glad she did."

Vincent didn't dare say anything. Not yet. Right now all he wanted to do was wrap his fingers around the man's neck and squeeze.

"Then I suppose I do owe you an explanation. Or did Ellie give you that, as well?"

"She told me," Vincent mumbled.

Lord Calvin sighed and removed his hat. "I had good reasons for doing what I did."

"I'm certain you did." Vincent turned toward the manor and took large steps, hoping to get inside soon and get himself that glass—or bottle—of brandy. "I don't think I would know what to do if there was a man trying to kill me, as happened to you."

"Yes. That's exactly what it was." Lord Calvin's strides were keeping up with Vincent.

"So tell me," Vincent snapped as he opened the door and stormed inside, "why did you come back?" He walked directly into the nearest room and to the liquor tray. "Why after all this time, did you return?" He poured a good amount of brandy into a goblet and tossed it down his throat.

"Well, you see, the man who was after me is caught and at Newgate Prison. That was when I decided to return home and start my new life."

Vincent threw his former friend a glare. "And what, pray tell, is that? Will you still be a spy for the Crown? Or do you plan on living the life as an earl, marry, and have children?"

Lord Calvin chuckled and walked to the window, moving the drapes and peering outside. "That is a good question. I hoped to pick up the pieces where I left off before leaving for battle, but…I'm not Adam Haddington any longer. Everything I've done since leaving you has shaped me into a new man."

Vincent arched an eyebrow. "You are certainly a different man now."

Lord Calvin looked at him and nodded. "I'm quite impressed with the changes I have made. Living in danger and on the edge definitely makes a man re-evaluate his life."

"I'm sure it does." Vincent took another deep swig of his drink.

"I almost miss it."

Vincent froze, holding his breath. What did he mean by that? "What do you miss, exactly?"

Lord Calvin chuckled. "There's a feeling of euphoria that shoots through one when one realizes one has cheated death yet again. I enjoyed the adventures of being a spy, and especially assisting in getting Napoleon sent to Elba."

"Yes, I'm sure that would be quite the accomplishment." Vincent scratched his chin. "I'm sure everything else you do seems not as important."

"Those are the very words I would use."

Feeling more in control, Vincent set his glass down and walked to a chair, running his hand across the back before sitting in the cushioned seat. "I would assume," he continued, "that returning to a normal life would be quite boring."

Lord Calvin shrugged one shoulder. "Perhaps a little."

Vincent crossed one leg over the other as he tapped his fingers impatiently on the armrest of the chair. "So tell me, why did you come to see me?"

"Can't a friend see another? It's been three years, but I still consider you a trusted friend."

"Do you now…" Vincent dropped his foot to the floor and leaned forward, resting his arms on his knees. "Or was it that you were worried about my being engaged to Ellie?"

The man's eyes widened and the color left his face for a few seconds. "I, um… Well, yes. I must say that I was quite shocked to see you and Eleanor engaged."

"Did she tell you why?"

Meekly, Lord Calvin nodded. "She did mention that you two were forced to wed."

"We were." Vincent stood and walked closer to Calvin. "Her father nearly caught us in a passionate embrace. However, he did catch us alone, hiding in a grove of trees at a party we were attending, and he heard us discussing our passionate kiss. You know that's enough to force a man to marry the duke's daughter."

"Yes." Calvin's voice was small.

"And I suppose"—Vincent paused, taking in a deep breath and exhaling it slowly, trying to calm his ire—"that you have returned to try to steal the bride. Am I correct?"

He couldn't read the other man's expression. Did Calvin want to marry Ellie, or stay with his former life of spying? Vincent didn't dare hold his breath as he waited for an answer.

"The last three years of my life have been a whirlwind of adventure and suspense from one day to the next. I never knew if I would live or die."

Nodding, Vincent listened without interrupting as he studied his old friend. Adam not only appeared different, he acted different. He was finally a mature man instead of the young pup that had left to go fight Napoleon.

"During those years," he continued, "I thought about Eleanor many times. Sometimes, my heart ached for her, but I knew it was right to leave her alone instead of bringing her into my world of secrets and spying."

"That was a wise decision," Vincent said. "But what about now? Are you still in love with her?"

"Part of me wants to return to the days when I was Adam Haddington and falling in love with the beautiful Eleanor Middleton." Calvin shrugged as he walked away from the window and toward Vincent. "But a larger part of me knew that if my new life came with a different identity, things would never be the same again."

Hope sprang inside Vincent. Did that mean what he thought it meant? Did he have a chance of winning Ellie's heart after all?

CHAPTER SEVENTEEN

ELLIE DONNED ONE of her lovelier gowns for the ball tonight. She liked how the lavender color enhanced her brown eyes, and she definitely liked the daring heart-shaped bodice that showed an ample amount of her bosom...enough to entice, anyway. When her maid had fixed her hair, Ellie couldn't stop thinking about Vincent and how he liked this style. He liked her hair flowing over her shoulders, too.

She had stayed cooped up in her room for three days, only because it took that long for her to stop crying and for her swollen eyes to return to normal. She didn't have an escort for this evening's event, but she didn't care. She definitely needed some time to figure out her own heart.

Descending the grand staircase, she listened for the voices of her father or Augusta, but the house seemed quiet. She assumed that Dominic was out. If she were a man and could leave the house any time she wanted, she wouldn't stick around to listen to Augusta's grating voice, like fingernails scratching down a chalkboard.

Ellie walked to her father's study first, but it was empty. Strange, since he was usually the first one ready for the night's party and waiting for the women to finish getting ready. But not tonight.

Curiously, Ellie wandered back toward the main hall, straining her ears as she listened for any sounds. Why couldn't she hear even the servants whispering?

Something wasn't right. Eeriness crept over her, churning her empty stomach.

Had her father and Augusta left without her? She hoped not. He knew she had been *under the weather* these last few days, but she was ready to get out and mingle now.

She moved outside and stood on the front porch, listening to the night's sounds around her. Crickets chirping was the main sound, but in the distance, an owl gave its night howl. Another sound captured her attention. Off to the right of the house in the trees, and through the night, came whispering.

Darkness had already covered the land, and she prayed she wouldn't be detected as she sneaked toward the trees. The closer she came, the louder the whispered voices were. She stopped behind a large tree and peeked around it. A man and a woman stood together in discussion. It was obvious the woman was Augusta, but the man…

"I will not have it!"

Ellie rolled her eyes. Now she recognized the other shadowed figure that paced the small space between the trees. Edgar Stone. Hadn't her father booted him out of the house two days ago? She was sure he had. So why was the idiot still here? Apparently, Augusta hadn't abided by the duke's orders.

"Edgar, you must know I'm trying everything I can." Augusta folded her arms across her large bosom. "Something has gotten into the duke as of late, and I cannot sway him like I have before."

He stopped and glared at her. "Then fix it. I don't care how you do it, but get *your husband* to allow me back into the house. How else am I going to get Ellie? This has been our plan all along, and I won't allow anything to stop it now."

Ellie hitched a surprised breath. *Plan?* What plan? And why did the imbecile still want her? How many times did she have to tell him no?

"Lower your voice," Augusta snapped. "I'll fix it, but you will have to help, as well. You have done nothing that we discussed, so this is your fault as much as it is mine."

Edgar marched to Augusta and grabbed her shoulders, shaking her once. "This is *not* my fault. *You* were the one who couldn't control your husband, which is why I'm not staying at the manor any longer."

The older woman pushed her palms against Edgar's chest to move him away. "Then tell me why you didn't follow through with the plan. You have been in the house for nearly a week. Don't tell me you never found the chance to sneak into Ellie's bedroom and climb in bed with her."

Gasping, Ellie slapped a hand over her mouth, hoping it wasn't heard. *He wouldn't dare...* But knowing Edgar, he *would* dare to do such a vile thing. But why? There were other women in town who were much prettier and more enjoyable to be around. However, she didn't think it was that. Could it be her large dowry? Yet why would all of this be based on money? Nothing made sense.

"I never had the chance to sneak into her room," he growled. "One of the maids was always lurking nearby. Or your stepson, Dominic. He watched me with eagle eyes, I tell you."

Ellie prayed she saw Dominic at tonight's party so she could convince him to stay home more often, if only to protect his sister.

"How am I able to accomplish that if I don't live here any longer?" Edgar asked.

"When we return from tonight's party, I shall leave the east side door unlocked. Sneak in that way."

Oh no you won't! Growling under her breath, Ellie hurried back into the house. Augusta would not win. Why she wanted her crusty nephew to marry her stepdaughter was beyond Ellie's imagination, but she would make certain their plans failed miserably. Even if she had to sleep elsewhere tonight.

Perhaps she could hide in the stable with the horses. Edgar would never search for her there.

She grumbled as she paced the floor in the drawing room. How terrible was it that she couldn't even feel safe in her own home? She could tell her father—however, that might upset him enough to shoot Edgar himself. She couldn't have her father doing that. He'd go to prison, and he might even have his title and lands stripped from him. No, she must deal with this issue on her own.

Before she could figure out what her plan was, Augusta entered the drawing room, followed by the duke. Ellie ignored the woman, but smiled lovingly at her father.

"You look absolutely beautiful tonight," he told Ellie. "I'm happy to see you are up and about now."

"Yes, well, I need to return to my normal activities. After all, I have a wedding coming soon."

"Indeed you do." Her father gave her a wink.

Augusta showed her faux smile and clapped her hands once. "Have we settled on a date yet?"

"Not yet," the duke answered. "I promised my wonderful daughter that she could take things slow or fast at this point. It is up to her."

"Oh." Augusta's forehead creased. "Well, then...shall we leave for the ball?"

Ellie followed her father out to their coach and climbed inside, sitting across from her father and stepmother. Thankfully, Augusta chatted endlessly about nonsense, and Ellie didn't care to add her opinion. She stared out the window during the ride, hoping to get to the party quickly so she didn't have to hear any more of her stepmother's mindless drivel.

They reached the party at Lord and Lady Smithton's estate. As soon as Ellie entered, she searched the crowd, looking for a familiar face—or two. Within minutes, she noticed Adam—um, Lord Calvin. It was as if he waited for her, because he stood next to a wall, staring toward the front door. When their gazes met, he smiled and pulled away from the wall, heading toward her.

Ellie's nerves shook and her palms grew moist underneath

her white, elbow-length gloves. He reached her side and bowed. She curtsied.

"Good evening, Miss Middleton. You are looking lovely tonight."

"I thank you, my lord." She smiled. "And you are quite dashing in your brown suit jacket and trousers."

"Would you accompany me to the dance floor for the first dance tonight?"

"Certainly." She glanced toward the floor as couples were lining up for a dance. Nervously, she placed her hand on his arm as he walked with her. They took their places across from each other.

Once the music began, she stepped in the correct rhythm to the country dance. He didn't say much, but neither did she. Her mind kept replaying the conversation they'd had a few nights ago. Part of her wanted to hate him for keeping his existence a secret all this time. The other part of her just didn't care. Knowing he was back in her life was good enough. Wasn't it? But if so, then why couldn't she get the anger and frustration out of her mind?

As soon as the dance ended, he took her back to her father. Lord Calvin exchanged pleasantries with the duke, but nothing was said about Adam's discovery. Then again, he wasn't Adam any longer.

It didn't take long before another man asked her to dance. Smiling politely, she walked with him out to the middle of the room amongst the other couples. The dance was another country dance, thankfully, and this man was as quiet as Lord Calvin.

She skimmed the crowd again, searching for the handsome face she had missed seeing these past three days. Her heart grew heavy as she remembered the way he looked at her that night in her bedroom when she told him about Adam. It was as though Vincent had stopped trying to pursue her. Sorrow had etched the lines of his face so perfectly that she wanted to cry all over again.

Was that why he wasn't here? Had he given up on her? Of course he had. He'd told her that she was finally going to marry the man that held her heart.

The dance ended before she realized, and soon she was standing beside her father again. This time, Lord Calvin wasn't there.

"How are you doing, my dear?"

She gave her father a weak smile. "The best I can, considering."

"I noticed you didn't talk with Lord Calvin much during the dance."

"No." She shrugged. "I think we are both being overly cautious. I don't know how to act around him anymore. He's a different person from the man I fell in love with."

"In a way, I suppose he is." Her father nodded.

Sighing, she rubbed her forehead. A headache had begun to grow the minute she stepped into the house. Actually, it had probably started when she overheard the conversation between Augusta and Edgar.

Her father's gaze moved behind her, and within seconds, his smile broadened. Just as she turned, someone tapped her on the shoulder. When her gaze locked with that man standing so close—and smelling so wonderful—her heart flipped crazily in her chest. *Vincent!*

"Good evening." He bowed. "Forgive me for interrupting, but I was wondering if you would dance with me."

Excitement leaped inside her, and she nodded. Her cheeks began to ache because of her wide smile. "Yes, I would love to."

She couldn't stop looking at him, even as he led her to the dance floor. He wore her favorite gray suit jacket and matching trousers, with the light blue waistcoat that made his blue-gray eyes shine.

Had she forgotten to breathe? Probably, since her lungs burned.

Slowly, she exhaled, trying to regulate her breathing before she swooned. When the music started playing a slow waltz, he took her in his arms, and they stepped in time to the rhythm. Being in his embrace again made silly little flutters of giddiness dance in her belly. Warmth spread through her, and she felt the urge to sigh in contentment, but she didn't know why.

"Ellie, I…cannot take my eyes off you. You're absolutely exquisite. I've never seen a lovelier woman in my life."

She licked her dry lips. "And you, my lord, are the most handsome man I have ever laid eyes on."

His smile relaxed. "How have you been? When I didn't get a missive from you, I wondered what was going on. Has your father decided anything?"

"No. He is leaving that up to me."

Vincent arched an eyebrow. "What is he leaving up to you, exactly?"

"He wants me to pick the man who holds my heart."

Vincent's expression softened as he pulled her a little closer. "Are you trying to tell me you don't know that answer yet?"

Slowly, she shook her head. "I've been very confused these last few days. But no, I have yet to come to a decision."

His mouth stretched wide again. "Let me know if I can help you with that in *any* way."

She laughed as her heart warmed. Hadn't she already made the decision? After all, she hadn't felt this comfortable while dancing with Adam, and her face didn't hurt from smiling so much with him, either. "Yes, I'll let you know if you can be of assistance."

Silence passed between them as they continued to dance, but heaven help her, she couldn't look away. Thankfully, he kept his gaze on her, as well. Her heartbeat hadn't slowed since she first noticed him. Happiness poured through her every second they were together. Wasn't this the answer she was looking for?

"How are things back at the manor?" he asked. "I worry about Edgar being in your house."

Her mind skid to a halt. *Edgar!* How could she have forgotten about that rotten rat? "Oh, Vincent," she gasped, and shook her head. "Things are worse, especially now. Earlier this evening, I overheard a conversation between him and Augusta."

Concern replaced his pleasant expression. "Tell me."

"Well, from what I gathered, they had some sort of plan figured out...even though I'm still stumped on the reasoning behind it. Nonetheless, Edgar wants to—"

The dance ended and couples left the floor. Ellie didn't dare continue, not now. She would find another time this evening to explain things to Vincent. It made her heart light knowing that he still acted as though he wanted to be with her. She trusted him completely. Undoubtedly, he would help her tonight.

CHAPTER EIGHTEEN

VINCENT COULDN'T BELIEVE their poor timing. Her eyes pleaded with him for another moment with him, but he couldn't dance with her twice in a row. Gossip would definitely spread like wildfire. But they were engaged. Didn't that make a difference?

She seemed hesitant to return to her father, and he really didn't want to let her go, either. She hooked her arm around his elbow, but instead of taking her back to her father, he led her out of the room and to the refreshment table.

He handed her a glass of punch before taking a glass for himself. He slid an arm around her back, resting his hand on her hip as he guided her toward a wall. They stood facing each other, but unfortunately, there were still people around who could overhear. That was what worried him.

"Vincent, I need your help," she whispered before taking a sip.

He glanced around them again before meeting her gaze. "What does Edgar want to do?"

"I heard him say he was going to sneak into my bedroom tonight so that he could create a scandal. He's desperate enough to do *anything* to marry me."

Hatred poured through Vincent like hot lava, and he tightened his grip on his drink. "Over my dead body," he grumbled, but not too loudly. He didn't want other people suspicious why he had suddenly turned angry.

Her face softened as a small smile bracketed her face. "I'll do *anything* to make sure that doesn't happen to you." She winked.

His heart grew light again. "Thank you for trying to be my protector, my precious Ellie."

"Just as you are mine."

His heartbeat quickened. "So tell me, how exactly does Edgar plan to accomplish this task?"

"Augusta is going to leave one of the back doors unlocked, since Father kicked him out a couple of days ago."

"Can't you just lock the door after she has unlocked it?"

She shook her head. "I could, but I don't know the exact moment when she'll unlock it, and when exactly he will enter."

"Very true." He sipped his punch, wishing it was a bit stronger right now. He couldn't let Edgar win. Or Lord Calvin.

Earlier this evening when he'd had a talk with Lord Calvin, Vincent realized the man didn't know if he wanted to marry Ellie or not because he missed the life he'd been leading for a few years. It was at that moment when something inside Vincent slapped him senseless, but woke him up to his feelings. He loved Ellie more than anything. He wasn't about to lose her. Not to anyone.

And he would do everything in his power to win her heart.

She took another drink and then lowered her glass. "I don't even dare go to my room this evening when we return home," she whispered.

"Then don't." An idea took root in his mind, making his heart hammer faster than before. He scanned around him before moving closer to her. "Come home with me. I'll always protect you."

Her breathing grew faster, deeper—evidenced by the quick rise and fall of her bosom. In return, excitement grew inside him just as quickly. Indeed, he'd meant every word. And he wouldn't back down. Not this time. Not ever again.

"Once you leave the party with your parents," he continued in a whisper, "I'll follow. I'll be the one who meets you at one of the back doors. Not Stone."

She smiled brightly. "Edgar will be going to the east door, so we can meet by the west door."

He nodded. "Yes. Good plan."

Her gaze moved slowly over his face, resting on his mouth. His heart jumped to his throat. Blazes, she was pretty, and right now if he kissed her, he knew the passion they had shared several times before would return, stronger than ever. Unfortunately, he couldn't kiss her right now. Too many eyes. But it made him ecstatic knowing that she felt the same way. She couldn't hide her happiness.

It also thrilled him to know she had asked *him* for help, even though she had danced with Lord Calvin already. Vincent had just entered the ballroom while they were dancing. It nearly tore his heart to pieces seeing them together, knowing that Adam had been the love of her life. But she hadn't smiled so radiantly with Lord Calvin. Nor had she really conversed with the man during their dance.

As Vincent watched them, hope had bounded in his chest. Feeling more encouraged that she hadn't totally pushed him aside, he decided he would let her know how much he still cared about her.

Now, as they traded whispers and heated glances, and as his heart rate skyrocketed, he knew she still held feelings for him. Did Ellie realize she was in love with him, not the other man? He would do all he could to make certain she knew it without a doubt tonight.

Silence had passed between them, and it hadn't become un-comfortable. As he stared into her magnificent brown eyes, he couldn't stop himself from wanting to hold her again and kiss her to distraction. He loved the way her gaze moved slowly over his face, from the top of his wavy hair, over his eyes, his nose, before coming to rest on his lips.

Vincent resisted the urge to take her in his arms and kiss her passionately. He wanted to forget that they were at a party, where so many pairs of eyes watched every little move they made. He wanted to forget that people would gossip and that he'd create a scandal if he showed such affections for her in public.

"Vincent," she said, breaking the silence. "Do you forgive me for jumping to conclusions the other night?"

His mind went blank for a moment. What was she referring to?

"I shouldn't have assumed," she continued, "that you had chosen Lady Livingston over me." She shrugged. "I was still very insecure. I suppose I'm still insecure."

"Why do you feel this way?" he asked.

"Because you've had so many lovers. How could I possibly compete with that?"

He shook his head and softly caressed her cheek. "There is no comparison, my precious. None of those other women can hold a candle to your beauty and class. When I'm with you, I don't think of anyone else. You are the only woman who has occupied my mind since you first ran into me when I came to visit your brother."

She chuckled. "That day seems so long ago, even though it was only a few short weeks."

"We've been through a lot."

"Yes." She sighed. "But I need to know you forgive me."

He smiled. "Of course I do. I sought you out this evening, did I not?"

"Well...yes."

"I don't do that for just anyone."

Her face reddened, but she didn't lower her gaze. He liked that.

Their private moment was ruined when a man walked up and stood beside Ellie. He bowed to her, and she curtsied.

"Miss Middleton, may I ask you for the next dance?"

Her genuine smile changed slightly. Vincent didn't know if others could tell, but he could. Even the light in her eyes disappeared.

"You may." She looked at Vincent, and the spark in her eyes returned. "Lord Trenton, would you excuse me now?"

"Of course." He bowed and watched her leave with the other man.

The evening seemed to drag after that. It reminded Vincent of the last time they had planned to meet after a ball. But this time would be different. He wouldn't let anything stand in his way of protecting the woman he was madly in love with.

He danced with Ellie one more time during the evening, but the music was much faster than he wanted. Still, she smiled so wide that he could see most of her teeth. Stars glowed in her big brown eyes, which made him beam with happiness. Lord Calvin had also danced with her another time, but her smile wasn't as lively as when she was with Vincent.

He liked that. No, he *loved* that.

"I'm relieved to see you haven't bowed out."

The voice behind Vincent startled him. He turned to see Ellie's father, his hands linked behind him as he rocked back and forth on his heels. The grin on the older man's face told the tale before he could say any more.

"Pardon me?" Vincent asked hesitantly, wondering if he really knew the reason behind the statement.

"I'm happy to see you didn't back off and let Lord Calvin win my daughter's hand."

Vincent's face grew warm from the compliment. It was good to know he had the father's acceptance. "No, I'm not backing down." He glanced across the dance floor to find Ellie, who was dancing with another man. "Your daughter is too special to lose."

Chuckling, the duke slapped Vincent's shoulder. "It does my heart good to hear you say that. She deserves a man who will put her first in his life, and I believe that man is you."

Narrowing his eyes, Vincent studied the duke's expression.

He didn't appear to be joking in the least. "Tell me, Your Grace, why do you feel this way? After all, you did practically force us to get married."

The duke threw back his head and laughed heartily. "Oh, my boy. The truth is I was helping you along. I knew my daughter was interested in you, just as much as you were interested in her. When I followed you outside into the grove of trees that night, I was just giving your relationship a little nudge. Neither of you wanted to believe you had feelings for the other."

Shaking his head, Vincent chuckled. "You cunning old man…"

The duke laughed harder. "True, but it worked. Correct?"

"Yes, it worked." Vincent sighed as he folded his arms. "However, now I just need to convince your daughter that she loves me."

"Do it soon." The duke nodded toward Lord Calvin, who stood against a wall, watching Ellie. "Because I fear that she'll think she's still in love with Adam. Although I really never believed she *truly* loved him. She hadn't been with enough men to know what love is."

How odd that Ellie's father would say such a thing. But Vincent was sure her father knew quite a bit about his daughter by this point in her life. "Well, Your Grace, I'll do all I can to win her heart."

The duke nodded once. "You're nearly there." He turned and walked away, still chuckling softly.

Vincent grinned. He hoped the old man was right.

Soon the time came when the duke ordered the butler to fetch their wraps. Vincent kept his eyes on Ellie, and she glanced around the room until their gazes met. She nodded, and he returned the gesture. *Follow us*, she mouthed, and he gave her another nod. Within minutes, the duke and his family left the party.

Vincent didn't wait more than five minutes before he hurried out to his horse and mounted. He followed, but at a distance.

There was no way he was going to let Lord Stone touch Ellie. He would rather rip off the man's head with his bare hands…and Vincent wasn't usually a violent man.

When Ellie's coach approached the drive to their estate, Vincent slowed his horse and waited behind a large tree. He watched them exit the coach and enter the house.

He urged his horse closer before dismounting, then tied it to a tree and crept toward the west side of the manor. He glanced around the area, wondering if he would see Lord Stone waiting. He almost hoped he spotted the man. Vincent wouldn't hold back. He'd love to use that insipid fool as his new punching bag.

He tried to find something to hide behind, and moved from one tree to the next, waiting and watching. A good ten minutes passed, with nobody coming or leaving the manor. The small window in the door showed that the hall behind it was dark. But he kept his eyes on the door.

Finally, a light flickered in the window. Holding his breath, he waited for Ellie to appear.

ELLIE COULDN'T BELIEVE how easily she was able to slip out of her room, down the stairs, and toward the west corridor without being spotted. It was as if leaving the house tonight was meant to happen.

This evening, she had wondered if her father knew what she had planned. The way he bade her goodnight with a twinkle in his eyes while grinning like a fool made her curious about his actions. Did he know she'd be sneaking out tonight? If only he could do something about that wife of his and her nincompoop nephew, Ellie wouldn't have to leave the house in fear.

Just as she had done last time, she changed her clothes so that she resembled a lad—even stuffing her long hair in the cap. She donned the same boy's shirt and breeches.

She tiptoed down the hall, listening for any sounds, especially voices. But none were heard. Dare she hope that everything would continue to go smoothly? No, that would be ridiculous. Bad luck was following her as of late.

Suddenly, the echo of a heeled shoe clicking against the hardwood floor broke the silence. Light began to brighten the area. Someone was coming her way. And fast!

Panicked, she quickly opened the door to the nearest room and hid inside. Slowly, she closed the door, but not fully, praying it wouldn't squeak and bring undue attention. Holding her breath, she peeked through the slit, trying to see who the person was.

Augusta! Ellie should have known. The older woman unlocked the door that Ellie would leave out of. Confused, she scrunched her forehead. This was the west door, not the east. Then again, Edgar was probably too stupid to really know the difference. Perhaps that was why she had unlocked this door. Would she unlock *all* the doors? Ellie rolled her eyes. Probably.

Augusta waited by the door, peering out the window. Ellie's heart hammered crazily. *Please don't spot Vincent.* Without a doubt, her trusted protector was out there—somewhere— waiting for her. But if Augusta noticed him, the night would be ruined completely.

After what seemed like several minutes, Augusta stepped away from the door and headed back up the corridor.

Ellie expelled her breath. Her hands shook as she slowly pulled the door open. She glanced up the hall to make sure Augusta was well enough out of sight. Relief swept over her when she saw darkness covered the corridor.

She took soft steps toward the door, her ears on high alert. She peeked out the window, but the half-moon's brightness didn't let her see much tonight.

Holding her breath, she turned the knob and slowly opened the door. A small wind blew from the trees nearby, rustling their leaves. A cricket or two chirped. Somewhere in the distance, an owl hooted.

She crept outside, pulling the door behind her softly until it clicked. Shadows were everywhere. Dare she call out to Vincent? No, that wouldn't be wise. But what if Edgar was somewhere close by?

Ellie moved slowly away from the house, her gaze darting all around. She inhaled deeply, trying to detect Vincent's scent. His intoxicating smell was unlike anything else, and it would be branded in her memory forever. Unfortunately, the wind wouldn't let her detect anything.

She didn't dare stay by the house, just in case Edgar stumbled across her, so she stepped toward the stable located down the slope of the yard. As she passed some bushes, a rustle came from behind. Before she had time to react, a man's hand clamped over her mouth.

Fear rushed through her. *Edgar caught me!*

CHAPTER NINETEEN

Ellie struggled against the man's strong grip. As he dragged her behind some tall hedges, she tried to pull his hand away from her mouth.

"Ellie, it's me," Vincent whispered in her ear.

Relief swept over her, and she relaxed.

Slowly, he removed his hand and looked deeply into her eyes. "Edgar is out here. I saw him not too long ago."

She nodded. "I was almost caught by Augusta when she unlocked the door. I thought they'd talked about Edgar going to the east door."

"That's where I saw him," Vincent explained. "However, we aren't alone. There is another man out here."

She hitched a breath as fear raced through her again. "Who is it?"

"I don't know. I've just seen a shadow of a man."

"Do you think he saw you?"

"I pray he hasn't."

She pulled her attention away from Vincent and scanned this side of the yard. "You don't believe he's after me, do you?"

"That, I couldn't say, but I think we need to be careful, just in case."

She blew out a frustrated breath, turned, and buried her face against Vincent's chest. "Why can't this just stop? I want a normal life again."

"Don't fret, my dear." He kissed the top of her head. "I will protect you."

Being close to him like this was so comforting. She never wanted to leave this man's side. It was strange how quickly she'd thought of him as her protector. "I know you will."

With her face against his chest, she could finally inhale his manly scent—the smell she loved. Smiling, she slid her arms around his waist, cuddling closer to him. Immediately, his arms wrapped around her, holding her tightly.

Ellie loved this. She loved...him. Always, and completely. Her heart soared from the knowledge.

There, for a while, she thought she'd been in love with Adam, but now, after being with Vincent for these past few weeks, she realized *this* was love. What she had with Adam had already disappeared from her heart, and her memory.

She released a quiet moan. "Vincent, you are so wonderful."

His chest rumbled with a laugh. "Why did you say that?"

She tilted her head back to meet his gaze. "Because I feel so safe in your arms."

A serious expression took over his face. "Then I shall never let you out of them."

Her heart melted. How could it not? His words had always stirred such passion inside her heart.

"Will you tell me something?" she asked softly.

"Of course."

"Now that you are a wealthy man, are you...do you..." She paused, wondering how to say the doubts that had filled her mind lately.

"What is bothering you, Ellie?"

"You have money now, which means you don't need me or my money."

Confusion grew on his expression. "What are you saying?"

She shrugged. "I need to know if you want to marry me because of my money or...because of me."

He cupped her face. "Money is not part of the bargain any longer. I don't care if I ever see your dowry. I want you."

She looked at his mouth as happiness burst inside her, wanting to kiss him now more than ever. Before she could change her mind, she leaned up and placed her lips against his. Groaning, he tightened his hold around her. He met her kisses with urgent ones of his own. Happiness grew inside her. Why couldn't it always be this way?

The padding of footsteps coming near them startled Ellie, and she broke the kiss. Vincent kept her beside him. She couldn't see through the bushes, but she figured he could see better, since he was taller and could peek above the branches.

"Who is it?" she whispered.

"I don't know."

"Can you not see him?"

"A little, but it's not Stone. Neither is it your brother. I honestly don't know who it is."

As the steps moved toward the house, Ellie felt brave enough to raise her head and look over the hedge. The man, wearing a top hat and long, dark overcoat, hurried to the door. He tested the knob before entering.

Irritation shot through her. "I would like to know who he thinks he is, going into my home uninvited."

"Shh," Vincent said. "Lower your voice. Stone could still be out here somewhere."

"But who was that man, and why did he go inside?"

"That, my precious, is an excellent question. But do you want to follow him in just to see where he's going?"

Sighing, she shook her head. "Of course not. That would be ridiculous and defeat the purpose of hiding from Edgar." She glared at the house. "I pray Father will find the man, or perhaps one of the servants will see him."

"Yes, let's hope that is what happens."

Silence crept upon them, but the night sounds were louder this time. Did that mean they were free to leave their hiding spot?

She sure hoped so.

"Do you think we should go now?" she asked.

"Yes. I think we are safe." He cupped the side of her face, tilting it up to look at her. "Do you want me to go inside and see who that man was?"

Her heart melted, again. Adam would have never offered to do something as daring just to protect her family. Vincent was exactly the opposite, and that was one of the many reasons she loved him.

"No, I'll let the staff take care of him. Right now, I have only one thing on my mind." She slid her hand slowly up his chest. "I want to get out of here so that Edgar doesn't see me."

Vincent grinned. "Your wish is my command, my precious."

Feeling like a night thief, she held Vincent's hand as they ran to a tree, hiding behind the large trunk before darting to another tree. Each time they stopped, he looked around the area, seeing if anyone had noticed them.

Finally, they reached his horse. Vincent mounted first before lifting her and setting her on his lap. At first, it was quite uncomfortable, but as he slid an arm around her, holding her against his chest, she realized this position was perfect.

During the ride, she kept looking over Vincent's shoulder to see if anyone was following. From what she could tell, they were alone on the road. The farther away from the house they rode, the easier she breathed.

She rested her head back against Vincent's muscular chest. The pounding of his heartbeat soothed her fears. Not only was she worried about Edgar, and about the strange man who'd entered her house, but now she thought about what would happen once they reached Vincent's home. They had hinted about what they wanted to happen a few days ago. Even though so much had occurred in the last two days, she still wanted to be with him. Intimately.

His manor came into view, and the rhythm of her heart quickened. He led the horse toward a new structure. Even in the shadows, she could tell what it was.

Gasping, she sat up straight. "Vincent! You have a new stable."

He chuckled as he stopped his horse inside. "I do. I still need to paint it, but at least it's erect and can give my horses a place to call home."

"It's beautiful."

He dismounted first before reaching up to lift her off the horse. She wrapped her arms around his neck, staring into his shadowed eyes. He smiled so lovingly.

"Actually, you are the one who is beautiful," he said before dropping a kiss on her nose and setting her on her feet.

Vincent quickly removed the saddle and bridle before walking his horse into the stall. He turned back to her and took her hand in his, leading them toward the manor.

"Vincent? Are your sisters here?"

"No," he said, looking down at her. "They were so upset by the fire, they decided to stay with their cousins for a while."

"Then we will have all the privacy we need," she whispered, her voice shaking.

Was she scared or just looking forward to their intimacy? Either way, she trusted Vincent. She knew he wouldn't hurt her. So far, he had been so very tender with her, and she knew he wouldn't change that.

She just hoped she would have the courage to continue what they had planned. After all, she was still very innocent in a lot of things.

Inside the house, a few lamps were lit in the corridor. He took one as he started up the stairs. Her heart jumped in her throat, and her limbs began to tremble. She cursed her body's weak reaction.

He glanced down at her and smiled, then lifted her hand and brought it to his mouth, kissing her knuckles. "My precious, you are safe now."

She nodded. "I know. I'm exactly where I want to be."

Another small lamp was lit in the corridor where the bed-chambers were located. Three doors stood on each side of the hall. The wait was nearly killing her.

He stopped in front of the last door on the right, turned, and faced her. "Are you ready?"

She swallowed the lump the size of a cotton ball that must have been lodged in her throat. "Y-yes."

He bent his head and captured her lips. She threw her arms around his neck, participating fully in the passionate kiss. He must have set the lamp down, because both of his hands were circling her waist as he pressed her against the wall.

They kissed this way for the longest time, and she wondered if he would ever take her inside his room. Did she need to be the one who suggested a more *comfortable* place to go in order to continue this moment?

His lips moved away from hers and trailed over her cheek and to her ear. Lightly, he suckled her lobe, bringing goosebumps over her flesh. He then kissed down her neck, to the collar of the boy's shirt she wore. Chills ran rapidly over her, warming her body very quickly.

Vincent pulled away and looked at her. His breathing was as heavy as hers. He stroked her cheek before moving away from her to open the door.

Finally! She tried not to grin too wide. He picked up the small lamp before taking her hand and pulling her into the room.

She glanced around...and stalled. This wasn't his room. There was nothing that indicated a man slept here. Not even his scent lingered. This looked more like a guest room.

He set the lamp on the bedstand before turning to look at her. "I hope this room is to your satisfaction."

Disappointment washed over her. Deep down inside, she knew he didn't have any intentions of being intimate with her tonight.

VINCENT HAD NEVER desired any maiden as much as he did Ellie. And being with her now, he felt like a nervous schoolboy. A few shadows danced in the room from the flickering lamp, but the discontentment on her expression shone through it all. His speeding heart clenched. What had he done? But in an instant, he knew the answer.

He licked his dry lips. "Forgive me for not taking you to my room. Because I've been busy building a stable, my room is filthy, and I still have dirty clothes lying around. I cannot afford servants yet, so I've been doing all of this myself." He glanced toward the bed before returning his focus on her. "That is why I brought you here. I hope you don't mind."

Her shoulders sagged, and a smile graced her face once more. "Oh, Vincent. I feel like a fool for being disappointed that you didn't take me to your room." Chuckling softly, she moved to him and slowly slid her hands up his chest. "I thought you were going to kiss me passionately only to tell me goodnight and leave me in this room."

Warmth from her touch melded with his clothes, making him wish he didn't have these barriers between them. He grinned. "My precious Ellie. Have you forgotten I was once a defiler of women? Why would I give up the chance to be with the maiden who holds my heart?"

Her eyes widened and her mouth dropped open. "I-I…hold your heart?"

He nodded. "Indeed you do. You, and none other." He removed her boy's cap, and her hair tumbled down her shoulders and back. She had the most glorious hair, and he cherished those moments he could caress it. Like now, as he took a lock between his finger and thumb. "I love you, Ellie Middleton. I don't want to lose you to Lord Calvin—Adam. Please tell me I haven't lost you to another man."

Her eyes filled with tears, and she slid her hands up his chest to hook around his neck. "Oh, Vincent. I do indeed love you, and I know I cannot live without—"

Love urged him into action, and he kissed her, silencing her words. Never had he experienced such elation. Finally, he felt complete. They would repeat their vows soon, but tonight, he would make her his forever wife.

He lifted her and placed her on the bed. She lay on her back, but propped herself on her elbows as she looked at him. He would take things slow…as slow as he physically could, anyway.

First, he started at her feet, removing a shoe one at a time and dropping it on the floor. Next came her stockings…a man's stockings, no less. He couldn't help but grin as he rolled them down her leg, one at a time.

She chuckled. "I know what you're thinking."

"You do?" He arched an eyebrow.

"Yes. You're wondering where I got these clothes."

"From a servant, I'm assuming."

She nodded. "But I knew I had to appear exactly like a boy if I was going to make others believe that as well."

Exactly? He held his breath as he reached for her breeches. If she wore the very garments a man wore, then she wouldn't have on pantalettes. His throat suddenly dried. All she would have on once he removed her breeches was the man's shirt.

Another panicky jitter rushed through him. How could he remind himself that *he* was not the innocent one here? But then, he had never taken an innocent girl to bed before, especially one he loved so much. He gulped down a hard swallow. This moment with Ellie became so much more important now, and he vowed to make it a special night for her.

He stroked her legs, hesitating on his next move. *You can do this, Wallace.* Taking a deep breath for courage, he reached for the band around her waist. Carefully, he untied the belt-rope she had fastened around her middle, loosening the breeches.

Suddenly, his hands trembled. *What's wrong with me?* Once

more, he silently told himself that he could do this, and that Ellie would not hate him. He just prayed her father still respected him in the morning. After all, Vincent would be defiling the duke's daughter.

Stop thinking about the duke. He didn't want to ruin the mood.

Vincent shook that thought out of his head as he pulled off her breeches. Just as he expected, she wore a man's shirt—and nothing else.

He had seen many women dressed in much less, yet seeing Ellie on the bed wearing only a shirt that fell to her thighs was the most sensual thing he'd ever had the pleasure to look upon. Tenderly, he ran his hand up her leg to where the shirt stopped just above her knee.

"Vincent?" she asked with a voice deeper than normal. "Are you going to join me?"

He released an awkward laugh. "Can you believe I'm nervous?"

"No."

"Well, I am."

She smiled and held out her hand for him to take. "Then we'll be nervous together."

He slid his palm against hers, and she pulled him on the bed. Before he lay beside her, he kicked off his shoes. Turning, he situated himself next to her, leaning on an elbow as he gazed down into her lovely face.

"I feel like an innocent schoolboy with you," he whispered, cupping the side of her face.

"Is it because you've never loved the women you bedded?"

"Never." He shook his head. "Not until now."

"Then tonight, my darling man, will be a first for both of us."

"Indeed." He moved up, lying on her softness only slightly, as he met her waiting lips with his own.

Tonight would definitely be a night to remember. And he would make it spectacular.

CHAPTER TWENTY

Ellie cuddled closer to the man lying next to her. The early morning brought a chill, and she didn't want to wake him up to build a fire. Being next to him like this was too enjoyable. She never wanted to leave.

Unfortunately, she must return home today. She must try to convince her father that she and Vincent needed to marry immediately. If it took confessing what happened last night, she'd do it.

Sighing, she smiled and pressed her cheek against Vincent's bare chest. Last night was wonderful. Magical. And she had never loved him more than she did now. He was so very loving, so very tender, and so very passionate. Choosing Vincent to be her husband was the best decision she'd ever made.

Vincent stirred in his sleep, rolling her onto her back as he lay halfway on top of her with his strong leg imprisoning hers. She chuckled. Was he dreaming about last night, too?

She kissed his neck as she rubbed her hands over his bare back. She'd come to realize last night how incredibly robust he was. He had muscles everywhere. Strange, because she never thought this way about other men she knew. Those others seemed frail compared to her brawny Vincent.

A low groan rattled from his chest as his fingers threaded through her hair, pushing the locks away from her face. Whether he was asleep or awake, at least she knew he was thinking of her and last night.

He bent his head and captured her mouth, suckling sweetly on her lips before delving his velvety, sweet tongue into her mouth. Goosebumps rose over her flesh again as warmth encased her very being.

After a few seconds, he broke the kiss and peered down into her eyes.

"That is a wonderful way to wake up in the morning." He smiled.

"I agree. Cuddling next to you brought a smile to my face."

He traced the tips of his fingers over her lips. "You have made me the happiest of men. Ellie, I love you, completely."

She sighed as her heart melted, again. "And I love you, my big, strong, protector."

His fingers trailed from her mouth, down her chin, and down her neck. Although they still needed to exchange vows in front of a minister, she felt like Vincent's wife *now*. Nothing would ever change that.

Fast footsteps sounded in the hall, growing louder as they neared the guestroom. Vincent stilled then lifted his head, glancing toward the door.

"Who is it?" she asked in a low voice.

"I think it's Dalton, my servant."

The door shook with the servant's hard pounding, making Ellie jump. Vincent sat up straight and pulled the covers fully around her.

"My lord," the man said from the other side of the door, "you have a visitor downstairs."

"Who is it?" Vincent asked.

"It's the duke—Miss Middleton's father."

Ellie trembled, but for different reasons this time, as fear shot through her. Yet she wanted her father to know, didn't she? Of course, she had hoped she'd be dressed when she confronted him.

"Tell the duke I'll be down momentarily."

"Yes, my lord."

Vincent met her gaze, and remarkably enough, he didn't appear worried in the least. That comforted her slightly.

"Get dressed, but don't come down just yet. I need to speak to your father alone first."

She nodded. "All right."

He smiled, and his eyes sparked with brightness. "Remember, my precious, we shall be married shortly."

"Yes, I know. I pray it's today."

"If I have my way, it will be." He winked before climbing out of bed.

As she watched him dress, she realized she'd never seen any-thing so fascinating in her life. Knowing that Vincent would be *her husband*, and no one else's, made it easier to watch. Her heart filled with more love, if that were possible.

Once he left the room, she quickly climbed out of bed and dressed. As she put on each article of clothing, she couldn't help but remember when he had taken these off her last night. Her smile would remain on her face all day, she just knew it.

It didn't take very long before she was completely dressed, but then she paced the floor, wondering if it was the right time to go downstairs. Would Vincent send Dalton up to fetch her? She wrung her hands. How would she know when Vincent was finished explaining things to her father?

Inwardly, she groaned. She hated feeling this anxious. She would wait fifteen minutes, and no longer. Hopefully, her father would be more understanding by that time.

VINCENT ENTERED THE drawing room, feeling more alert and ready to meet his soon-to-be father-in-law. Before coming down, he'd rushed into his room to comb his hair and splash a little cologne on his face. His clothes may be wrinkled, but he didn't have time to change completely.

The duke stood in front of the window looking out with a frown on his face. When Vincent entered, the floor creaked, which made the older man swing around. The duke's gaze swept over Vincent as he walked toward him.

"Lord Trenton, please forgive me for intruding on your early morning, but I need your assistance." Panic laced the man's shaky voice. "My daughter is missing."

Nodding, Vincent held up a hand. "I know. She came here last night."

The duke's eyes widened, and in an instant, his face flamed red. "She did *what*?"

"Your Grace, please let me explain." Vincent took a deep breath as he collected his thoughts. "Last evening, she overheard her stepmother and Lord Stone discussing a plan in which the man could finally get Ellie to marry him."

The duke's eyebrows twitched, but he remained silent.

"Apparently, Lord Stone was going to sneak into her bedchambers and create a scandal which would force you to make them marry."

Fury shone in the older man's eyes and created wrinkles around his mouth.

Vincent continued, "Ellie was afraid to say anything to you for fear you wouldn't believe her."

The duke shook his head. "Why wouldn't I believe her?"

"Because of your wife…because that is her nephew."

Sighing, the duke nodded. "Indeed. The woman I mistakenly married would have been able to convince me otherwise." He groaned and scrubbed a hand over his face.

"Last night at the ball," Vincent continued, "Ellie approached me for help. The only way I knew how to help her was to have her stay here, with me." He shrugged. "That was the only way I could protect her from Lord Stone."

Ellie's father arched an eyebrow. "Do you realize I will now have to quicken the wedding plans? I will have to get the two of you married by tomorrow."

Vincent grinned. "Yes, Your Grace. We were both aware of that, which is what we wanted anyhow."

The older man chuckled and pushed his fingers through his thinning hair. "I should have suspected. I was once very much in love and couldn't wait to marry Ellie's mother. I understand fully."

Vincent held in a laugh. He suspected the duke may have done this very thing with Ellie's mother, too.

"So, Ellie is still here? She is all right?"

"Yes. She is in the guest bedroom. Would you like me to go get her?"

The duke nodded. "Yes. I shall take her home, and then I'll have a nice long talk with my *wife*."

Vincent left the drawing room and headed up the stairs. His mind buzzed with different thoughts, especially about why the duchess would want to do this to her stepdaughter. Ruthless people always had a motive. So what was hers? *Why* did she want her nephew to marry Ellie so badly?

Another thought entered Vincent's head. Who was the man that he and Ellie had seen entering the house uninvited last night? Obviously, he was invited by the duchess, since she was the one who had unlocked the door.

There was another mystery he needed to solve.

As he approached the guest room, the door opened and Ellie stepped out. Her mussed hair hung around her shoulders, making her more desirable than he was prepared for. Then again, after she'd stirred passion inside of him this morning, how could he not think this way?

Worried eyes looked up at him, so he swept her in his arms and kissed her soundly. She clung to him, answering him just as eagerly as he wanted. Unfortunately, nothing could be done about their desires now.

"My love"—he pulled away—"we must stop before I carry you right back in that room and have my wicked way with you."

She chuckled and pressed her face against his chest. "Forgive me. I just couldn't help myself."

"I couldn't either." He kissed the top of her head. "But your father is downstairs. He came here seeking my help to find you, so I told him what happened last night."

She snapped her head up, her wide-eyed gaze locked with his. "You told him *everything*?"

"No. Just enough to satisfy his curiosity. All I told him was that you were staying in the guest bedroom."

Her body shook with a silent laugh. "How very cunning you are, my lovely man."

"He is going to take you home. I suggest you tell him everything about your stepmother and Lord Stone. I think he will listen now."

She nodded. "Did he say anything about our wedding?"

"Yes." Excitement jumped inside of him. "We will get married tomorrow."

She released a little squeal and threw her arms around his neck. He held her tight, just to feel her supple body against his one more time. *Tomorrow.* It would seem like forever before they were together again.

Taking her by the hand, he walked her down the stairs to her father. When she saw him, she moved to him and hugged him.

"I'm sorry, Father."

"No, I'm the one who is sorry. I didn't realize that Augusta was making your life so miserable." He kissed his daughter's forehead. "But between the two of us, we will make things right."

She peered up at him with teary eyes. "Promise?"

"Yes. For you, I'll do anything."

Vincent's heart softened as he watched father and daughter. Within a few years, he'd be a father, too. He hoped that he would be understanding and loving, just as the duke was.

Ellie turned back to Vincent. "I shall see you later."

"In fact," the duke quickly added, "you will come over for dinner tonight."

"Of course, Your Grace."

Vincent walked them to the door. The duke and Ellie climbed in the family-crested coach, and it drove away.

Sighing, Vincent leaned against the doorframe. This time tomorrow, he hoped to be married. Well, probably not this early, but no later than midafternoon. Then he'd be able to keep her in his arms forever, just as he had promised her.

Yawning, he realized how exhausted he still was. That wonderful, passionate woman had kept him up most of the night. He stretched his arms and turned to go back inside the house, but something in the yard caught his attention.

He blinked and rubbed his eyes. Was he seeing correctly? Was that someone sneaking around the thicket of trees—the same trees where his horses had been when the stable caught fire? Irritation festered inside of him, ready to explode. Was someone trying to destroy his new stable?

Growling, he marched out of the house and bounded down the porch steps, heading for the trees. A movement flashed inside. Whoever it was wore a long black coat—just like the one who'd entered Ellie's house last night. That color would be difficult to see at night, but this morning it shone like a beacon in the sunlight. Vincent wouldn't lose the imbecile this time.

He quickened his steps until he'd entered the area. He stopped and listened for any sounds. The person was still here. He just knew it.

A scent wafted through the air. It smelled as if someone was sweating profusely and hadn't taken a bath for a few days— mayhap longer. Vincent crinkled his nose. This person should be easy to find now.

From behind him came the rustling of bushes mere seconds before something hard struck him in back of the head. Dizziness assailed him and darkness entered his vision. All the sounds around him echoed—like he was in a cave. He fell to the ground and his world turned black.

CHAPTER TWENTY-ONE

PAIN SLASHED THROUGH Vincent's head as he struggled to open his eyes. With his blurred vision, he ascertained two things. It was still day, and he was in some kind of makeshift hut. The strong scent of hay, mixed with the smoke from a fire, burned Vincent's senses. His head throbbed, but as he tried to lift his hand, he also realized both of his hands were bound together behind his back.

What the devil is going on?

Closing his eyes again, he tried to listen for sounds. The snapping of wood told him there was a fire somewhere nearby, but the small amount of heat against his face let him know it wasn't a large one. There was an opened window because the chirps of birds drifted into the hut. And by the stiff, smelly substance poking against his cheek, he knew he was lying in hay.

So was this a barn or stable instead of a hut? Yet why would someone have a low-burning fire in a stable?

Once more, he tried to open his eyes. The pain slicing through his skull tried to keep him from this goal, but he fought against the stinging discomfort.

The squeak of a door made Vincent still his efforts. He focused on the sounds. Footsteps came near him. A boot knocked against his shoulder. He bit his tongue against the pain.

"You can open your eyes. I know you're alive."

Alive? By that remark, Vincent assumed that the man wanted him dead.

He opened his eyes and tried to adjust his vision. Beside the small fire, a man sat, leaning up against a rock. Apparently, there wasn't furniture in this little shack.

The longer Vincent concentrated on the man, the more his face came into focus. *Edgar Stone!* How had that mousy man captured him?

The back of his head throbbed harder. Now he remembered. The fool had crept up behind him and smacked his head with a large, hard object. That would be the only way to take Vincent down.

Stone chuckled. "By your expression, I see you are surprised that I was the one who brought you here."

Fighting against the pain, Vincent adjusted himself on the floor made of hay in order to glare at the other man. "I'm very surprised. But I'm more surprised at myself. Your stench was detected quickly enough. I should have known a weasel like you would attack a man without his knowledge."

Stone's brow creased as he threw Vincent a scowl. "What is that supposed to mean?"

"That means, you fool, that you are not man enough to fight me face to face."

Chuckling, Stone leaned back against the rock. "I'm a lover, not a fighter."

Vincent rolled his eyes. "Why is that hard for me to believe?"

"Listen, you little slip of a man." Stone pointed his finger at Vincent. "I would have been able to convince Ellie to marry me if you hadn't been in the picture. I am quite charming, you know."

"Is that before or after you have bruised a woman's face?"

Stone lifted a haughty chin. "I only strike women when they deserve it, but normally, I'm a charming man. Ellie would have eventually fallen in love with me."

"Ellie cannot stand the sight of you," Vincent snapped, even though the rush of words made his head pound harder. "She has better taste in men."

"Like you?" Stone threw back his head and cackled. "Well, let me assure you that I will change her mind quickly. She *will* marry me."

"What makes you think that?" Vincent struggled again, but managed to sit up fully. "The only way she will marry you is if I'm dead. Is that what you have planned?"

"Once more, you have guessed correctly." Stone nodded.

"And once more," Vincent replied cynically, "you are going to take the spineless way out and kill a man that cannot fight back." Shaking his head, he tsked. "That doesn't say very much about your character. Wouldn't you like to be able to actually fight a man...and win, without using these childish tactics?" He turned slightly, raising his tied hands.

"You are playing with my mind, aren't you?"

"No. I'm just encouraging you to fight like a real man. Or do you just feel empowered when you beat women who cannot defend themselves?" He tilted his head as he narrowed his eyes on the other man. "Now that I know your true character, I'm willing to bet that you were the weasel who set my stable on fire the other night."

Stone scratched behind his ear. "You would like to think that, wouldn't you?"

"It all makes sense," Vincent continued. "You have made it clear that I'm the reason you don't have Ellie, so you are slowly trying to take out the competition. And a weak man like yourself would have no qualms about setting fire to another man's property."

Edgar rose to his feet. Fire blazed behind his eyes as he glared at Vincent.

"I am *not* a weak man." His nostrils flared. "I choose to use my intelligence instead of my fists."

Finally, Vincent was getting the man almost where he wanted him. "But you are weak. I am still tied up. If you want me dead, do it the right way. Untie me and we'll fight to the death like *real* men. Or are you afraid that I might break one of your bones and it might actually hurt?"

Growling, Edgar whipped out a knife from his boot and pointed it at Vincent. He held his breath. Had he gone too far? Or would Edgar fall for his trickery?

ELLIE WORE A permanent smile as she wandered through her mother's flower garden—which, thankfully, Augusta had decided to keep after becoming the duchess. Finally, after two harrowing weeks, Ellie felt at peace. After the talk she'd had with her father during the drive back to the estate this morning, he promised that he would send Augusta and her vile nephew to the winter estate in Essex. Ellie just wished her father had a good reason to divorce the woman. England and the church frowned upon divorces, yet living with a woman like Augusta would ruin anyone's life.

While her father arranged for tomorrow's wedding, Ellie had taken a nap. The much-needed rest had refreshed her, as did the bath afterward, and now all she wanted was to see Vincent again. She wanted to be in his arms and kiss his tender lips. She wanted to gaze into his dreamy blue-gray eyes, and thank God how lucky she was to have found him to marry.

That first day when her father had told her she had a month to find a husband, Ellie was prepared to enter a loveless marriage. Now she was grateful that she wouldn't have to.

She stopped by the red roses and bent to take a sniff. These flowers, out of all of them, reminded her most of her mother. Sadness crept into her heart as she relived the heartache of losing her parent to sickness. The physician couldn't say what had killed her mother, but thankfully, she hadn't been sick for very long before the good Lord took her up to heaven.

Her mother had loved tending the rosebushes, instead of having the servants do it. When Ellie was young, she recalled taking walks through the garden with her mother as she clipped the dead leaves.

Her attention was pulled to something sticking out of the ground. Ellie bent and pushed back the dirt. A letter was stuck between two rocks. How long had it been here?

She brushed the soil off the old paper and carefully unfolded it. Immediately, she recognized Augusta's handwriting. Ellie gritted her teeth as she read the letter.

My dearest Edgar, our plans will soon come together, and we will finally be able to live a life of love, just as we have always wanted. I made certain that the Duchess of Primberry was given the poison. She will soon meet her maker, and I will continue to get close to the duke in his time of grieving and convince him to marry me. Soon, his daughter, Ellie, will be ready to marry, and you shall ask for her hand. Between the two of us, my dearest Edgar, we shall have the duke's fortune and lands. We will finally be able to love each other as we have dreamed of doing. It won't take much to see that the duke and his daughter's deaths are quick and painless. Until then, we shall continue to convince people that you are really my nephew, and that I am your aunt.

Always yours, Augusta Long

Shock vibrated through Ellie and her stomach twisted with nausea. Before she could stop it, her breakfast jumped from her stomach to her throat. She darted toward the nearest tree to vomit.

Anger shook through her trembling body as she clutched the letter, fearful that she would lose the only evidence that showed her mother had been murdered...and that she and her father were next. Augusta was indeed an evil stepmother, and Ellie was determined that the woman would not win. Neither would Edgar! Ellie would see to it that both were thrown in the gaol...or hanged.

She gripped her middle, feeling that her stomach still had

more to release. Tears swam in her eyes. Hatred for *that woman* and her evil so-called nephew grew quickly inside her. She wanted to wrap her fingers around the woman's throat and squeeze…

No. She wouldn't take a life. She wouldn't sink to *their* level. Ellie would let the law do their job and arrest the two frauds.

Poor Father! He would want to kill his own wife, too. But Ellie would try to convince him that wasn't the proper thing. Taking a life for a life was not the answer.

She stood and moved on unsteady legs toward the manor. Her stomach continued to rumble, but she fought back the feeling and concentrated on making it to the house to find her father. Tears swam in her eyes, making her vision blurry. No matter how many times she wiped away the moisture, more would come.

"Eleanor!"

She stopped and turned toward the man hurrying toward her, waving his arm. She blinked again and recognized Lord Calvin. She swiped the wetness under her eyes again, hoping to finally remove the tears dampening her face.

"Eleanor, something awful has happened—" His words stopped when he stood in front of her. "What is amiss, my dear?"

Raising her shaky hand that still held the letter, she presented it to him. "I…just found this."

His forehead creased with worry lines as he took the letter and opened it. He scanned the contents and his eyes widened. "Augusta killed your mother?"

She nodded. "Yes, and as you can see, she wants to kill me and my father as well."

Lord Calvin stepped closer and took her in his arms. She rested her head against his chest. Immediately, she realized he wasn't anything like Vincent. Still, it was nice of him to try to comfort her right now.

"There's actually more," he said in a low tone.

She raised her head. "More?"

"Yes. That is why I'm here. Edgar has kidnapped Vincent and plans to kill him, but I don't know where he has taken him."

Anger rushed through her again. She pushed away from Lord Calvin. "Did you see Edgar take him?"

"Yes, but I was on foot and Edgar was on horseback. All I know is that they must be somewhere near your estate."

Panicked, she couldn't think straight. Vincent was in trouble, and she needed to rescue him. Her head throbbed with frustration as she tried thinking of where on her father's property the madman could keep her beloved.

Groaning with uselessness, she rubbed her forehead. *Think, Ellie!* Her gaze rested on Lord Calvin's attire—long black coat and top hat. Realization smacked her from out of nowhere.

"Lord Calvin? Were you at my house last night? Did you enter through the west wing door?"

Lord Calvin scowled. "Eleanor, we don't have time for this. You need to help me find Edgar before he kills Vincent."

She couldn't understand any of this, and her mind swam with confusion. Why was Lord Calvin hellbent on trying to find Edgar? What was the man's purpose? To save Vincent or to catch Edgar?

Her questions needed to be answered quickly, before she went insane.

CHAPTER TWENTY-TWO

ADAM GRASPED ELLIE'S arm and tugged as he started them back around the house. Irritation inside of her overrode the moment, and she stopped short, jerking her hand away from him. "I'm not going another step until you tell me what is going on."

Inhaling through his mouth, he pinched the bridge of his nose.

"Tell me the truth, Adam."

His eyes darkened with his scowl. "I'm Lord Calvin. Will you please remember that?"

She rolled her eyes. "Just tell me the truth, please?"

He sighed and folded his arms. "Remember when I told you I was a spy for the prince regent?"

She nodded.

"One of the men I have suspected of treason for a while now is Edgar Stone. I followed him here. That is the real reason I came back."

"So all of this was just an assignment?"

"Yes…although I'm glad I told you the truth about my identity."

She shrugged. "Go on."

"I suspected Edgar was working with someone, but it wasn't until I met your stepmother that I knew who that person was."

"Augusta?"

"Yes. She and Edgar have been supporters of Napoleon Bonaparte from the very beginning. They rob people of their money as a way of getting back at the Crown. Every person that the prince has awarded—like your father—Edgar and Augusta are determined to ruin their lives. They have chosen your family now."

"By killing my mother," she shouted as tears sprang to her eyes.

"Yes. That was Augusta's first mistake. I assure you, she will be arrested, along with Edgar, who has plenty of crimes under his belt."

Finally, things started adding up in Ellie's mind. No wonder she hadn't fully trusted Augusta. Now it made sense why she didn't like Edgar from the moment she met him. Was her guardian angel mother trying to protect her? She liked to think so.

"So why would Edgar take Vincent?"

"To get him out of the way so he can marry you." He pointed to the letter he still held. "Remember, that's part of their plan."

"Make sure you keep that letter safe, Calvin. That's the only proof we have of Augusta killing my mother." Her voice broke.

He stepped toward her and gathered her in his arms. "Eleanor, you can trust me to do just that. Consider it a way of apologizing for all I have put you through." He pulled back and looked into her eyes. "I do still love you, but...things have changed. I no longer wish to marry you."

She managed a small smile. "Do not fret, dear Calvin. I don't wish to marry you, either. I'm completely in love with Vincent."

"I know. I could tell last night at the ball. You never looked upon me as you did him last evening. I'm glad you found someone to be with."

Sniffing, she pulled away and wiped the tears off her face. "All right now, let me concentrate on where Edgar would have taken Vincent. Are you sure he took him somewhere on my father's property?"

"Yes. I'm wondering if he is going to kill Vincent and make it look like your father did it."

She snorted a laugh. "What an idiot. My father loves Vincent and cannot wait until we are wed."

"Edgar doesn't know this."

"True." She paused, thinking of where the evil man might have taken her true love. Immediately, she recalled seeing an old shack on the property. It was one of the first shacks built that housed the servants many years ago.

"I think I know where he is."

⟫⟪

VINCENT STOOD WITH his unbound hands folded across his chest, watching with humor as Edgar danced around him. The man looked like a cross between a boxer and a dancer. But he was serious as he hopped around, holding up his fists. He had yet to throw the first punch.

Thankfully, Vincent's criticism had worked. Edgar wanted to feel like a real man and fight. But if something didn't happen soon, Vincent would think the man wanted to dance with him instead.

"I say, Trenton," Edgar said, "you stand there as though you don't expect me to clobber you."

"You know, Stone, for once, you're right."

Edgar stalled as confusion etched his dimwitted expression. Vincent would bet good money the man was thinking over what had just been said.

"So, you aren't going to fight me?" He shook his head, still holding up his fists. "Perhaps *you* are the one who isn't a real man."

Vincent sighed and lowered his arms. Edgar's frame stiffened, and he lifted his hands higher.

"I suppose," Vincent said slowly, "that I shouldn't feel guilty if I hurt you."

"Ha!" Edgar spat at him. "I daresay you are stalling. Now I can see *you* are the weakling."

Vincent rolled his eyes. The insipid man had asked for it, and he was going to get it.

In one quick movement, Vincent fisted his hand and punched Edgar square in the nose. The sound of bones crunching rent the air. The man didn't even have time to block the punch.

Edgar screamed like a child and covered his bloody nose. He stumbled backward, tripping over his own feet and landing on the ground. He then fished in his pocket and pulled out a knife, pointing it at Vincent.

He wanted to laugh. Did the man actually think that was going to scare him? He shrugged and, in another swift movement, kicked the knife out of Edgar's hands. The sound of bones crunching pulsed through the air again.

Swearing—and crying—Edgar cradled his injured hand and his broken nose. The pathetic man curled on the ground and rocked back and forth. A chuckle escaped Vincent's throat. At least the man had tried to prove he had a spine. Sadly, though, he didn't succeed.

"I swear this to you now," Vincent said with tight lips as he glared at the pathetic weasel. "I will get in touch with the magistrate and have you arrested for kidnapping me. I'll also have him look into your lineage, because I highly doubt you are a real *lord*. Gentlemen do not act this way, I assure you."

Vincent turned to leave but decided he'd better tie Edgar up. After all, the man was a coward. He'd run and hide to keep from being arrested.

Vincent searched the floor, looking for the ropes that had bound his wrists together. They were in the corner of the room. A movement from outside pulled his attention toward the door just as Augusta entered. She held a pistol and pointed it at him.

He stood still, waiting and wondering what she'd do next. Her gaze shifted to the floor where Edgar was curled in a ball, whimpering like a baby. Her expression hardened, and she whipped her attention back to Vincent.

"What have you done?"

He shrugged. "Edgar wanted to fight me like a man, so I let him. As you can see, he didn't win."

"Get off the ground," she snapped at Edgar.

"I-I cannot. He broke my nose, and I think he broke my hand," Edgar whined.

"Augh!" She marched toward him, still trying to keep her pistol on Vincent. "You sniveling little fool. What made you think you could fight a man like Lord Trenton? He's twice your size."

Instead of answering, Edgar covered his face, continuing to rock back and forth.

"You were supposed to kill him. Trenton is the only one standing in our way right now. You cannot marry Ellie while *he* is still alive."

"Actually," Vincent said, lifting a finger, "Ellie loathes the very ground Edgar slithers upon. She would never marry him, and I'm quite certain the duke won't force this coward upon his only daughter, either."

"Silence." Augusta aimed her scowl at Vincent. "You have no idea who I am or what abilities I have, do you? I will be able to convince the duke to give Edgar her hand in marriage."

Anger boiled inside Vincent. He'd had enough of their games. Indeed, both of their minds were in an alternate world, and he was exhausted of trying to discuss things with these insane people. If he could only just turn and leave—but the duchess still held a pistol. He was sure she knew how to use it. If only he could play with her mind as he'd done with Edgar's, then perhaps Vincent could leave here unscathed.

"Forgive me, Duchess," Vincent said. "You are correct. I don't know what abilities you have. All I know is how absolutely charming you are, and also how lovely. I'm sure you have persuaded many men."

She lifted her chin haughtily. "I have."

"Just as I suspected." He smiled, hoping to pour his charm on her. "And because of that, I wonder why you have chosen to associate yourself with a weakling like Edgar."

She arched an eyebrow as she threw a glare toward the man on the ground. "Edgar and I have known each other since childhood. Because of our different backgrounds, we were never able to unite our love as we wanted."

Warning bells went off in Vincent's head. *Love?* What in the devil was she talking about?

Her shoulders sagged as a frown touched her face. "For years, I tried to convince people that we were related and that I was his only family. That was the way to keep him close."

"Edgar isn't your nephew?" Vincent asked warily.

"Of course not. As soon as we can find a way to get rid of the duke and his daughter, Edgar will then become my husband and we'll have all the money and lands that we've been trying to obtain for years."

Years? None of this made much sense, and Vincent now felt as though he was the one who had gone insane. Although he surmised that he was dealing with two people who had lost their minds a long time ago. Could he really talk himself out of this now?

"Might I make a suggestion," he said hesitantly. He needed to do something to divert her attention from him so that he could lunge for the weapon in her hand.

"What, pray tell, is that?"

"For a woman as powerful, lovely, and charming as yourself, I think you should find a man who is your equal." He glanced at Edgar, who peeked at him through the fingers still covering his eyes. "As you can see, this weasel is not worthy of you."

Her gaze bounced to Edgar, and then back to Vincent. She didn't say anything for a few moments, and he was glad she at least thought of his suggestion.

Augusta eyed him up and down before a smirk twisted her mouth. "Pray, are *you* applying for this position?"

Vincent nearly laughed out loud, but he bit his tongue to hold it in. She must be insane to think that he would want her over someone as perfect as Ellie. "Oh no, Your Grace. I cannot even measure up to someone as refined as you. I will never be able to fill the duke's boots, either."

She shook her head. "Anyone can fill his boots. He is almost as pitiful as Edgar sometimes."

"Then why do you waste your breath on a man like him?" He pointed to the wretched man who now glared at him with so much evil in his eyes, his whole face turned red. "As you can see, he is not worth your energy."

"That's enough," Edgar shouted as he fought to stand while still coddling his broken nose. "You speak of me as though I've lost my hearing." He limped to Augusta. "And you, who has been the love of my life since I was ten years old, should be more respectful of my feelings. As of two nights ago, you were lying in my arms, pouring out your devotion and love. Tell me, were they untruths?"

"I-I—" Augusta stumbled over her words.

"Can't you see what this man is doing?" Edgar asked, nodding toward Vincent. "He is trying to trick you with his words, just as he did with me. I was a fool and fell for his tactics, but I beg you, do not be as weak as I was. This man cannot win, or all of our hopes and dreams will have been for naught."

Vincent held his breath. Apparently, *he* wasn't the only sweet talker in this room. He needed to keep Augusta's mind focused on Edgar's faults. That was the only way he could get ahead in this game. And the only way he could save his and Ellie's lives.

CHAPTER TWENTY-THREE

ELLIE RODE ALONGSIDE Calvin. She'd thought she knew the location, but when they reached the spot, she had discovered she was wrong. Now, as she and Calvin scoured her father's lands, her heart sank with dread. Would they arrive too late to save Vincent? She couldn't think of her life without him.

"Eleanor, please don't fret. We will find him." Calvin offered a sympathetic smile as if reading her thoughts.

She nodded. "I cannot help feeling this way. So much bad luck has come upon us as of late, it's hard to look past that."

"Keep in mind"—Calvin scanned around them—"that most of this misfortune was brought on by Edgar and Augusta."

"Very true."

"They are both greedy buggers, and I plan to see them arrested immediately."

As she stared at Calvin, she couldn't believe he was the same man she'd been engaged to not long ago. He'd acted like a boy still in his youth when he left for battle, only to return a headstrong man who took chances. She admired him for that.

"Why are you looking at me so strangely?" he asked with a crooked grin.

"Because you are not the same person now as when you left me."

"I have changed."

"And what about your heart? Has it changed as well? Did you ever love me?" she wondered aloud.

His grin disappeared. "I think I did love you. I mean, I entered into battle hoping it would make me a hero in your eyes—and the eyes of Society—and hoped it would make me some money in the process. I knew I could never afford the lifestyle you are used to, but I wanted to try." He shrugged and turned his gaze away from her. "However, over the years I realized I enjoyed being one of the prince's spies. You were in my mind those years, but you were not utmost in my heart." He glanced at her. "Are you upset at me for admitting that?"

"No. Although I did mourn for you, so in a way, I feel cheated. I didn't want to meet any other man for fear he would erase the fond memories I had of you."

He was silent for a few moments before he sighed heavily. "Fate has a strange way of working out, don't you agree? If I had returned to marry you, would we have been truly happy? If you hadn't mourned for me, could you have fallen in love with Vincent so deeply?"

Warmth spread across her face. Calvin's words held so much meaning. He was correct. If these things had not happened to her, she wouldn't have given her heart to Vincent. And truly, she loved him so very much that she ached.

"Yes, Calvin. I see now that mourning for you helped me."

They rode for another few minutes before he pulled his horse to a stop. Grumbling, he scrubbed his hand over his goatee. "Perhaps Edgar didn't take Vincent anywhere on your father's property."

"But didn't you see them go this direction?"

"Yes, but he could have gone farther, and I wouldn't have seen that."

Her mind replayed everything Calvin had said about being an agent and what he suspected of Edgar and Augusta. "You mentioned that Edgar would kill Vincent on this property to make it appear as if Father was to blame."

"Yes."

She shook her head. "But that doesn't make sense. If Augusta and Edgar did that, my father would be stripped of his fortune and lands. The duke's family would get nothing."

Calvin narrowed his eyes on her and nodded. "You're correct." He paused again, appearing that he was in deep thought as he stared at one spot toward the horizon.

She tried to recall everything she knew about Edgar, but she really didn't know him. He had always just been Augusta's nephew. There were no stories on how they were related, exactly, or where he'd come from. She didn't know a lot about Augusta, either. When had her father met the woman? What was her life like before she married the duke?

Finally, a memory broke through. Augusta had bragged about her family owning some land just north of here. Ellie realized now how much she had lied, but would the woman lie about this? Ellie hoped not, because this was their only shot of finding Vincent.

She searched the land before pointing north. "Let's go in that direction. If I recall correctly, one of the ways Augusta used to get close to my father was telling him her family owned some land not far from here."

Calvin nodded and pushed his horse faster. Having ridden sidesaddle since she was a young girl, she knew how to ride with the best of them. She tightened her leg around the horn, ducked slightly, and urged her horse faster.

It didn't take too long before she noticed a worn-down hut amongst some sparse trees. Calvin must have seen it as well, because he straightened and led his horse toward the structure. When they came closer, both she and Calvin slowed their animals to a trot.

He turned to her and placed a finger to his lips, hushing her. She nodded. Two horses stood near the pitiful shack. Her heart pounded against her chest as fear clawed its way through her. Had they made it on time?

Please, Lord, let Vincent be alive.

Calvin stopped his horse first, and she halted Pegasus right next to his animal. He helped her down before taking the reins and hooking them around a tree, then reached in his saddlebag and withdrew two pistols, handing one to her.

She looked down at the weapon in her hand. Shock froze her limbs when she realized just how dangerous this situation was.

Calvin held a stern expression and gave her a nod. "Don't worry. I won't allow them to hurt you."

Taking a deep breath, Ellie tried to prepare herself. Calvin would know how to use a pistol, but she didn't. Hopefully, she wouldn't get the chance to do it today.

⇶⫷⫸⇷

ALTHOUGH VINCENT WASN'T certain how he was going to get out of this mess, a calm feeling came over him. Help would come soon, he had to believe it. But now he needed to stall Edgar and Augusta and convince them not to kill him.

Augusta seemed perplexed as her gaze darted between him and Edgar, who was still holding his bloody nose. Vincent wanted her to doubt the man she proclaimed to love. As long as she had reservations about Edgar, she wouldn't shoot Vincent.

He tsked. "Your Grace, please reconsider. I'm thinking of your happiness. If you believe Edgar's words, you will be forever in misery. He isn't the man he's led you to believe all of these years."

More doubt crept into her baffled expression. Her eyes narrowed on Vincent, which worried him slightly. But he liked the way she threw Edgar a glare every now and again.

"Are you calling me a fool for believing that Edgar can make me happy?"

"No, Your Grace," he quickly said. "I do not blame you. I blame Edgar. He is cunning, and he cannot tell the truth if his life depended on it. You are just a victim."

"Listen to me, you little sliver of a man," Edgar snapped as he continued to hold his nose. "I demand you stop talking this instant. All you are trying to do is gain your freedom, but I assure you, it's our plan to kill you. It's been our plan all along."

Vincent raised an eyebrow. "Let me take a wild assumption here. By chance, are you the one who put sticker weeds under my horse's saddle when Miss Middleton and I went for a ride in the park?"

Edgar lifted his chin haughtily. "That was I."

"How very inconsiderate of you, especially since someone could have seen you do it, and it would have reflected on the duchess. Do you wish to ruin her good name?"

Augusta's eyes widened, and she aimed a heated glare toward Edgar. "That was *you?*"

"Um… Well, yes, my dear." He touched her arm, but she yanked it away. "You see, love, I was trying to get Lord Trenton out of the picture. I was trying to make him look like a weakling in front of your stepdaughter. I even tossed a rock through his window as a means to stop him from seeing Ellie."

Vincent folded his arms across his chest and shook his head. "Your antics didn't work. It made Ellie admire me even more."

Edgar huffed. "I have had enough of your arrogance." In a flash, he bent and picked up the knife from the ground. "It's now time I end your life."

Vincent silently scolded himself for not retrieving the knife the first time he'd kicked it out of the idiot's hand. Warily, he watched Edgar to see what his next move would be. The man lunged, and Vincent moved out of his way, making him stumble into the wall.

With both arms in blocking position, Edgar circled Vincent, who sidestepped him. Knife or not, Vincent was not going to let this weakling draw any blood.

After the two men circled the room a few times, Vincent chuckled deep in his chest. "I thought you were going to end my life. After all, you must impress the duchess."

"Oh, I will. Mark my words."

"Not before I lay you flat, you miserable excuse for a man."

Edgar shouted and lunged toward him, pointing the knife in the direction of Vincent's chest. Vincent grasped the man's hand in his crushing grip. Edgar struggled to compose himself, but the pain in his hand must have been too much to bear…even in front of the woman he professed to love.

Edgar screamed and sank to his knees. The knife dropped to the ground. This time, Vincent didn't hesitate to remove the weapon from the other man's reach.

"Actually," Augusta said, raising her pistol to Vincent's chest one more time, "you can give me the knife now."

Vincent cursed under his breath. Could he get ahead in this battle of wits? "Of course, Your Grace. I'm not going to use it against you." As he handed her the weapon, he prayed she would soon come to trust him. That would be the only way to win. "But it's clear that Edgar shouldn't be trusted with a knife, or anything harmful." He glanced at the man on the ground. "He just cannot handle it."

"Yes, Lord Trenton, I believe you are correct." She threw a disgusted glare at Edgar. "Now I'm very upset that I spent so much of my energy giving in to this man's wishes. He has never wanted my happiness, only his own. I see that now."

"Your Grace," Vincent said hesitantly. "What is it that you want? What will make you happy?"

She stayed silent for a few awkward moments as her eyes glazed with unshed tears. "For years, I wanted wealth and power. Now that I have married the duke, I have the money, but I still don't have the power."

"Pray, how exactly do you plan on getting the power?"

Edgar adjusted on the ground, sitting up slightly. "She wants recognition for taking over the money that the prince regent issued to some of the lords."

"Edgar, hush!" Augusta shrieked, and aimed the pistol at him. "You have said too much."

Vincent reacted quickly. He grasped Augusta's hands and pushed her aim away from Edgar. She cried out again and struggled, but just like Edgar, she was no match for Vincent. He finally yanked the weapon out of her hands. She crumbled beside Edgar, sobbing.

The floor behind Vincent creaked. He swung the pistol in that direction, ready to protect himself, again. Lord Calvin rushed inside, holding a pistol as well. His gaze left Vincent and dropped to the two on the floor before he pointed his gun at Augusta and Edgar.

Seconds later, Ellie hurried into the shack. When she looked at Vincent, she sighed tearfully and ran to him, wrapping her arms around his waist.

"I was so worried. Thank the good Lord you are all right."

"Alexander Claremont?" Augusta gasped, pointing a finger at Lord Calvin. "What are *you* doing here?"

Confused, Vincent frowned. Why did the duchess just call Calvin a different name?

Lord Calvin grinned. "Yes, Augusta, it's me, although that's not my name. I lied to you about my identity."

"But…you are dead."

Vincent arched an eyebrow. How many times did Adam have to fake his own death?

"As you can see," Calvin said, motioning up and down his body, "I'm very much alive. I made you think you killed me so that I could keep an eye on you. Too bad you disappeared before I could stop you from marrying Ellie's father." Tsking, he shook his head. "I see you didn't learn your lesson the first time."

Vincent gasped. There were other times?

"Calvin." Ellie pulled away from Vincent and looked at the other man. "What is she talking about? You had another identity?"

"Yes. I've had many, in fact."

"Wh-what more has Augusta done?"

"My dear Eleanor," Calvin said, frowning as he shook his

head. "Your stepmother has married many men for their money and become a widow within a year. I took on the name Alexander Claremont, pretending to be a close friend of one of her husbands. She thought she had killed me, too."

Ellie gasped and slapped a hand over her mouth. Shaking her head slowly, she glared at her stepmother. "You…you are a liar and thief!"

Augusta rolled her eyes. "I tell men what I think will help me win them."

Ellie rubbed her forehead. "Is there anything else you haven't told me?"

"Yes. Probably." Augusta shrugged.

Vincent moved to Ellie and wrapped her in his arms. She turned and held him, pressing her cheek against his chest.

"Augusta," she said in a tight voice, "I have never approved of you, and I'm happy to know my first instinct of you was correct. I will do everything in my power to ensure my father divorces you."

"He won't do that." Augusta snickered. "I have him wrapped around my little finger. He's my puppet now—not yours."

"Actually, that's not accurate."

A man's strong voice boomed through the shack. Vincent snapped his attention to the door. Ellie's father walked inside, folding his arms across his chest as he aimed a glare at Augusta. She gasped and fell back, looking upon the duke with wide eyes.

"Lord Calvin has enough evidence against you to have you thrown in the gaol. And I will arrange it with the Crown to have the proper documents written up to start our divorce."

"Father!" Ellie tore away from Vincent and ran to her father. "I'm so sorry you had to witness this."

"Not as sorry as I." He cupped his daughter's face lovingly. "Forgive me for not listening to you sooner."

"There's nothing to forgive." Ellie smiled as her lips quaked.

The duke took a deep breath before turning his focus on Calvin, and then to Vincent. "My lords, if you don't mind, please tie these two traitors up and take them to the magistrate. I need to return home with my daughter. We have a wedding to prepare."

Vincent smiled and nodded. "I'll be very happy to assist, Your Grace."

As he watched his soon-to-be wife leave with her father, Vincent smiled. Finally, good fortune appeared in his future.

EPILOGUE

ELLIE SAT ON the end of the bed, staring at the low-burning fire in the hearth as she brushed her wet hair, trying to dry it before retiring for the night. Her thoughts drifted back to the past month, and especially the past few days. Her humdrum life had turned into a whirlwind of excitement, adventure, terror, and surprise—but also, most importantly, love. Everything she'd heard and seen these past few days had left her stunned. She still couldn't believe what she had heard about Adam's new life. No wonder he wasn't in love with her any longer. He was too busy catching traitors for the Crown.

And Augusta—it was a great relief to find out about her past and that the duke could finally obtain a divorce from the evil woman. Ellie knew her father had never truly gotten over his wife's death, and discovering the news of how she'd died nearly sent him insane. Thankfully, Vincent and Calvin helped her father understand. Soon, he would be back to the loving, supportive parent she'd always had.

As for Vincent...

She peeked over her shoulder as he walked out from the bathing chamber, heading toward her. His hair was damp as he patted a towel to his wavy strands. He wore a velvet black robe, tied around the middle, and his bare, muscular legs were the only visible skin that showed on her husband.

My husband…

Ellie smiled. She had thought that day would never come. Thankfully, before the news broke about Augusta's arrest and the duke filing for divorce, Ellie and Vincent were married in a small ceremony in front of their closest friends and family. That was exactly twenty-four hours ago, and this day had been spent lying in each other's arms, making love to their hearts' content, and planning out their future.

Could it get any better than this?

Dropping his towel over his shoulders, he bent and kissed her neck, nuzzling her skin. Shivers of delight coursed through her.

"Good evening, my lovely wife. Are you ready for supper? I'll instruct the cook—"

"No, I'm not hungry." She took his arm and pulled him down beside her. "All I want is you."

"Hmm…" He arched one eyebrow higher than the other. "That is considered cannibalism, and is frowned upon in most countries."

She laughed and rolled her eyes. "You know what I mean, you handsome devil."

Chuckling deeply, he slid his arms around her waist, pulling her closer. "Indeed I do. I just enjoy making you laugh. Am I wrong for wanting to see your eyes light up like stars against a darkened sky?" He kissed the tip of her nose. "I never want to be without seeing your twinkling gaze again."

She groaned softly and kissed his exposed neck. "You shall never be without it, I assure you."

He sighed heavily and peered into her eyes. "Are you ready for tomorrow?"

Confused, she shook her head. "What is tomorrow?"

"That is when the news will break about your stepmother being arrested, and all the crimes she has committed." He stroked her cheek tenderly. "I want to make certain you can handle it."

She nodded. "As long as you promise that you'll stay right by my side, I shall be able to conquer the world."

"Undoubtedly." He smiled. "You aren't going to get rid of me that easily now that you hold my heart."

She sighed and leaned into him. "Do you know how happy you've made me already?"

He shrugged. "Are you anywhere near as jovial as me?"

"More so." She winked and cuddled closer. "And to think, when I first offered you that silly bargain, I was prepared for a loveless marriage."

"Yes, about that bargain…" He cupped her chin and lifted her face toward his. "I want the truth now."

"The truth? Have I not been truthful with you?"

He grinned. "You have known me for years, and you knew what kind of scoundrel I'd been lately. Correct?"

"Correct."

"So tell me, my precious, did you honestly believe that you would have never been happy with me? Did you honestly believe you would never come to love me?"

She lifted her fingers to his throat and trailed them down the opening of his robe. "At the time I was foolish and thought my heart belonged to Adam. I didn't think I would ever find a man who could replace him." She smiled wider. "But after our first kiss in the carriage, I honestly wanted you to love me. I wanted to feel the excitement in my body only you could create. Adam never made my body quiver like that. Only you."

"So, you can honestly say I've been your first in many things."

She nodded. "My first, now and forever."

He stared at her for a few long moments. His eyes darkened with desire, which made her heartbeat quicken considerably. She wanted to push him back on the bed and have her wicked way with him.

"I'm very grateful," he said slowly, "that you had patience with me. I didn't know I was looking for a woman like you—until after I found you. I'd convinced myself I couldn't have a relationship, but then I realized I couldn't bear to see you with any other man. I became possessive. I was going to make you love me if it was the last thing I did."

Her heart tripped with excitement, and her love grew. Funny to think how much she'd had this reaction since meeting him.

"I love you, Vincent Wallace."

"And I love you, my beautiful, precious Ellie."

She sank back into the mattress, pulling him with her. As he covered her body with his, she anticipated the pleasure he'd bring. She also looked forward to her life as his wife. She couldn't wait to show England just how a husband and wife were supposed to act. And when they brought children into the world, she and Vincent would be great examples to them, so that they would want to find the perfect mate as well.

Sighing, she kissed her husband deeply. Indeed, life was wonderful. Just as it should be.

THE END

READERS—find the whole series here—
www.authormariehiggins.com/love-s-addiction-regency

Join my newsletter
www.authormariehiggins.com/newsletter

Find more of Marie Higgins' books here—
www.authormariehiggins.com

About the Author

Marie Higgins is an award-winning, best-selling author of clean romance novels that melt your heart and have you falling in love over and over again. Since 2010, she has published over 100 heartwarming, on-the-edge-of-your-seat romances. She has broadened her readership by writing mystery/suspense, humor, time travel, and paranormal, along with her love for historical romances. Her readers have dubbed her "Queen of Tease" because of all her twists and unexpected endings.

Website – www.authormariehiggins.com
Facebook – facebook.com/marie.higgins.7543
TikTok – tiktok.com/@author.mariehiggins
Instagram – instagram.com/author.mariehiggins
Bookbub – bookbub.com/authors/marie-higgins